HOUSE OF DOORS

War widow Ruth Taylor arrives at RAF Morwood, the great house formerly known as D'Esperance, hoping that nursing badly wounded airmen will distract her from her sorrows. But almost as soon as she enters the house, she experiences strange visions and fainting spells, and the almost overwhelming sensation of her late husband's ghostly presence. For D'Esperance is a place of shadows and secrets - and as the strange occurrences become increasingly menacing and violent, Ruth is forced to confront a terrible possibility: that her dead husband might be the cause...

* available from Severn House

HOUSE OF DOORS

Chaz Brenchley

Severn House Large Print
London & New York

This first large print edition published 2012
in Great Britain and the USA by
SEVERN HOUSE PUBLISHERS LTD of
9-15 High Street, Sutton, Surrey, SM1 1DF.
First world regular print edition published 2011 by
Severn House Publishers Ltd., London and New York.

British Library Cataloguing in Publication Data

Brenchley, Chaz.
   House of doors.
   1. War widows--Fiction. 2. World War, 1939-1945--War
   work--Fiction. 3. Great Britain. Royal Air Force--
   Airmen--Nursing home care--Fiction. 4. Haunted
   hospitals--Fiction. 5. Horror tales. 6. Large type books.
   I. Title
   823.9'2-dc23

   ISBN-13: 978-0-7278-9941-5

Severn House Publishers support The Forest Stewardship Council
[FSC], the leading international forest certification organisation. All
our titles that are printed on Greenpeace-approved FSC-certified paper
carry the FSC logo.

Printed and bound in Great Britain by the
MPG Books Group, Bodmin, Cornwall.

ONE

She had never really believed in the car.

There'll be a car to meet you at the station. It was an absolute promise; but even in peacetime, it had been Ruth's experience that other people's promises were ... contingent. Never her own, she was scrupulous about that. A promise was a promise. Even Peter, though, whom she had loved and trusted beyond measure, beyond reason: even he had made certain promises that turned out to be worth less than she had hoped.

And now, after Peter, in this world of war – well, she had apparently become someone to whom promises could be made carelessly, heedlessly, with no real intent behind them. A woman, a widow, a nurse. There was nothing in her life or situation, nothing in herself to give her weight or influence. Nothing in her sense of self. She had no family to back her and no money, no position, no authority. She didn't care about any of that, but she did wish that people would not make promises they had no intention of keeping.

No possibility of keeping, in wartime. Travel arrangements across half the country, for someone so insignificant? No, she had never believed in the car. Even before her train north had been delayed and delayed: shunted aside to let a troop-train by, re-routed away from a marshalling yard that billowed smoke, stranded in a siding for hours with no explanation. Night had come before Leeds, her expected connection had been and gone long since.

She ended up sitting through the darkness on Darlington station, a rug around her knees and her eyes on the sky. No searchlights, no balloons; no distant fires, no firefly-spark of aeroplane exhausts, no ack-ack. No sudden flares of death dealt out. Only clouds and stars and the waning moon. She could spot all the constellations that Peter had taught her and make up others, tell herself their stories, try not to dwell on the train she had missed and the car that would never have been there anyway.

Try not to wonder just what it was that she was travelling to, what blind commitment she had made now. What all her promises might mean, to herself and to others in the weeks and months to come.

She no longer thought in years. Months were enough, surely.

It had been an odd interview that fetched her here, unforthcoming even by wartime standards. She hadn't actually applied for a transfer, even, only mentioned in the canteen that she was thinking of it: 'I suppose I'd feel more useful overseas, where the men are fighting. When they need a nurse right there, right then.'

'We're needed here, now.' This was at the end

of a long night, half a dozen of them clustered around a table with mugs of tea and cigarettes, their voices blurred with exhaustion. Almost too tired to go home, when home meant only a quick wash and a tumble into bed, a few blessed hours' sleep and then back into uniform and back to the ward, back to work again.

'Of course,' Ruth said quickly. The raids were worse than ever. London was burning all about them, and most of these girls were Londoners. 'The home front is as important as anywhere else. Just – well, we can't win the war from here. Only survive it. I want to help win it. And that means nursing soldiers, not civilians.'

'That'll mean the *QA*s, then.'

'I suppose so, yes.' The Queen Alexandra corps, military nurses: almost a regiment in themselves.

'Sooner you than me, Ruth. All that marching and saluting – if I wanted to be a soldier, I'd join the *ATS*. But I don't. Why would you?'

'Because the *QA*'s full of posh girls, of course,' another voice, too weary to be bitter. 'Posh like her.'

'That's not true,' although it was, of course. Both parts of it. The *QA* was scrupulous in selecting girls from good families, and Ruth would fit right in.

'You leave her alone, Maisie. She does her share; that's all that counts these days. Go on, though, Ruth. Why would you?'

'Oh, you know,' she said vaguely. 'I'd like to get away, find some sunshine. The desert might be nice, Egypt or Palestine, but that doesn't really matter. Anywhere but here.'

'And live in tents and be shot at?'

'It's no worse than living in digs and being bombed.' She was trying to make light of it, trying to sound superficial. Flighty and, yes, posh. Not making a very good job of that, she thought, but no matter. So long as no one picked up what she really meant. *I'd like to find a bullet, if there's one out there with my name on it. As all these damn bombs keep missing me.*

The following week, she was called into Matron's office.

'Sit down, Taylor. I hear you're thinking of leaving us.'

Matron famously heard everything. Either she had a spy network that rivalled whatever Hitler could achieve, or else her own chilly spirit pervaded the entire hospital, noting every sin and listening in to every whisper. Certainly that was what the probationers believed. Ruth used to laugh at the silly young things in their awed terror. It didn't seem quite so funny now.

'I've been considering it, Matron, yes. I haven't quite decided yet.'

'Indeed? Well, you may find that the decision is not entirely your own to take. This is wartime, you know.'

Ruth blinked. In anyone else, that would have been nothing but bluff. Wartime, of course yes, but nursing was a reserved occupation and she wasn't proposing to leave it. Only to leave here, a grey and hopeless hospital in a grey and hopeless city. If her new path led to a quick sunlit death in a distant land – well, that was her own affair and no great loss to her country, no great loss to herself. No loss at all to anyone else. She wouldn't throw her life away, but she must be allowed to risk it.

She shouldn't need to say that, any of that. Only, Matron didn't bluff...

They weren't alone in this little cubicle. A man sat in one corner, on a chair that must have been fetched in for him, cramped awkwardly between Matron's desk and her filing cabinet. His felt hat was perched jauntily on a plaster bust – of Aesculapius, Ruth rather thought – that was as unfamiliar in here as the chair or the man. He was soberly suited, middle-aged, crisply shaven. It was odd to see such a man without either the white coat of a doctor or the uniform of an officer; in honesty, though, it was odd to see a man at all in Matron's bailiwick.

Matron hadn't introduced him. That was odd, too.

He stirred now, said, 'Why the Queen Alexandra mob? Looking to be with your own kind?'

It was the same question, the same accusation; she hadn't expected it here. *'No!'* she said. Really she wanted to say *it's none of your business*, but Matron had scared her now. Perhaps she – or he – really could stop her going. 'Not that,' she went on more steadily, getting a grip, understanding this to be some kind of interview. 'I just feel that the war's ... elsewhere. I know that makes no sense when the bombs are falling every night and we're treating people in corridors because we don't have enough beds, but

9

even so. There's nothing we can do here but suffer. I want to, to make a difference. To be closer. To help the men when they need it most.'

All her justifications, trotted out to order. They sounded thinner than ever to her own ears, where she most needed them to carry weight. When she was done she felt oddly breathless, pent up, waiting.

He said, 'Hmm. You're a widow, I believe?'

It was easy for him. Herself, she still struggled to believe it sometimes. *I'm twenty-nine, and Peter—*

Twenty-nine, and Peter. Yes. They were almost the two facts of her life now, the twin poles that defined her. Twenty-nine seemed quite long enough in the circumstances, and Peter...

Peter had always been enough. And still was. No need for more now, no.

'Yes,' she said: the coldest, bleakest word she knew. *May I have my bullet now, or will you really make me wait?*

He said, 'If I asked you to consider something else, would you do that?'

Consider. It was her own word, unfairly used against her. She couldn't conceivably say no.

He said, 'We need experienced nurses, adults. People who have seen the worst of life, and death too. The worst of death.'

Oh, Peter...

Ruth said nothing aloud. She was revising her first estimate of this man. A doctor *and* an officer, she thought now. Who else could be quite so ruthless?

But then, they were all soldiers now. She had

10

said it herself, *the home front is as important as anywhere else*, and she could be ruthless on her own account. With her patients, and with herself too. Which was what this man was looking for, what he was seeing, what Matron had presumably promised him.

Ruthlessness and honesty went hand in hand, each drawing from the other. She said, 'You're not going to let me join the *QA*s, are you?'

'I think it would be a waste,' he said. 'Society girls doing their bit, bandaging troops and keeping up morale, squirting the mosquitoes. You're worth more than that. Come to me, I'll give you a job to stretch you to the limit.'

Yes. He would use her and use her, she could see that; he would use himself just as hardly. Not married, she thought. Not ever likely to marry. Like herself, now. *Oh, Peter...*

She said, 'Where is it, this job?'

'I can't tell you that.'

'Not overseas, though?'

'No. A train journey, no more.'

No bullets, then. And probably no bombs either. He had dressed for town, but she thought that was a rare event. He had the air of someone who had come a long way. The shadows under his eyes were nothing, everyone was tired these days, but not everyone had a soot smudge on their face and an overnight case tucked beneath their chair.

His shoes were scuffed, and she thought his feet hurt from pounding pavement.

She said, 'What is the job?'

'I can't tell you that, either.'

His own reticence amused him. She had to struggle a little not to match his smile with her own. To remember that this was not what she wanted, a challenge from a challenging man. A swift release and a sudden end, that was what she wanted. Yes.

'Nursing, though?' she pursued, just for the sake of it, just to appear calmly ordinary. As though her mind had never turned to thoughts, to hopes of death.

'Oh, yes. Nursing, absolutely. And the chance to make a difference to the war, that too. I can say that much. It's more important work than you will find anywhere else.'

That stymied her, perhaps. It took her credibility away. Nevertheless, 'And if I say no, if I go to the *QA*s anyway?'

'You might find that they won't take you. Despite your impeccable credentials. You might find that there is no way to come closer to the war, except through me.' Just for that little moment, his eyes were stone hard, absolute. *No bombs, no bullets.* As though he knew her inner self entirely. Then he smiled again, and said it again. 'Come to me. We'll give you a promotion, ward sister, how about that? You give us your best for six months, and if it doesn't suit, then I promise the *QA*s will swallow you up gladly and waft you away. You can have your pick of postings, as close as you like to the front. Just, promise to give us a fair try first.'

She had, apparently, promised. It felt now like a deal with the devil. No – even at the time, it had

12

felt like making a deal with the devil. It wasn't charm, exactly, but he had something irresistible in his manner, or more deeply embedded in himself.

He had gone away with his hat on his head and the bust of Aesculapius under his arm. She rather thought he might have been whistling as he went.

And now she was here, chilled and stiff on Darlington station as night faded into dawn, waiting under the milk-stained sky for the milk train to take her forward in pursuit of a promise she had not wanted to make and would keep regardless. Six months. She could do that, yes. And then a different uniform, a posting, the war, that relentless pursuit of a bullet. Yes.

The milk train came and carried her through a succession of valleys, hills that grew steeper and darker against the day, bleak moors and tangled woods.

At last one more station, yet one more, and the kindly guard there to hand her case down to her, to be sure she got off where she was meant to.

She stood in a watery sunlight and eased her back and gazed about her, understanding how the town, such as it was, spread that way along the river – *eastward, Peter, yes, towards the risen sun* – while all the valley else looked entirely grim. Unlifted by light. She shivered, scolded herself for being fanciful and turned away from the view, turned her mind to practical matters. She'd need a cab, she supposed. She had written orders to say where she should

13

report, but of course no map and no notion of how to find her way.

Here was the station forecourt, and of course no taxis. Only the one car waiting, a landaulet with the hood folded back and an officer drowsing in the driving seat. If the RAF had taken to moonlighting as cab drivers, she hadn't heard of it. She might have asked him whether there was any point her waiting, any chance at all of a cab's arriving; but he was at least half asleep, his back to the thin sun and his cap pulled low across his face. She really didn't like to disturb him. Especially when the answer was almost sure to be no. Petrol was short everywhere. She'd just go into town, ask directions and steel herself to walking. However far it might be, and however heavy her case.

Behind her the train was pulling out, giving a peremptory blast of its whistle at a level crossing. The sound was unexpectedly raucous, trapped here between the valley walls and echoing off the slab side of a mill. The man in the car startled, and sat up straight.

Ruth smiled, and thought she would still not bother him with pointless questions. She turned, hefted her case in her hand and began to walk the other way ... and was arrested by a sudden voice, cracked and hoarse but strong enough to carry.

'I say, excuse me...!'

Still expecting nothing, she stopped and looked back over her shoulder. He was half out of the car, almost falling over himself in his hurry. A very young man, she diagnosed. As so

14

many of them were.

Catching his balance, he was suddenly almost graceful as he came towards her. Not quite. There was something wrong: something in the way he held his right arm, awkwardly unmoving at his side. He didn't wear driving gloves, which any young man might not, but this particular young man, she thought, probably could not. One useless hand would leave the other necessarily bare, unless a friend helped out. Or he could use his teeth, perhaps, to draw a glove on, but...

She was surprised, a little, that he could drive at all. That was all but drowned, though, in a far greater surprise. Here was her promised car after all, at the wrong time on the wrong day and quite unlooked for. And her driver – well. She would never have expected this.

Even before he lifted his head and met her eye to eye, letting the sun strike in under the peak of his cap. She would still never have expected this much just for her, a flying officer with the kind of car her brothers liked to jaunt about in before the war. Even so: his injuries suggested some kind of recuperative treatment; his uniform said he was still on active service, which would justify the hush-hush nature of her appointment here; and his determined chasing implied that he was here to pick up a female. All in all, she did think this was her car.

Then she saw his face, and all doubt fled away.

He blinked, which was a thoughtful, almost an effortful process, nothing natural; and said, 'Miss Taylor?'

15

'*Mrs* Taylor. But yes.' She had been Miss Elverson once. That seemed a long time ago. Then she had been Peter's, and he marked her with his name. Now she was no one's, but she kept that name like a banner. She wore that and his ring together, not to let him pass from the world entirely before she must, before she did. Until that bullet found her, she would be Mrs Peter Taylor. A promise was a promise, after all.

'Of course. I'm sorry. Sister Taylor, I suppose you'll be, once you're settled and togged up. I like that better, I like to call pretty girls Sister...'

He was, of course, just talking to cover the double awkwardness, his and hers.

She couldn't offer to shake hands unless she did it leftwards, as she used to with the Girl Guides, long and long ago. That might be awkward too, unless he'd been a Scout himself. She opted for sternness instead, the widow scolding the insouciant boy. 'You really shouldn't talk nonsense. And yes, you should call me Sister, but not till I'm on duty. What should I call you? Flying Officer...?'

'Oh, Tolchard is my name, Michael Tolchard, but no one uses it. The fellows mostly call me Infant, but to the nurses I'm Bed Thirty-Four.' And then, heartbreakingly, 'Please, you mustn't mind my face. I don't, so why should you?'

He must have been endearing once, with all the attractions of youth and charm and very likely money too. Blond, she was guessing, though the evidence was sparse: no eyebrows to speak of, and his hair hidden under that cap. Pale hairs on the back of his left hand, as he reached

16

to take her case.

'Don't do that,' she said sharply. 'I can manage perfectly well.'

'So can I,' he said. And did, lifting the case and turning back towards the car, perhaps deliberately giving her a moment longer to recover. Very well. Nice manners, and she would take advantage of them. She could curse Aesculapius for not telling her more, not warning her of this at least. Two minutes in Michael Tolchard's company and she already knew far more about her new job, but she would rather have been prepared.

Be Prepared – that was the Girl Guides again. Some things clung. Perhaps she should have shaken his hand after all. Why did this boy make her feel so young, when in truth she was so very, very much older than him? Not only in years. Marriage and widowhood had accumulated layers of experience, enough to leave her drearily tired of life.

Tired until now. Now she was just exhausted, after a long wakeful night on a platform bench. Exhausted enough to make her foolish and gauche and over-thinking everything.

Michael Tolchard. Infant. Bed Thirty-Four. Very well. He was a patient, no more than that. Flying Officer Tolchard: a fighter pilot, surely, Spits or Hurricanes. She couldn't see him in a bomber crew. He'd have wanted the solo glory of a fighter, devil-may-care.

Wanted it and got it, of course. Gilded youth, he probably got everything he wanted. Until he chased one Messerschmitt too many, stray-

17

ed too far from the squadron, took on a fight he couldn't hope to win. And so the dreadful screaming plunge to earth, the struggle with the cockpit canopy, at last the blessed tumble free and the snap of the 'chute to arrest his fall and perhaps for a moment he thought the nightmare was over. Until he realized that the smoke and the heat had come with him, came from him, his clothes and hair still afire.

Perhaps he tried to beat the flames out with his hand. His right hand, of course, the good one. That was not much more than a claw now. Not useful to him. He had to put her case down to open the boot left-handed, before he could lift the case again and swing it in.

'Oh, just put it on the back seat,' she protested, too late. Surely he didn't mean to play chauffeur and make her ride behind him?

His eyes flashed a smile at her, across his shoulder. He had good eyes despite the swollen horror of the lids above, still showing the marks of their stitches. He had probably learned, probably had to learn not to try to smile any other way. It was a surprise to her – in this hour of surprises, but at least this was a *professional* surprise – that he could talk so clearly, with such a brutal slashing mockery of a mouth. His voice was damaged, to be sure, and that would be from smoke and flame inhaled as he struggled to breathe in the blazing fury of his plane, as he struggled to escape; but the sounds were clear despite the scarred throat behind them and the stiff clumsy semblance of lips he had to shape them with.

He said, 'I would, but we're picking up a couple more fellows on the way home. I hope you don't mind?'

'Not at all. Of course not. In truth, I never expected to be met. When I missed the train last night...'

He shrugged. 'Happens all the time. Or else the bally thing's cancelled, and people are stranded anyway. If we're expecting a person and they don't show up, someone always comes down to meet the milk train. Couldn't leave you to walk, we're in the next valley. There's no other way to get there, no bus, and it's a dreadful trek with luggage. And if a car's coming in early, there's always someone wanting a lift for this or that, so I get to play bus driver. It's usually me.' He opened the passenger door for her, saw her settled, walked around the long sleek bonnet to the driver's side. 'The car's rigged for me, d'you see? What with the hand and so forth. Deuced clever, but it's awkward for anyone who doesn't know the system. Easier to drive with one hand than two, actually. And I can make myself understood, at least, better than some of the chaps. Though I do still scare the horses. And the nurses,' he added with a sidelong glance.

'Oh no, young man,' Ruth said, 'you don't scare me. Startled me, I confess it, I wasn't expecting...'

'Frankenstein's monster? All sewn together, out of dribs and drabs?'

'You're no monster.' Though very possibly he had been as a child. Spoiled rotten, she speculated, his mother's own precious white-haired boy; redeemed perhaps by that charm that clings to the fortunate, and ultimately saved by war, by the need for sacrifice. He had given too much, she thought. And wondered what his mother thought of him now. Whether she came to visit, or only wrote.

Ruth scolded herself for leaping to conclusions in all directions at once. She took a grip internally, and scolded him aloud. 'As I said, it was the car I wasn't expecting. Don't take everything personally, you can't afford it and neither can I. You're not the only patient in the hospital. In fact, you don't seem much in need of a hospital bed at all.'

'The nurses do complain I'm never in it. I'm down for more ops, though, so I take advantage while I can. I'm a sort of guinea pig, do you see? What with the face and the hand, Colonel Treadgold gets to try all sorts of new techniques on me. I'm his lucky mascot; everything works, everything takes. It's a bit of a bind, to be honest.'

'Oh? How's that?'

He only shook his head. Perhaps driving took more concentration now than the carefree skills of yore. She let the question by – for now – and watched with a species of wonder how he worked the heavy car. The gearstick had been removed entirely; there was only a handbrake between the two front seats. She could hear the car's motor growl and shift from one gear to another, none the less. At last she understood that he was achieving that with a kind of wand that emerged from the steering column, that he could knock

20

up or down with the same hand that held the wheel while his feet danced between the pedals. She couldn't begin to imagine how much work and thought must have gone into this car, rebuilding it from the engine outward. Peter would have known immediately, instinctively – but she didn't want to think about Peter. Particularly she didn't want to start this new job with her mind focused on the past, past losses, the only loss that could ever matter. It would seem dishonest. She had promised six months, after all.

The car nosed its way through narrow streets to a cobbled marketplace. Tolchard sounded the opening bars of a tarantella on the horn, and two figures appeared from the doorway of a small hotel. They carried a crate between them; she wondered if she was being made the excuse for a smuggling expedition, contraband beer fetched in under the cloak of fetching her. Did she need to play strict Sister Taylor before she'd even reported for duty?

Apparently not. Tolchard was too sharp for his own good, or else her face was too revealing. He said, 'That'll keep the old man happy. The colonel's Devon-born, and he does miss his cider. Mrs Melcher has it shipped up specially. He'll offer you a glass tonight, but do say no. Unless you can't stomach beer under any circumstances, I mean.'

'Oh, I like beer well enough,' though it hadn't figured largely in her life, nor in her expectations. Nor at all in any hospital she knew. *Start again, Ruth Taylor. With a cleaner slate this time.*

The cider bearers were taking their time. One walked with a curious stiff gait, from the hips, unbendingly; the other needed both hands on the crate, and had to shuffle sideways as they came.

'Should we ask if we can help, perhaps?'

'No, no. Absolutely not. We only get an exeat for tasks we swear blue that we can do. It's really important, you'll find, to let us do them.'

'You mean they'd be humiliated by the offer.'

'Utterly. Brutally. They're fine as they are. Doing well.'

'Well, then. As we have a little time to wait, why don't you tell me something about RAF Morwood?'

'Well, I could do. That name's a fiction, for a start.'

'It is?' It was the destination marked on all her papers: blandly uninformative, not in any gazetteer she could find.

'Utterly. It must have been designed to confuse the enemy, if any enemy comes sniffing after us. I suppose they're bound to, sooner or later. When they do, they'll be looking for an airfield and find a big house; and then they'll find that the house is just a convalescent home for badly injured aircrew, with a genius surgeon attached. As witness.'

As witness himself, he meant, and his two friends who were even now heaving their burden on to the back seat. Introductions followed, while they squeezed themselves in on either side. Donald Carter-Fleck – dragged from a crashed plane with a shattered pelvis and largely

22

rebuilt from the waist down, as he told it, still learning to walk again – and Rupert Ronson, whose hands were savagely twisted in towards his wrists. 'My fingers look like boiled prawns,' he said, examining them ruefully. 'The Infant's my dry run, you see, my stand-in. The old man is practising on him, and once he gets that hand right, he'll work on mine. I wish he'd hurry up, to be frank.'

'Patience, Methuselah.' Tolchard might perhaps be a year younger than Ronson. 'Never rush a doctor, a sapper or a ... whoops. Beg pardon, Sister.'

'Don't worry. Infant,' using the absurd nickname deliberately, to let him hear the truth of it. From his point of view, she likely seemed very old indeed: married and widowed both, two stages ahead of himself. She wanted to keep that distance. 'Anything you've heard, I've heard worse.'

In fact the versions she'd heard had been different, and none of them had started with a doctor. The sapper was common to them all; Royal Engineers dealt with bomb disposal. The third element, the one he'd elided: the politest version she knew had a good-time girl in there, but they were all variations on a whore. Which she could probably say in mixed company with a deal more comfort than he could, and a deal more experience too. She'd treated some so often they were almost friends. She doubted he'd ever actually encountered one, beyond the occasional shouted exchange in the West End when he was out with his brother officers. In the old days, before his catastrophe. He wouldn't do that now.

She didn't want to be cruel, but if he ever grew too outrageous, she might accuse him with his own virginity, in front of his brother officers. Just to quiet him, and to see if his patched-up face could still blush.

Quiet in the car meant that she had a minute or two to pay attention to the world beyond. That long aristocratic black bonnet thrust between high banks and stone walls as they climbed, erupting at last onto open moorland. Sheep scattered across the road ahead, then abandoned it altogether as Tolchard played out another intricate rhythm with the unsubtle blast of his horn. He had been musical once, perhaps. She supposed he still would be, talent didn't burn away. But he'd have no singing voice left in him, and one-handed instruments were few. Perhaps he could learn to play bugle or cornet, trombone even, if he only had the lips to make an embouchure. After another surgery, perhaps. They couldn't mean to leave him as he was, surely, with that oddly articulate savage gash of a mouth.

'I tell you what's odd,' said Ronson from the back, 'these sheep – have you noticed how they never come over to our side of the hill? There's nothing to stop them, but they won't come.'

It was probably just as well. These restless young men would only use them for polo ponies, or some other outrage. Ruth was on the very verge of saying so when she was forestalled.

'Hefted,' Carter-Fleck said, 'that's the word. I knew a shepherd once, and he says a flock is hefted to their own land, and won't leave it. They're territorial.'

'Like cats, you mean?'

'Not much like cats, no. But still. If they're born on the land, they won't stray.'

'So much for the school chaplain and all his homilies. Another metaphor bites the dust.'

The height of the moor was marked with a tumble of exposed rock that the Devonshire colonel would no doubt call a tor. Now they were coming down into the next valley, and no, there were no sheep. She was learning an unexpected respect for sheep, just on this one brief journey. If she were free to roam, she thought she'd not roam in this direction. Of course it was just the angle of the sun and the slope of the hill, the dark of the woodland below, but she felt suddenly embraced by shadow and distance, very far from town or comfort.

'Now this is genuinely odd,' Tolchard said beside her. 'Never mind Rupert and his curiously static sheep. If you owned this land and wanted to build yourself a stately pile, wouldn't you put it somewhere up here, up high, for the view?'

'Yes,' she agreed. 'I suppose I would.'

'Quite. But you can't even see the house from here; it's hidden behind that bluff; and by the time the lane brings us around, we'll be down among the trees and seeing nothing.'

'Just as well, really,' from Ronson. 'In the circumstances.'

'Well, perhaps. But whoever built it, they weren't building for these circumstances, were they? I say it's downright strange, such a grand place being built so secret.'

Ruth wanted to ask what circumstances he meant, why a convalescent hospital might need such degrees of discretion. But by definition, such a question would be unanswerable. The wary practices of wartime held it back in any case, stifled in her throat. She would learn soon enough. Anything she wasn't authorized to hear would be common knowledge in the nurses' staffroom.

Random stones on either side of the road grew less random, grew into walls; and here were the trees, ancient and overhanging, so that the way seemed to sink between them. It was fanciful surely to think that this valley was both older and colder than its neighbour, but Ruth thought it anyway. Again and again those dry walls were broken by tree roots or leaning trunks, as though they'd been built up in a slowly desperate attempt to hold back the forest. Desperate and doomed, and perhaps by now abandoned.

They drove too far, she thought, in the swallowing shadow of the trees. At last they did have to come to a gate, though. Logic demanded it, and here it was: a new gate, indeed, of welded steel and coiled wire cruelly barbed, spanning an old rutted drive. The gate seemed pointless, given the slumped condition of the walls on either side. Likewise the armed guards hurrying from their sandbagged redoubt to haul the gate aside and salute the car through.

'This is actually the back way,' Tolchard said. 'There's a proper gatehouse at the far end of the valley and a better road, but we all use this. No point driving all the way down, only to come all the way back again. The old coach-road used to run over there, you see, before the railway came.'

And then the town would have grown around the railway, and the road must have turned to accommodate the town, and so the house found itself facing the wrong direction. Not actually moving, but ever more remote. She supposed that would be true of dozens, maybe hundreds of great houses, that they were caught in stasis while the world shifted around them. The war might even be a blessing, perhaps, finding advantage in that isolation, bringing purpose back...

Nonsense. Houses don't have purpose. Only people do that, and her own purpose was quite unaltered. These young men might have a brittle attraction and a deeper need that drew her deeply, but they were not irresistible. Nor was she irreplaceable. They would find other nurses to tease and amuse and depend on. She would serve her six promised months and be gone, once and for all, irrevocable. Yes.

She hadn't expected a sudden lake among the trees, it would have been almost the last thing she looked for, but here it was. Patently man-made, dug no doubt by a generation of navvies and fed from some high spring through a network of buried piping, it was long and straight and square-cornered, stone-lined. Above it were no more trees, only the terraced ranks of an old formal garden, given over now to vegetables between its paths and ponds and hedges.

The drive skirted one narrow side of the lake, giving her just time enough to lift her eyes up the broad flat steps of the terraces and find what stood above, darkly weathered and bleakly impressive, the house itself.

Just for that moment it lay in her gaze entire, all the height and the stretch of it, three storeys of old stone with attics over, and all its proportions wrong. The portico was minimal against the extravagant length of the house, the door it sheltered too tall, the windows all too small.

Then it was lost behind hedges as the drive took them up beside the gardens. She could see the house only sidewise and in glimpses, in the gaps. Knowing the military mind as she did, she was a little surprised that no one had troubled to trim the hedging; it would be a useful way to use up youthful energies and the heavy hang of time. The system that had men all across the empire whitewashing stones to line parade grounds should never blink at a little topiary.

Perhaps the CO here thought that fetching in his cider counted for more. But that was only one trip for one carload, an hour out of a day. There were people at work in the gardens, the orderly rows of greenstuff testified to that and she'd glimpsed uniforms through the rampant shadows of the hedge. And with patients as

28

ambulatory as these, then surely...?

Well. She'd find out. And it wasn't for her to be finding make-work or occupational therapy for bored convalescents.

Unless it was, of course. Unless that did indeed form an aspect of her job. She'd find out. For now she could only speculate. And here they were running past the east wing of the house, more of those small windows in a broad flat fascia unrelieved by Georgian balance or Victorian extravagance. She couldn't imagine what had happened in the owner's head, or the architect's. Nor how later minds and hands had ever made this place, ever *thought* to make it into a hospital.

Well.

The drive turned around the great bulk of the house, and behind was a courtyard framed by that long front elevation and two matching wings. The rear of the house was no more ornate; *just as brutal*, she wanted to say. In these parts perhaps they'd call it blunt, or honest. She thought it incomprehensible. Whoever built the house must have had money in quantity, surely enough for a little indulgence, a little decoration somewhere.

A separate stable block made the fourth side of the courtyard. That at least looked traditional: brick with stone facings, an archway through to the cobbled yard, a clock tower above. Whether there would be horses in there now, Ruth couldn't guess. She rather hoped there were. Airmen and cavalry were joined almost seamlessly in her mind, like squires and the hunt. These boys were all public school and old families. Horses must have been an intimate part of their childhoods, as they were of her own. She thought it would do them good to ride, those who could manage it.

Besides, she'd be glad of the chance herself, now and then. It had been too long.

But the courtyard here was full of motors, from Army lorries to tractors to motorcycles and an ambulance. Perhaps the stables were too. Horses might be seen as an extravagance; no room for them in wartime, unless they pulled a cart. If she thought them therapeutic, that might only be her own soul's yearning to go back, because she couldn't go on.

She might be alone. As alone as she felt, in this as in all things, abandoned, bereft. Betrayed.

Tolchard parked the car with a flourish of gravel, hard by a door into this near wing. Gazing at it, for a moment Ruth was simply lost to her own body. She sat where she was, quite still, because there was nothing more that she could do.

Not fear, not dread. Not acceptance. Some deeper feeling inhabited her, and she could not move against it until her young driver had made his cheerfully noisy way all around the car, opening doors for his friends on either side, finally reaching hers and holding that wide, bowing low like a footman, his appalling face glimmering with humour as he rose.

'Welcome to Morwood, Sister Taylor.'

He gave her the cue, and she found that she

could act on it. Because she had to, therefore she could: step out of the car, straighten her back, square her shoulders and confront this new dispensation. A new job, no more. It was never as bad as a new school, and would be over sooner. It was nothing like as important as a marriage – for example – although that had ended far too soon, *oh, Peter...*

'Thank you.' She didn't know what to call him, quite. His nickname was for his friends, his surname was for his superiors, his rank would be absurd. His bed number – well, if that was truly the custom here, she could fall in with it, but not yet. Not until she knew everyone else's number too. For now she elided the difficulty with a smile.

He knew, she thought. And did nothing to help her out, because he was young and wicked, amused, a boy: hurt in adult games too hard for him, but still a boy beneath.

Besides, if he offered a solution it would be a callous one. *Call me Mikey, as my mother does.* She was no one's mother, and never would be now. And he wouldn't know, wouldn't think, wouldn't understand the hurt. Being a boy, and so forth.

So, no. Let it stand, for now. She'd find her answer from the other nurses. She took a step towards the rear of the car, but he blocked her. 'Never mind your case, one of us will take that up for you later.'

'No, no, I should—'

'What you should do,' he said firmly, taking her arm in his, 'is come with me to meet the old

31

man. Report in. Salute and so forth. Do nurses salute? I don't know, but I'm sure you must...'

He was talking nonsense but his intent was nothing but practical, as he led her up two steps to the door. She went along because again she didn't have the option.

It was a plain plank door, unpainted and possibly as old as the house it inhabited. Not iron-bound or studded, nothing grand. This was a servants' way to come and go. Servants and children, perhaps, visiting the kitchens on a detour between nursery and stable. Not for family in the proper sense, not when they were being proper. These days perhaps it was a door for staff, and not perhaps for patients.

There was no handle and no escutcheon, only a keyhole deeply recessed, a cavity she could have slid three fingers into, three with ease. She wondered briefly how Tolchard meant to open it, with his one good hand so solidly clasping her elbow; then she saw the scuff marks and streaks of mud that adorned its lower planking and knew, even before he lifted his foot to kick it wide.

That seemed disrespectful, both to the door and to the house it guarded. She lifted her gaze, not wanting to watch. Lifted her chin too, stubborn in the face of defeat, fighting back a wave of dull exhaustion with the world. *Six more months, just six months. My promise and no more.*

She couldn't remember now why she'd ever made that promise. All she could see in front of her was the door, a flat barrier, dark and un-

32

promising, unadorned. It seemed appropriate.

Then her eyes found forms within the ancient wood: a knot here, a whorl of grain there, a scar from some injury long ago. They looked almost like eyes and a mouth; that was almost a face beneath the varnish of centuries.

It was a face, of course. It was Peter's face, emerging from the wood just at her own height as it properly ought to be, she was tall for a woman and he not for a man.

His face, wreathed in the smoke of his disaster, screaming.

Tolchard kicked the door open and she saw Peter fall away from her, falling and falling.

Tolchard stepped forward and took her with him, and she felt herself follow Peter, falling and falling.

TWO

'Well,' a voice said, 'I've known young women come fainting across my threshold before this, but I don't expect to find it in my nurses.'

She had, of course, expected Aesculapius.

This was someone else altogether. A burly man, balding, with a luxuriant silver moustache to compensate. His voice rumbled like a cannon-ball in a barrel; his hands were huge and un-expectedly subtle. She could feel the strength in them as he lifted her up, the delicacy with which he checked her pulse.

'Feeling better?'

'Ye–yes...'

He eased her back against something firm but yielding, the rising arm of a couch. She blinked a little dizzily, and lifted her head from its seductive solidity. It smelled of comforts, leather and tobacco. She could see the dark deep-but-toned back of it stretching away, her own body laid out along its length. Her shoes were miss-ing. No doubt she should say *where am I?* or *what happened?*, in her new unexpected role as a fainting female. But she knew exactly what had happened. She was quite clear about that,

34

she remembered it distinctly. The door...

No. She wouldn't think about the door. Better to focus on the professional shame of this moment; better yet to distract both herself and her interlocutor. She turned to look about her, and there *was* Aesculapius. Not the man, the bust. Set now in an alcove that might have been designed for him, where she might have assumed he'd stood for a century or more if she hadn't seen him being carried about London just a week ago.

Nothing else in this room suited it half so well. She couldn't guess, quite, what its proper purpose had been, before. Perhaps one would need to have grown up in those circles, to see a room with all its proper furniture stripped out and still tell at a glance the butler's pantry from the housekeeper's room from the nursery toy-store. Ruth's parents had been well-to-do, but never quite part of the country-house set.

Peter might have known – but actually she thought perhaps one would need to have grown up in this particular house, to know this particular room. Plain white wainscoting, with the plaster painted institution green above. That told her nothing. Nor did the off-square shape of it, nor the window that lacked a sill, nor that curious solitary niche in the wall. There were cupboards hidden behind the wainscot, she could see keyholes and fine brass hinges, but again those had nothing to say about what they were designed to hold.

Whatever its original use, the room had been taken over by a man with a whimsical practicality. This couch had surely been salvaged from somewhere else in the house. That desk likewise, a massive Victorian edifice with a bank of drawers in each pedestal. At this moment, the desktop was bare but for a stopped clock, a stiff-backed lamp and an elderly teddy bear who leaned against it, much as a drunk might lean against a street light.

The shelving on either side of the desk was new and utilitarian, burdened with books and files in that kind of tumbled disorder that speaks of constant use. The floor was uncarpeted, the window rather shockingly uncurtained. It was a sign of how war retrained the mind, Ruth supposed a little ruefully, that she could come round from a faint and gaze around an unfamiliar room and find herself thinking of the blackout.

If that was what it took to keep herself from thinking about the faint, about the door, about Peter – well.

Perhaps she should ask about the blackout. This might be remote country and far from any ARP wardens, but the law was still the law. Planes get lost, lights attract bombs; this was a military establishment. And more than a home for convalescent pilots, there seemed no doubt about that.

Good, more things to think about. To ask about, perhaps, if only to earn a snub in response. She was here to nurse, after all, not to interrogate senior officers about their other occupations.

Aesculapius watched from his alcove. Benignly, she thought. She wanted to think.

She was sure she knew whose office this was. Not this man's who sat above her now, in the chair he'd drawn over from the desk. Who watched her with a less benign eye, perhaps.

Whose moustache twitched hypnotically as he spoke, but best not to focus on that or she'd get the giggles and find herself in disgrace on her first day. More disgrace than she was in already.

'Want to tell me what happened?'

No. Aloud, she said, 'I'm sorry, sir, it's my own stupid fault. I can't remember the last time I slept properly, and I haven't eaten since ... oh, sometime yesterday. I should have thought to bring something, sandwiches, something. But I haven't been thinking any too clearly in recent days, it's all been such a rush to get here. Spending the night on Darlington station must just have been the last straw. I didn't try to sleep, I'm afraid. And then the motor made me feel sick, a little, and stepping out – well, I came over all dizzy,' *and the rest you know.*

That should do.

'Hmm. Nothing to do with young Tolchard's looks, then?'

'Oh.' In honesty, it hadn't even occurred to her – but of course he would think that. Wonder about it, at least. 'Good lord, sir, no. If a damaged face could make me pass out, I wouldn't have worked through the Blitz. I've seen worse than Flying Officer Tolchard. And no one so well patched up, either...'

He snorted. 'Flattery cuts no ice with me, young woman,' but she thought he was pleased none the less. Pleased that he needn't send her back, at least, as unfit for his purposes.

'Of course not, sir – but I look forward to watching you at work. Assisting in theatre, if I'm allowed to.' And then, determinedly bright and sitting up, 'Is this your office?'

'Not mine, no. M'colleague's, Major Dorian. Trick cyclist. You met him. He's not here today, but this was the best place to bring you. Otherwise it was treat you where you lay. Couldn't take you into one of the wards, let the men see their new ward sister flat on her back. Bad enough that those boys who fetched you saw you go. I've sworn them to secrecy and they'll keep their word, it won't be all over the hospital, but even so...'

'It will, you know.'

'Beg pardon?'

'It will be all over the hospital. By now, most likely. By lights-out, most certainly.'

'No, no. They gave their word.'

'And they'll keep it, I know – but even so. Did you carry me in here yourself?'

'Yes, I did. That Tolchard boy fetched me at a run, and...'

'And then you sent him off to, where, to the kitchens to fetch a glass of water or a cup of hot sweet tea, while you carried me however far this is from the back door? So the kitchen staff know that something's afoot, and so does any nurse who saw us in the corridor, and any orderly who was plying a mop in the vicinity. And this is a *hospital*, which is worse than boarding school for simple gossip. No one has literally anything better to do here than talk about other people.'

He blinked, slowly, as he thought about it. Then he said, 'Well, I didn't see an orderly. That means nothing. You're quite right, of course. There may have been faces in doorways, and scurrying footsteps. You'll just have to deal with it, as best you can. Come!'

That last was not to Ruth. Rather it was bellowed at the door, in response to a hammered tattoo.

It was, of course, Flying Officer Tolchard. With reinforcements, because he couldn't both knock and carry.

In this same house, in another world – before the war, that was – his drafted assistant would have been a housemaid, no doubt, or a kitchen maid. Perhaps the chance would come again. In the meantime, in this world, she wore another kind of uniform and would no doubt have saluted if she hadn't had both hands full of tray.

'I did ask for brandy, sir,' Tolchard was explaining, a little incoherently, trying to justify himself and his companion.

'I sent you for water,' the colonel observed, quite mildly.

'Yes, sir. I, ah, amended your suggestion.' Of course he did: young man with a reputation and no experience, dismissing water out of hand, wanting to do better by her. Fainting females required brandy, everyone knew that. Brandy or smelling salts, and only virgin aunts carried those. He wouldn't even know what they were. 'But Cook interrogated me – you should give that man to Major Black, sir, he's a natural – and then he wouldn't give me any brandy. He sent

39

soup.'

'So I see.'

So did Ruth see. Indeed, she couldn't see anything else, couldn't take her eyes from the covered bowl. Wisps of steam escaped the tin lid, filling the room with a savoury aroma, flooding her mouth with saliva. She hadn't been hungry, all night or all this morning; she had barely had an appetite for months, indeed, not since Peter...

Not since Peter. That was an absolute division, and it was still a surprise sometimes that the rest of the world didn't acknowledge it, didn't seem quite to understand quite what had been lost that day.

She was hungry now. Ravenous, apparently. The *ATS* girl was monstrously slow, deliberately tormenting her, laying the tray on the desk out of reach while she fetched a little side-table to the couch here, while she set a place with spoon and knife and napkin. Lifting lids aside to reveal first a plate of bread with a knob of butter, real country butter on the side; and then at last the bowl, the soup, brought to her.

It was just a broth, beef broth with vegetables and little dumplings floated in it. It might have been the most delicious meal she'd ever confronted. She barely paused to murmur an apology to the two men standing above her, 'I'm sorry, I hope you don't mind if I—' and then she did, she started whether they minded or not.

She was, dimly, aware of a conversation above her head.

'The man's a genius.'

'Yes, sir.'

'Did you actually tell him that she hadn't apparently eaten for two days?'

'No, sir. I didn't know. I suppose I should have thought, but...'

'Not paid to think, eh, Tolchard?'

'No, sir.'

'No, nor I. Just as well, in the circs. Nor Cook, of course, officially. Perhaps he knows these things by instinct.'

'Perhaps so, sir. Though I believe I did mention that she'd been all night on the platform, waiting for the milk train. I suppose one could deduce...'

'Yes. If one's mind moved that way. Better soup than brandy, one might think.'

They sounded curiously satisfied, for two men who had conspicuously failed to think any such thing. Ruth didn't care. She had soup. And bread and butter, but mostly soup. Soup was a miracle, all unheralded: working from the inside out, spreading a sense of well-being through all her tissues, warmth in her belly and comfort in her bones even before it made its insidious healthful way to her headspace. There would be no more visions of Peter's face in woodgrain, no. No more Marley-like visitations. No more passing out as she passed over a threshold. This was a regular hospital in a regular house and all it offered her was work. Work and soup. She would be grateful for that, for both of those. Work at a distance from all that had gone so sour down south, soup at a distance from any ration book.

She supposed she should hand over her ration

41

book to someone, at least for the gesture of it. And her other papers, the orders that had brought her here. That should have been first business on arrival. Ready now – and not going to wipe this last crust of bread around the bowl, no, not under two cynical, amused pairs of eyes – she straightened and set down her spoon, moved the table a little to one side to demonstrate how fit she was for work now, lifted her head to meet the colonel's smile and his strict instruction.

'Bed,' he said. 'I'll make that an order if I need to. Tolchard here will take you up. Your case should be there already, or I'll know the reason why. Lie down for an hour, give your body a chance. Then find my secretary. She'll see to the paperwork, and hand you on to Matron.'

'I say, I really am most terribly sorry.'

Of course he was, he was still a boy behind that dreadful face. Soaking up guilt like a sponge, as he would soak up any feeling else that came his way. She knew.

He didn't, of course. He was a boy; he had no notion of himself as the watching world might see him. Only what he saw in the mirror, that face and the constant need to outclass it, to be better than that. All ego, and all suffering, and all shame. She smiled to take the sting out of her words even before she said, 'Don't be ridiculous. If I didn't know myself that I was hungry, how should I expect you to divine it?'

'No, but I might have thought. Damn it, such a dreadful journey, and of course you wouldn't have found anything to eat on the way. Never mind being stuck overnight. You *told* me that, and...'

She couldn't console him, only distract him. 'I suppose this is the servants' wing, then,' as he led her up steep and narrow stairs, uncarpeted.

'I'm afraid so, yes.' That should have been tossed casually back over his shoulder with a quirky smile, a laughing glance, the flick of a floppy blond fringe. Another world. He kept his face turned forward, into the shadow of the stairwell. He was most sensitive, she realized, when they were alone. *Young man, do you have no sisters?*

She might guess the answer to that – *Mummy's white-haired boy, the one and only, spectacularly spoiled beneath his veneer of charm; spoiled on the outside now, and who knew what that might do?* – but she couldn't ask, of course. Not directly, at least. For the moment, she didn't need to. He was seizing the chance she'd offered and running ahead with it, distracting himself.

'What used to be the servants' and the family wings, they're staff and patients now. In that order. I'm afraid we do better than you. Our rooms are luxurious in comparison,' whereas here was hers: down a bare corridor, sisal matting underfoot, one door among half a dozen. At least she had it to herself, which was relief of the basest sort, a foundation to build upon. A single iron-framed bed, made up with military conformity and military blankets; a bedside locker, a toilet table and a chest of drawers all squeezed together where there was barely room for two out of the three. She would have to sidle in and out.

She didn't mind that. She didn't mind anything much, this whole adventure was just distraction for her – though she was trying not to wonder about the bathrooms. Old country houses were notorious for their lack of plumbing. She had visions of a pump in the scullery, shuddering morning scrubs with a queue behind her, hard soap and hard towels and hard bitter water.

'We're the Other Ranks, you mean, while you're the officers?'

'Something like that. Although you nurses count as officers, you know. And of course the doctors are all this side, even the old man; and actually not all of us patients are officer rank, officially. We have sergeant pilots too, and a few I'm not sure about at all.'

He was floundering, a little. She could be kind, she could move him on. 'So if this is the staff wing and the other across the courtyard there is the patients'–' with a nod out through her high mean window, no far views for her – 'what happens in the main house in between?'

'Oh. Ah. I, um, I can't tell you that.'

'Not even yet? Now that I'm actually here?'

'You'll have to ask the old man. Or, well, just keep your ears open. You'll pick it up.'

Was that shame again? Something was keeping him averted: from her, or from the truth. From confession. Something he didn't want to say.

Goodness. Well, as he said, she would find out soon enough. Directly or otherwise. And for

44

now: 'You get your head down,' he said, like a little boy instructing his nanny. 'Doctor's orders. You'll feel better for a sleep.'

Damn him, it was true. She chivvied him out – she only needed to sit on the unyielding bed and slip her shoes off again and he was gone, and yes, he could still blush – and submitted to the solitude, the silence, the great weight of the turning world. Lifted her legs on to those harsh khaki blankets, laid her head down on rough laundered linen and barely had time to wonder one more question – why was everything here so resolutely Army, when it was called RAF Morwood and devoted to the aftercare of pilots? – before discovering that in fact her body had greater weight than all the world together, was dragging her down and down...

'Well. You'll feel better for that, I make no doubt.'

The voice was firm, as unyielding as the mattress beneath her; its owner was in her room. Her private room, but of course nothing was truly private any more. Except what she kept in her head, her secret determinations. *Six more months.*

The invader was a short, stocky woman, dressed in darkest blue. Ruth opened her mouth to protest as she clicked the light on, closed it abruptly as her eyes focused. The cap and veil of a nurse; the insignia of a matron. This was Ruth's own most senior officer. She dragged herself to her feet, and almost saluted. Almost thought she ought to.

'How ... how long have I been sleeping?'

'Long enough. It's time for tea.'

That wasn't tea she'd brought, though. A broad enamel bowl, rather, and a ewer of steaming water. A bar of soap, a towel.

'Have a wash, and bring yourself downstairs. Just follow the noise, you'll find us.'

'Oh. Ah, do I have time to change...?' She felt suddenly that everything on her body had been there for too long.

'Yes, of course. The longer you take, mind, the later you'll be.' *And the more chance everyone will have to stare at you, when you come* – that went without saying. She knew institutions of old.

'I'll be quick. Uh, Matron...?'

'Well?'

'Thank you for bringing these yourself. You didn't need to do that.'

'No, of course not.' She could have sent anyone with washing water and a summons. 'I wanted to introduce myself. I'm Elizabeth Ingliss, matron here at D'Espérance, and that's probably the last time you'll hear my – why are you staring like that?'

'I beg your pardon, Matron, but *what* did you just say?'

'Oh – D'Espérance? I don't suppose it's the last time you'll hear that. It's the old name for the house. No one here uses it officially, but Cook always does, and so of course do the locals. I think the change of name is meant to be more secure,' but she clearly wasn't convinced.

I don't understand, why does it need to be

46

secure? What are you protecting here? Ruth did actually take a breath to ask, but habits of secrecy were too ingrained, questions were impossible. That was Peter's influence again. Of course it was, everything was Peter. They were one flesh, indivisible, death not enough to part them; and she was all the flesh he had now, so naturally whatever she did would be coloured by his choices.

She let the words die in her throat, and earned herself a little nod from Matron. Was she really so obvious, were her thought processes written so clearly on her face? Did that mean that Peter shone through her, those times that she so clearly heard his voice...?

There was no telling, and still no way to ask. Matron left. Ruth poured water into the bowl, stripped off her blouse and rinsed grime from her face, wishing only that she might shift her weary resignation as easily.

The clouded water showed her nothing as it stilled. No reflection. There was nothing to be learned in any case, of course, no art to read a woman's future in her face. Peter had taught her not to believe in omens; she tried to cling to that. She did try. It was just ... unfortunate ... that earlier lessons lay deeper, at the heart of her. And that his own death had been so ominous, trying to teach her other lessons yet.

Teacher, instruct thyself. But he had done that, of course, he had lived and died believing in the physical world, whatever he could determine and measure and control; and in the idea of

England, more than just geography; and in her. More than anything, she thought, he had believed in her. More than grateful, almost desperate, he had clung to her even in the hollow fragile peace, restless and uncertain, struggling to find or make something solid and dependable in a time of shift.

They had struggled together, built it together, a marriage that could endure. And then the war came, as it must; and then more than ever he had needed her, and she had been his rock. So busy doing that, perhaps neither one of them had noticed actually how much she had needed him.

All her presentiments, all her anxieties were natural, of course, in a young wife in wartime. Proven right too, but there was nothing unusual in that either. Young men do die, and their widows will look back and see those deaths foreshadowed. And feel guilty, blame themselves. If only they had said this or not done that, not let him go at the last, everything would have been different and some other man, some other woman's husband would have died in his place, and that would have been better, yes.

She couldn't live without him, there wasn't any point. She couldn't live with herself, it was too distasteful.

She couldn't see anything in the water. There was nothing to be seen.

She straightened, and turned away.

For a wonder, there was a glass in the room. Hung of course in the darkest corner, small and square, the mirrored door of a little cabinet. Hung of course too low for her, but no matter, she could stoop. And she need only make herself presentable, pull a comb through her hair and be sure her cap was straight.

Just a glance, no more. It wasn't as though she cared, only that Matron was safe to be a stickler for neatness. That was laid down in regulations, that all matrons must be tartars.

So, a stoop and a squint, leaning one-handed on the chest of drawers with her other hand reaching already for her toilet bag to rootle out her comb, and—

And that wasn't her face peering out from the shadows, no.

Blessedly, not Peter's either. Just for a moment the world had faltered again, she'd been afraid.

Not a face at all, nothing peering. She saw a blankness, a pale blur, and thought the mirror somehow fundamentally broken, its silver fogged, as unreflective as the wash-water.

Until she understood that it was *turning*, that pallid wash of light. It was not quite featureless, and she could see it spin within the glass. Spin and rise, as though it reached to engulf her.

Or no, she must be spinning as she fell because now she was falling into it. Even standing entirely still in her room here, she could feel the sudden chill, the damp as it soaked her through and through. She could feel the sick giddy spinning, even while she felt the utter solidity of the furniture beneath her hands, the floor beneath her feet.

And now she had fallen entirely through the cloud and there was the land below her, the patchwork fields of England that he loved even as he plunged towards them, and she could feel the weight of the parachute on his back and the stubborn treachery in his hand as it didn't and didn't and didn't pull the ripcord, as he fell and fell and...

I am not going to faint.

Not going to.

Not.

Not again. She was oddly determined about that, even as her own world spun dizzily about her, as her gaze was drawn down and down into that sucking well. She was not going to faint again. That was all that mattered.

Almost all.

She might die, she thought. She might be found dead. That wouldn't matter, except that it would be a bewilderment – her bones all broken, as though she had smashed to ground from miles high, just here in her own room beneath a plastered ceiling – and she really didn't want to attract any attention to herself. It wasn't about her, really not. Only the impossibility of living on, the dreadful dragging weight of it day after day after—

Not going to, and so she didn't faint.

Neither did she die.

Gradually, the fixedness of furniture and floor drew her back into her own body. Her swirling mind rediscovered rootedness, that sense of presence, *here I am*. With that came *who I am*, not Peter, and so not falling, no.

The mirror ... failed. Today. No promises for tomorrow. But today she stood firm and was strong, and that spinning chaos faded and was blank again, and then was nothing but ill-silvered glass and she could just see her own face in it, if she stooped and peered.

Actually she could just see her own face in motion as she twisted away, looking anywhere but there. Wanting to pull away entirely except that she needed to lean hard on both hands still, *here I am*. Trembling through to the bone of her, prickling with sweat all over, sick and dizzy again with the reaction.

She was late, then, in finding her way downstairs. Very late, perhaps. She wasn't sure. Her watch had stopped, at about the same time that she fell – no, that she *didn't* fall into the mirror.

She had washed again, despite the scummy water. And had put on her old uniform, for lack of a new one yet; and had barely troubled with her hair at all, determined not to look again into the glass. Perhaps no one would notice, with the wrong cap perched so blatantly atop. Perhaps they would all busy themselves with telling her how very incorrect her dress was, and what to do about it.

Follow the noise, Matron had said. In fact she followed an orderly with a trolley, but she really didn't need to. There was rather a lot of noise.

And that was before the orderly used his trolley to nudge open the green baize door at the end of the passage. The trolley was weighted with a steaming urn, which she guessed to be reinforcements, a second round; but it wasn't only sound that washed around the orderly to greet her, as soon as that door swung wide.

51

There was an aroma also, instantly distinctive. Not tea.

No hospital she knew would tolerate such a racket from its staff, no matron of her acquaintance would condone it for a moment. And that was beer that she was smelling, impossible and unmistakable, a heady tang that caught her throat with memory and yearning. *Beer...!*

She would have hesitated, even in full sight on the threshold there, only the orderly just barged straight in and she seemed to be caught in his wake, to have no alternative but to follow.

In the passage, that weight of sound had overflowed her like a wave released. In the doorway it would have been a wall, that solid, it would have stopped her entirely if the trolley hadn't broken through ahead of her.

She felt it none the less, every brick of it, every separate voice. Her head dropped just a little, her shoulders hunched, as though she were walking into a wind. One step, two steps—

Then she realized. And stopped dead, right there, two paces into the room; and straightened her spine, squared her shoulders like a soldier on parade, lifted her head and looked about her.

This was a hallway, seemingly, or should have been. An open area between the servants' wing and what must be the main family rooms, with a stairway leading up – the East Staircase, she supposed they would call that – and doors in all directions.

They couldn't conceivably be short of space in this enormous house, and yet they had chosen to lay this hallway with trestle tables and eat their meals here. She would have called it the staff canteen, except that some of these men were very clearly not staff. The rowdy ones, for example: some in uniform of one description or another, uniform and dressings, some in dressing gowns and slippers. Those were surely patients.

She might have called it a dining hall, then, set aside for walking wounded – and she might have been casting about already for a glimpse of Bed Thirty-Four, young Lochinvar, young Tolchard – except that some of these, men and women both, most certainly were staff. There was Matron herself, presiding at one of the tables. Presiding over dressing gowns and uniforms together, all mixed ad hoc; and some of those uniforms were nurses, some orderlies, some officers. Ruth was confused already, even before her eyes were drawn again to the rowdy congregation around the piano.

A piano, standing at the heart of all this noise. And a congregation, a *singing* congregation, half of them with pint mugs in their hands. Doing that thing that men do, wrapping their hands around the body of the glass rather than use the handle.

The other half couldn't manage to hold theirs, by the handle or otherwise. Their drinks were lined up on the piano top, with paper straws.

Two men shared a bench at the piano. She could barely see through the packed bodies, but they weren't playing a four-handed melody. She thought perhaps they played one hand each.

She thought she knew where Bed Thirty-Four might be found, if she cared to push her way through the crowd.

There was no question of that. Among the singing congregation, one voice in the multitude, a man in an overcoat between the dressing gowns and the blue serge: that was Aesculapius. *Major Dorian*, she reminded herself sternly. Already she thought he had noticed her. Indeed, he was tilting his mug towards her in a greeting, in a toast.

She ignored him magnificently, stalking over to Matron's table to ask where she should sit.

'Why, here today, Sister. With me,' and the short woman reached out to touch an empty chair on her left. 'Another day, you'll take a table of your own; another again, you'll move around. You'll find us ... not so much informal as irregular. In many ways. One day you may even join the choir,' with a nod towards the piano, where those two invisible hands were breaking down catastrophically over *Greensleeves* in waltz time. 'Today, though, I thought you'd likely have questions, and I'm your best hope of an answer.'

Meaning *I want a closer look at you, young woman, I want to see what Aesculapius has sent me.* Ruth wasn't fooled for a moment.

Still, she did indeed have a flood of questions, all dammed up. Better to loose them than turn inward once again, towards that sucking void at the heart of her. Far better, so long as Major Dorian had his eye on her. Beer or no beer.

She opened her mouth, then, to ask the first of them, and—

'No shop!' It was a curious parrot-squawk of a

54

cry, rather terrible, and it came from the man sitting opposite her. Half the skin of his face was drawn pale and sheer, like greasy silk, in brutal contrast to the vivid colour of the other half. She thought one eye was glass. It was as though he wore a demi-mask, as though he could be two men in one, depending which way he was facing.

The voice suited neither one. Its clarity was almost obscene, given how far it was from human. Birds, she thought, should not have voices; certainly should not gift them to men in their extremity.

'Squadron Leader Jones,' Matron introduced him, trying perhaps to quell him at the same time.

If so, it was a hopeless endeavour. 'Tubby,' he said, 'people call me Tubby around here,' and once perhaps it had not been ironic. Certainly the jacket he wore had been cut for a wider man. He looked almost gaunt within its loose folds as they fell around him. The sick burn fat, as do the sorrowful. She had been plump herself, once, it seemed an age ago. *Blame the ration, and never worry.* What did she need of flesh?

Besides, he was still talking, distraction, what she was here for: that dreadful voice, savage and precise. 'No talking shop in the mess.'

'Squadron Leader Jones.' Matron was professionally sharp, conspicuously not calling him Tubby, and not actually repeating herself even though each word was the same. This was a conversation, unless it was a ritual dance, each step prefigured and familiar.

'You can say what you like, Matron–' even if that was just his name, apparently – 'but rules are rules—'

'And rules change, when you cross the border.' That was his neighbour on the other side, another of these too-thin young men in ill-fitting uniform that might once have shown his frame to advantage. 'We've been over this, Tubby.' Over it and over it, Ruth was guessing. 'This isn't your mess, it's Matron's tea table. We don't wear our own ranks in here.' Which was true, she realized, and one of the things that jarred: bare epaulettes on all these uniform jackets. 'And we don't fetch our own rules either.'

'Matron flings our ranks around willy-nilly.'

'Not willy-nilly. Only to scold. Isn't that right, Matey?'

'I'll thank you, Flying Officer Kaye, not to call me Matey.' But she said it with a glimmer of humour around the purse of her mouth, and it raised a grin in him. He was lucky, he could still grin. His damage was elsewhere. Ruth couldn't see it immediately, and she wasn't going to peer, nor pry, no: but she was sure that it was there to be found. To be learned about. As and when. There were orderlies down the table, but orderlies had their own proper uniform, RAMC fatigues, familiar in any military hospital from here to Timbuctoo. Every military hospital Ruth was familiar with put their walking wounded in uniform too, *uniform* uniform, regulation and distinctive. Something was different, apparently, here.

No, *everything* was different, apparently, here.

56

Driving out into the world, Tolchard had worn a normal uniform jacket, with insignia. So had his friends fetching cider for the colonel. She was starting to think that perhaps they had only a few such, which they shared between them on exeats. Here in the house, the patients wore their own old uniforms, but stripped of rank. That was only indicative of something that ran far deeper and mattered far more. Something that she kept glimpsing, but could not seize.

Something that she wanted to blame on Aesculapius, whether or not that was fair. She wasn't stupid; she was fully aware that it wasn't only the most obvious patients around this table who exhibited damage. If she were bolder, she might wonder what Matron's secret was.

Though she'd never be bold enough to ask.

There were other questions, though, and she'd been invited to ask those. The uniforms were easy, were obvious; and there was her own uniform too, not regulation, she needed to ask what to do about that. She opened her mouth and was interrupted by a blast of singing that would have drowned out last orders in an East End pub, and she could barely hear herself as she said instead, '*Beer*, Matron? At teatime?'

In a hospital? – but she wasn't of course going to add that. And didn't need to, because it was absolutely inherent in her tone of voice, in her question.

Matron's face was eloquent in its response, and actually more informative than what she said.

'By special dispensation, yes. It's supposed to

be reserved for Major Black's boys, except on special occasions, but of course they exploit the privilege. And their senior officers connive with them–' her eyes finding out Aesculapius, Major Dorian, who had been away for the day and come in and not even shrugged off his overcoat before he joined the communal singing – 'so of course everyone takes advantage, as soon as they can shuffle from the ward to the piano. That seems to be the major's definition.'

Which major, and his definition of what? Who is Major Black, if he's not the surgeon and not the psychiatrist? What goes on behind those doors there, in the central block of the house?

Her mind was abuzz with questions, her tongue tripped over them. She was too slow with any. The squadron leader squawked across the table: 'Matron, you know we love you and fear you and would do anything to please you—'

'Just so long as I don't come between you and your beer, am I right?'

'Of course. But I'm drinking tea today, just so that I can sit with you.'

'Young man, you are drinking tea today because your friends have heard your singing voice and they won't let you join in. How naive do you imagine that I am?'

He smiled down at his plate, glanced sidewise at her, didn't answer. She snorted, and turned back to Ruth.

Who managed, if not quite a question, at least a step towards one.

'I don't believe I've met Major Black yet.'

'No, likely not. He doesn't trouble himself

58

much with the nursing staff. He's not interested until a boy's ready to leave my side.'

Any hospital was an exercise in territory and hierarchies, just as the military was. Even so, this place was beginning to remind Ruth of nothing so much as a boys' boarding school. At least as far as she understood them, from the stories of Kipling and *Tom Brown's Schooldays* and what Peter had told her of his own.

Matron kept her patients as long as she could, and then handed them over – reluctantly – to this Major Black, for whatever purposes he had in mind. With Major Dorian's clear consent, indeed, with his collusion. There was more to it than beer and a sing-song. She glowered at the piano troupe, and found herself once again eye to eye with Aesculapius, across that gulf; and blushed, and turned her head away, back to Matron's bird-bright gaze.

'When may I see the wards?' It was nothing but defiance, to declare her proper loyalty. *I belong on your side.*

'After tea. You can join the colonel on his rounds, meet your patients at last.' *Mine,* her voice declared, *until I have to let them go.* 'No more than that, mind, I'm not having you on the duty roster until tomorrow. You've come a long way, and that little sleep won't be enough to set you up for the work you have ahead. Especially if you don't eat. You haven't touched your cake. I won't let you lift a hand, you know, until I'm satisfied that you're ready.'

Ruth gazed down in mild startlement at the slab of dense sticky gingerbread set before her.

'I, I'm sorry, Matron. You know, I can't quite remember the last time I saw a cake like this?'

In truth she had lost the habit of cake, almost the habit of eating. Except what was necessary, enough to keep her going from one day to the next, not to be a nuisance or make an exhibit of herself.

She thought the little tyrant on her right was not fooled for a moment. What she heard was a snort, and, 'Well, it'll do you no good looking at it. I want to see a clean plate, my girl,' for all the world as though she was herself back at school again, a gawky adolescent with too much else on her mind to worry about the minor things like keeping body and soul together.

'Yes, Matron.' Meekly, not to be a nuisance. Picking up her fork.

THREE

In the end, because she wouldn't – *wouldn't* – catch his eye again, Aesculapius came to her.

'Well, Sister Taylor? Settling in?'

'Yes, sir. Thank you.'

'Well. Take your time, don't rush things. It'll all be a little strange for a while.'

The sharpness of her answer surprised herself, perhaps, more than it did him. 'I'm here to work, sir, not to take things easy.' *I'm not a convalescent. Not one of your patients. No.*

'Of course. Nevertheless. Tompkins, if you're done with that chair...?'

The orderly sitting at her other hand had conspicuously not finished his tea, but the major's word had him draining his cup in one throat-aching swallow and running off with a wedge of cake still clenched in one hand, trailing apologies as he went.

Major Dorian chuckled, and annexed the vacated chair. 'You're thinking that wasn't kind,' he observed, uncannily accurate. 'Tompkins is a lingerer. If he's late on duty one more time, he'll go down in his sergeant's report as a malingerer. He needs chivvying. It's kinder in the long run, to be a little unkind now and then.'

'He's afraid of you.'

'Yes. Yes, he probably is. Most people here are, a little.' He considered this, as though it were simply another datum; and added, 'You're not.'

'No.' In honesty, she was afraid of very little now. Except her dreams, some nights, perhaps. There might have been a reason why she didn't stretch out on a bench at Darlington station and try to sleep.

Here she seemed to have waking dreams; Peter was everywhere.

Well, but what did she expect, coming to a hospital full of pilots?

They didn't tell me...

No, because something here was top secret, something more than a hospital full of pilots. Aesculapius must have known, she thought, how Peter died, he must have seen her file. He must have known how she would feel coming here, or what else was a psychiatrist for, what use was he?

He must, surely, have known; and yet he had approved her anyway.

Ruthless. It had been her first impression, and she saw no cause to change it now.

Ruthless, but...

Ruthless but careful, that would do for now. He would use whatever came to hand, use it and use it but not – she thought – damage what he might need later. A man who looked after his tools. He said, 'They tell me that you fainted on the doorstep.'

As I stepped across your threshold, Aesculapius. Make of that what you will. She herself wanted to make nothing of it, she wanted it to mean nothing that she had seen Peter in the door's wood, falling.

Of course they had told him, though. She had been carried to his own office, laid out on his couch. Perhaps he thought that she belonged there. One more patient to be analysed, one more skull to examine from the inside.

She said, 'Yes. I'm sorry, it was stupid of me. No food in far too long, and a wakeful night. Not even nurses can run forever without refuelling. As Matron has been reminding me,' with a firm turn of her head to draw in that redoubtable woman, and a forkful of cake to busy herself with.

'Hmm,' he said, utterly unfooled. Unpersuaded. 'Well, if it happens again – despite Cook's generosity, which is unbounded, and Matron's watchfulness, which is legendary – come to see me. Don't try to carry on regardless. The work here will take it out of you in any case, as much as you have to give. If you start with something missing, you'll end up taking harm, and I won't have that.'

'I'm perfectly all right,' she said. And then, a little belatedly, 'Sir.'

'To be sure,' he said. And then, after a wicked pause that just matched hers, 'Oh, to be so sure...'

He left her feeling small and young, diminished. It wasn't fair – it wasn't kind, no – when she had worked so hard to be the other thing, mature. Complete. Done with the world now, ready to move on.

Unexpectedly done with her plate too. She'd been afraid that the gingerbread would sit like lead in her stomach if she managed to swallow it at all, but she had seldom been more wrong. It melted somehow on the tongue and filled her with a warm benevolence, a sense of well-being that was almost frightening, it was so utterly unfamiliar.

She looked to Matron for consent to leave the table, and saw a looming figure behind her, Colonel Treadgold. His the voice she might have missed from the sing-song around the piano, if she'd only been paying attention and thinking straight. His bluff manner and mustachioed splendour made him a natural, surely. A bass baritone, most likely, laying down the path that the lighter tenors walked. And quaffing beer – no, cider, he was a cider man, but quaffing with the best, surely...

No, again. Something else to remember: he was on duty. So was she, now. Ward round, and he was here to collect her.

'Ordinarily,' he said, 'staff cross the courtyard from one wing to the other, coming on and off duty. Rain or shine. Tonight you have a special dispensation; you're with me, and so we may trespass in Major Black's domain. Besides–' in a pantomime whisper – 'he isn't here just now, he's stood his team down till tonight, so the coast should be clear.'

64

'Colonel...'

'Hmm?'

'Who *is* Major Black?' *And what's he up to, and why do you all tiptoe around him, why does he get first claim on anything? This is a hospital, and you're senior surgeon. And a colonel. You outrank him every way you can.*

'Ah, you'll meet the major soon enough. Let that happen in its own good time.' *No need to dash to damnation,* he seemed to be saying. Which was no answer at all, and only left her the more frustrated.

Which he knew, of course. She thought the moustache was hiding a smile as he opened a tall door and ushered her through.

No suggestion of servants' quarters now, suddenly everything had changed scale. She stepped into darkness and couldn't sense walls or ceiling, anything, until he touched a light switch by the door.

'Oh. Goodness...'

Electric chandeliers glowed into life, high overhead.

Shuttered and stripped, silent and empty of life, this was still a magnificent space. The wide parquet floor was sprung beneath her feet; every window bay held an upholstered seat beneath the barred shutters; above the chandeliers, the ceiling was an arch of glory, a masterpiece of plasterwork and colour.

'It's a ballroom, surely?'

'It was a ballroom, of course. Not for a while now, not for a long time. It wasn't we who killed the dancing. Perhaps it will be a ballroom again,

65

but that is out of my stars. For now – well, as you see.'

Major Black's domain. Yes. She saw, and didn't quite understand what she was seeing. Trestle tables collapsed and set aside against the long wall, they might be used for anything. Stacked chairs explained themselves. The gouges in the floor, the ruined varnish – well, heedless military occupation, of course they wouldn't trouble with the varnish, any more than they trimmed the hedges.

Ammunition boxes, stacked beside the chairs. Again, they might hold anything. She didn't want to think of this beautiful room being used as a rifle range. The sandbags piled up against the far end, though – and the sand that had spilled out of them, all across the floor there – did make her wonder. Did make her sniff the air, and frown, and, 'Surely they don't...?'

'Oh, they do. Indoors, outdoors. Popguns and worse. Night and day. You'll grow used to having your sleep disturbed. Oh, but you've been in London, of course. You'll be used to that already.'

I'm a nurse, Colonel dear. I have been a wife in wartime. I am very, very used to that already. It wasn't only shooting that went on in here. There were tailors' dummies marked with arrows that had little or nothing to do with tailoring. *Punch here*, she guessed, *to disable, here to silence, here to kill*. There were man-sized silhouettes painted on the walls and pierced with many gashes in the plaster: St Sebastian in effigy, except that she thought that the damage

66

probably had more to do with flung knives than arrows.

She did wonder what the owner of the house might have to say about such wanton vandalism, when he reclaimed it after the war. Assuming that he did so, assuming that he survived and England too, that it wouldn't be the Nazis who were next to requisition his property.

She followed the colonel from one room to the next, and found herself apparently in a world that contravened her own assumptions, that tracked her own thoughts. Here were Nazi uniforms racked and ready, for when those invaders came.

If that was the ballroom they had just traversed, this must be the supper room, smaller and less stately, still grand. Repurposed now as a robing room for German officers: regular army grey and SS black, summer and winter weights, overcoats in wool and leather, boots on shelves and a library in Gothic black letter print to browse through while they waited for a fitting.

They did, all too obviously, wait here for a fitting. There were chairs and footstools, coffee tables, signs of use. Shoehorns on long handles – boot horns, she supposed. Tailor's chalk and pincushions.

Ruth blinked, and realized it had been a while since she'd done that.

Realized she'd been standing, staring, quite a while now.

Lifted her eyes to his, ready to apologize; saw his smile, his quick shake of the head.

'Don't worry,' he said, 'and don't ask. Mum's

the word, yes?'

She nodded mutely, followed obediently.

Out of the supper room, and here was another, grander hallway. Here was the front door at last, with its two leaves and heavy bolts; here was the main stairway, dividing overhead and sweeping down in two mirror-image curves that met again in the last flight. Like a swan's wings, she thought, grace and power embodied in a line.

Here was a racket, all unexpected, footsteps thundering overhead and voices raised in an incoherent whooping.

Here was something stranger, a shadow that flickered in and out of vision as she lifted her eyes, a shadow that seemed to turn and tumble in that great open space overhead, between the light and her, *oh, Peter...*

She might have thought he was coming down to find her, only that he wouldn't make so much damn noise about it.

It was hardly possible to be sure of anything, but she was sure of this at least, that he wouldn't have screamed as he fell. Not her Peter. As long as he wasn't burning, as long as the fall had put the fires out.

In any case, this was no haunting. This was young men on the ramp: hurtling downstairs, yelling their heads off, doing ... something with all that height and air, and—

Oh.

Oh, yes. Of course.

Feeling slightly foolish, she stood beside the colonel and waited while his errant charges came charging into sight and down this last long flight, still making noise enough to wake the devil, while their failed experiment clattered down to earth ahead of them.

She probably didn't feel as foolish as they did, these three boys, when at last they lifted their heads and saw Nemesis waiting for them.

'Oh, lor',' one of them breathed, as they stumbled to a halt on the fine floor, stood almost to attention. As straight as they could, perhaps, with their various hurts on parade. The one who'd spoken was perhaps the only one who could actually speak; the others she guessed had been contributing their share of noise, but shapelessly.

Even now, she thought, they were expecting leniency. They thought it was their due.

They were probably right. The colonel raised an eyebrow, but not his voice at all. He said, 'Gentlemen. *Strictly* necessary?' in a voice that expected the answer yes.

Expected it, and duly got it.

'Oh yes, sir. Training, sir.'

'*Training*, Barrows? Do enlighten me,' in that tone of voice that says *I'm looking forward to this, but you should probably not be.*

'Sir. All sorts of things you can do with a kite, sir, in the dark. The major's had us practising with them for weeks now. And then we had to go up top to fix the blackout, sir, after last week's storms, so of course we took advantage—'

'Yes, of course you did—'

'Of the *opportunity*, sir, to practise with the kites from the roof there. And then, well,' he

69

sounded suddenly a little less sure of his ground but carried on regardless, 'then it just seemed the thing to do, to see if we could make a kite fly in the stairwell here, if we could get up speed enough as we came down, and—'

And conspicuously not, but conspicuously that didn't matter any more. The colonel had lost that hint of shared amusement, any sense that they were all lads together underneath.

He said, 'Wait. Stop. You have been flying kites, from the roof?'

'Well, yes, sir...'

'Is anyone still up there?'

'Yes, sir. Dumpty's there. He said he wouldn't come down with us, on account...'

'On account of the severe vertigo, I expect?' The colonel's voice had become something unexpectedly complex, dealing in justified dread as well as fury. 'I thought there was one of you missing, and of course it must be him. So you left him up there, did you? On his own?'

'Uh, yes, sir. He wouldn't be left behind, when we went up. But, but, he's quite comfy where he is, quite safe. And he won't try to move without us, he's not a fool...'

True or not, the assertion came too late. The colonel was already on the move, brushing men aside as he headed up the stairs.

He was a big man, and determined, but not fast on his feet. Ruth could overtake him, while the men below were still wondering whether they ought to.

In honesty, she wasn't really certain why she should. But vertigo on a roof did not sound good, and the colonel thought the case serious enough to haul his bulk up flight after flight, as fast as his legs might manage it. Really, that ought to be enough. It was enough. Here she was, ahead of him. On the first floor, and going higher. The staircase not so striking now, all beauty spent; but still grander than anything she'd seen in the way of stairs so far, because this would be where the house guests strayed uphill.

Up, then, up and up. It was hard, taking stairs at a sprint. Nursing toughened the body, though, as much as the spirit. She could do this. This, at least, she could do. And look up as she went and see a circle of dark, which must have been a fabulous skylight before the war, as wide as the helix of the stairs, a complex circular frame of glass and wood meant to send daylight tumbling downward.

Now it was all dark, blackened from the outside because how would you fix a blackout from within? But there was a ladder on the top-most landing, rising to a hatchway, a door to the outside. To the roof. And that door was standing open, despite the fact that lights burned below and there was no curtaining, no screen. That would be a reason to fall on the errant patient, scathing and imperious: *don't you know about the blackout, how could you stand here and let this shine up for any passing bomber...?*

It was always good to have an excuse, to disguise anxiety as anger. Bash them about a bit, exhibit some righteous indignation, keep them abashed.

Even so, Ruth wasn't about to erupt through the hatchway like an avenging angel, justified or otherwise. Not if the man out there was uncertain in his balance. She was horribly aware of all that glass, and the plunge beneath.

Swiftly up the ladder, then, but slowing at the top. She could hear the colonel at her back, beneath her, hauling himself up that last turn, breathing hard. So was she, though, breathing hard: which gave her an excuse the other way, to pause at the head of the ladder, just her head pushing up through the hatchway into open air. She could look like she was blown, no more than that, while she looked about, and—

Ah. There he was, and yes, well stowed for a man with vertigo. It was stupid, of course, being a man with vertigo, being on a rooftop at all. But young men could be stupid, and young airmen more than most. They seemed addicted to risk. If warfare didn't or wouldn't put their lives in danger, they'd seek it out elsewhere. Peter had been a test pilot when she first met him. War was almost a substitute for that, she had thought sometimes, not quite up to the mark.

If you'd been through war and come out scathed – and come out with vertigo, which was odd in itself for an airman, surely something deeply significant, something to ask Aesculapius about – then of course you'd want to sit on the roof and fly kites. Even if you needed a boost from your mates to get you there, and would be stuck where you were if they abandoned you.

Stuck where he was, he was still flying kites. A

kite, at least. Probably he used to call his aero-plane a kite, back when. Now he was a man like any other here, bad face and bad hands, barely able to hold a string between them. But he sat against a convenient chimney stack with his legs spread out across the leads of the roof, and he played tug-and-come-again with both hands on his kite string, and seemed quite happy at it although his face was hard to read.

Until Colonel Treadgold coughed heavily, significantly, on the landing below her. Too much the gentleman to be discourteous, to start up the ladder before she was safely off it – or simply too much of a man, not trusting his weight and hers to the same frail risers – and far too much the gentleman to hurry her up directly, he fell back on the audible nudge. Which was audible to kite-flying Dumpty as well as herself, because so much body of course had power and resonance beyond his reckoning.

Which brought Dumpty's head flying round to find the source, and finding her. And scrambling to his feet any old how, despite injuries and vertigo and all; and letting go his kite string in the process, and realizing a moment too late and making a despairing grab at it anyway; and his eyes and hers following the kite as it soared away beyond reach, beyond limit, bizarrely into the midst of a flock of starlings wheeling to-wards their evening roost.

That frantic snatch had overtoppled him, so that his arms were wheeling for a balance no longer there. The fatal suck of the skylight hung below him, black-coated but still glass in all its fragility, all its threat. Ruth could see it happen in her mind's eye, how he would fall and fall through in a terrible shatter, how he would fall and fall.

He was falling already, except that she was there. Drawn by his need and her duty, impelled by the colonel from below, she felt almost translated from the hatchway to the rooftop all at once. Just in time, her experienced arms caught hold of him, loaned him the balance he lacked. It's a nurse's knack, to keep a heavy man on his feet at need.

His head lifted to find her, perhaps to thank her. She couldn't tell, he never came that far. For a moment his eyes looked over her shoulder, to where she could hear the colonel puffing through the hatchway. Then they clouded abruptly, as though a storm had rolled into his skull. His body lost that grateful cling and he slumped utterly in her arms and now she really couldn't hold him but she wouldn't let go, so that they were both teetering on the edge of calamity, that long drop calling to her. Just a tumble, a shatter she'd never feel, and there would be Peter waiting for her; and wasn't that better than a bullet...?

Apparently it wasn't allowed her, even now. She could feel herself, both of them going, the dead weight of the body in her arms and the living struggling body that was herself not giving up, not even now, but going anyway – and then suddenly there was a third beside them and a strong grip on her shoulder, something to lean on, solidity.

And that was the colonel, and she might have sagged in his arms if she hadn't had a sagging body in her own and his voice in her ear, 'Steady, now. Just lay the man down. Do you need help?'

'No, no,' she gasped, meaning *yes, yes, don't let go* ... But he took her at her word, and apparently she was right, or he was. He could let her go and she wouldn't fall, not now.

She lowered the unconscious airman to the leads, just by the curve of the glass there but safely so. She felt most extraordinarily safe herself, crouched beside the great trunks of the colonel's legs. They were like pillars between her and the fall. She could put that from her mind and do what she was meant to, nurse the sick.

Loosen the airman's collar, check his breathing, try to bring him round. Vertigo, was it, that made him faint? Well—

Something struck her head, and tangled in her cap.

She didn't scream, it was too strange for screaming, but she sat back on her heels and reached up. And touched stiff spikiness and warm softness both at once, and felt the flutter of life in it; and snatched her hand away and almost did scream then, only not with the colonel standing there. And would have reached back determinedly to pluck the thing out regardless, except that just then there was a shadow on the gray matt of the leads beside her, a dot that grew startlingly. She barely had time to glance up before here it came, a bird, a starling falling out of the sky.

Falling, or plunging. Hurtling. It seemed to come down faster than it should. And hit its own shadow hard, hit the leads and broke in some way, horribly, and barely moved again.

And here came another, and another, hitting the roof to left and right, dying or dead already. She risked one more glance upward and nearly lost an eye, barely had time to bat the thing away from her face. It fell like something dead already, but so fast...

And the sky was dark above it, dark with birds; and she barely had time to duck down again and cover her head before they hit like hail all about her.

She heard the colonel swear, then heard his bellow: 'You men! I need you, two of you up here, two at least...'

They would be for her patient, to carry him down out of this. For the moment she could crouch over him on all fours, feeling the impact of the birds on the arch of her back like thrown snowballs, stinging hard. Soon enough there were new voices, raised and roughened with shock, emitting strange oaths. That must be the kite flyers come to the rescue, wading through dead birds as they came. And then, 'All right, Sister, we'll take him now, if you'll just...'

She crawled backwards to be out of the way, and came up against the chimney stack and that was welcome, something almost shelter. She could huddle against that and peep through her fingers to see them hoist their unconscious colleague and bear him away, manhandle him down through the hatchway while they tried to shield themselves and each other against the rain that kept on coming, the constant fall of birds.

The colonel had pulled his jacket up over his head, for what protection that could offer him. Now he came pacing over, almost like a bird himself, like a heron spreading its wings to cast a shadow over water: except for the sheer bulk of him, nothing bird-like in those legs.

'Come now, Sister. Your turn, let's have you out of this.'

'Colonel, what—?'

'I don't know. Some freak electrical discharge? Ask the boffins. I swear some of these birds are *smoking*. I'd say lightning, but there's been none. Come *on*...!'

He took her under his wing, as literally as he could manage, and they stumbled through birds ankle-deep as far as the hatchway. Still bombarded all the way, more and more birds plummeting helplessly, thrown down. Once she was on the ladder his bulk above her served as protection, and there was no courteous nonsense in him now, no waiting. She had to move fast to avoid his big feet coming down on her fingers on the rungs.

There was a scatter of birds on the landing too, those that had fallen through the open hatch. Only a scatter, though, and she could ignore them all, except the one that wasn't quite dead yet, that hauled itself over floorboards at her feet. There was something infinitely creepy about that, and she couldn't keep from backing away. She should go with her patient, but the men were well ahead of her, a turn and a half down the broad wind of the stairs. It was only polite to wait for the colonel to come to ground, before she went down with him.

He fussed for a moment on the ladder, pulling the hatch closed, shutting out that storm of birds, and then huffed his way to the bottom. And looked at her, saw where she was and what she was doing – and somehow that great foot of his just happened to come down blindly, firmly on the crawling bird.

Ruth shuddered, and lifted her eyes to find him as bereft of words as she was. Overhead, they could still hear the impact of bone and feather striking on the great glass skylight.

Afterwards, she wondered if perhaps they shared a telepathic moment, she and the colonel. Some transient touch of foreknowledge, that had them both finding each other by eye and then moving together, still speechless but backing away from the open well, his arm sheltering her again as they huddled against the wall as that shatter came at last, and—

Oh, Peter...

—there was a shape in all the falling glass and she thought it was him, she thought that he had come for her. Only it fell apart as it fell and no, not him: only an aggregate of dead birds and black glass, though it really had looked like a man coming down and she had every reason to scream, every reason in the world.

Nor was she the only one. Voices of shock came

echoing up from below, something to hide her shame in; the colonel's arm was something to clamp on to until it became a reason to let go, to find her self-control and wield it strictly.

To pull herself erect and clip smartly down the stairs to where staff and patients were milling about, only waiting for someone – her – to take charge; to organize them in such a way that her own ignorance and newness didn't matter, sending some for brooms and bins, mops and cloths and soap and water, some to seek out tarpaulins for the roof.

When Matron came, she could hand all that over and have someone show her to the nearest cloakroom, where she could finally wash the filth from her own hands and emerge to find the colonel unexpectedly waiting for her.

'We were interrupted,' he said, deliberately bathetic, forcing her to laugh. But he was right, of course. Every patient was a priority; ward rounds must still go ahead, whatever the excitement elsewhere. In London, they happened with the air full of cordite and dust. She brushed a feather from her uniform, suppressed a shudder, carried on. The fainted man would be in bed by now, and thoroughly doctored. Neither of them mentioned or needed to mention a flock of birds mysteriously dead.

Here was a passage with fine rooms leading off; here was something to talk about, a question she could legitimately ask, or she thought so.

'Why not use these–' drawing rooms and dining rooms, high and wide and handsome – 'for your wards?' Why make the nurses walk so far from their own accommodations, why walk so far himself? 'They're large enough, surely, you could fit ten or a dozen beds in each, with lockers and cupboard-space in plenty...'

'Too large,' he said. 'Our lads, they're better in small rooms, three or four together. No more than that, and sometimes that's too many. You'll see. Besides, Major Black has a lien on this corridor as well, for the other aspect of his mysteries. Lectures, training, tests. Interrogations.'

He shrugged, but she thought only because he'd steeled himself to do it. He was not by nature in the shrugging vein. A shrug might be dismissive, or it might be defeated; Colonel Treadgold was neither. If she could be sure of one thing, she was sure of that.

Who is Major Black, what is he, that you should try to shrug at him? Unconvincingly?

This walk had taught her one thing, given her one part of an answer: he was teaching these damaged men to fight again, with whatever weapons they could manage.

That wasn't enough, though. Not to justify all this space and all this secrecy, Nazi uniforms, guards at the gates. Not to make a Regular Army surgeon shrug as though he didn't care, as though it didn't matter what Major Black did with his boys. Whether or not he was done with them himself.

Ruth did think that might be an issue, that the colonel would not want to give his patients up. Not hand them back to the chaotic force of war, after spending so long and working so hard to make them whole again. Imperfect, marked for life, but ready for the world: just, not the world of Major Black. She thought.

She'd not yet met Major Black, and already she was lining up with the colonel in some fancied war of possession. No surprise. It already seemed obscene to her that so many people should give so much to heal the young men of this land, only to see them sent back to the bullets and shells of the front. As though they were lorries and tanks and aeroplanes, in for swift repair and swift return. It was why – one reason why – she had worked in civilian hospitals, until cold despair overwhelmed her.

It was the one great argument between herself and Peter. Even before his plane had fallen from the sky, fallen away from him, left him to fall and fall.

Another smaller hallway, another staircase, the West Stair no doubt; and the colonel took her up, only waving an arm towards the ground floor of this wing. 'Through that doorway? My surgery, your treatment rooms, the pharmacy. If this house is a hospital at all, that's where you'll find it.' His territory, he meant; his last redoubt, she heard, against the depredations of Hitler on the one hand and Major Black on the other. War and the revival of war, and only him to hold the dreadful space between. 'We stow the boys upstairs, purely for the staff's inconvenience. The men are fine, there's a sort of dumb-waiter affair, a paternoster that takes them up and down on stretchers or even in their beds, those who aren't on their feet yet. I'm afraid it's the stairs for us...'

He was, she thought, just talking. Not from nerves, or not his own. In anticipation, rather, trying to grind her edges down, to leave her a little numb from the simple constant flow of words, the soft weight of his voice like a cushion between her and what he meant to show her.

It was a kindness, no doubt, but quite unnecessary. She knew what she at least was here for. She knew her job, and she was good at it. There was nothing in nursing that could make her blench. She was no silly probationer, to scream at the sight of maggots in a wound, or a skin sloughing off with its dressing, or...

It was just as well she felt herself prepared. Her own pride lent her a stiffness, a rod in the spine that carried her – just – from room to room in Colonel Treadgold's wake. Every step she took, every conscious turn of her head, every nod and every word stood as a reminder to herself that she could do this, see, here she was doing it, step and turn and speak. So of course she could do it again, why not? Again and again, a step, a word, another glance. Another horror, laid out like a specimen and to be treated the same, just a specimen. Don't think of him as a person, as a boy, no. No. Don't think of Peter, oh no, not at all.

That should have been easy, really. After all, Peter had never made it this far, to visible damage and a hospital bed.

But he had been with her all day, all unannounced; and none of these boys was him but he might have been any of them, if he'd only had

82

the patience and the nerve.

She seemed to see him everywhere. Not this time in knots of ancient wood or the broken silver backing to a mirror, no. Still inside her giddy head, alas – but at least she was looking at flesh-and-blood young men, and knew it. And knew that she was only drawing inferences, drawing Peter's lines on their abused bodies. This wasn't madness or illusion or deceit, only a terrible regret: *I have lost my man, he is dead, when he might have been like you. I should have preferred that, but it was his choice in the end.*

Here were men in the raw, Treadgold's material, untouched as yet by his subtle knife. Men with disfigured faces and twisted limbs, ruined once under fire and then again by nature as she strained to make good what was far beyond her healing. Ruth knew. Her eyes were brutally experienced, and half of what they saw in bed after bed – the worst distortions, the extremities of pain – was what happened after the bullets, after the shrapnel, after the fire. When bone tried to knit to bone, whatever shattered bone there was; when muscle lost its memory, flesh forgot its purpose, skin grew over any open wound it could and battlefield medics were glad to see it happen, called it recovery, signed off their patients and passed them up the line.

To Treadgold and men like him, whose first work would be to undo that rough impatient healing. Cut through fresh skin and muscle tissue, break new-knit bone apart. She knew. She'd seen it in her own wards, again and again. Civilian bodies healed themselves as well as military ones, or as badly. She'd seen joints dislocated by their own ill-laid muscles working against them; she'd heard men scream with pain when they tried to walk or lift a weight, when their skeletons betrayed them.

She thought she'd seen it all – but these were only the new intake, candidates for surgery and treatment.

Here was another room, nothing in the corridor to distinguish it from its neighbours. A typewritten sheet was pinned to one panel of the door, listing the names and ranks of its occupants. By their bed numbers, Ruth noticed with a private smile. *Where are you, then, Bed Thirty-Four? Not this corridor, I'm guessing.*

Inside, four beds, drawn up two and two on either side of the windows. Not patients fit to wander, these, not up for tea, for beer and a singsong. Each bed was occupied. An uncanny silence hung in the little ward, nothing to do with this sudden incursion of a senior officer; there had been no noise coming through the door, and there was none of that sense of sound swallowed, the abrupt hush of a dormitory almost caught in sin. These men lay wrapped rather in their own silence, trapped in stillness, rapt.

One, the nearest, had his arm flung up across his eyes. Not a gesture against the light: the shutters were closed, and only a single dull bulb burned to light the nurses their way from bed to bed. It took Ruth a little time, a little too long to see how a tube of flesh grew like something alien and strange from the inside of this man's elbow, reaching out and down to engulf his

84

cheek. His arm was tied in place with bandages, but actually it was his own flesh that bonded it.

'All well, Johnson?' The colonel's voice was hushed in deference to the gloom of the room or the possibility of other patients' sleeping, or else simply by professional practice. Even a whisper had impetus, though, with that much mass behind it and that much sheer intent. Colonel Treadgold was a rock, a mountain, rooted deep in the earth's crust. He murmured, and everyone stirred. Ruth hoped never to hear him shout.

'Tickety-boo, sir.' The patient – she should probably stop thinking of them as boys, but it was almost irresistible; in tousled hair and pyjamas they looked younger yet, mere children – peeped up from beneath his bent arm. He might have been smiling. It was almost impossibly hard to tell, in the weave of shadow and surgery.

'Not too uncomfortable, the arm?'

'Hideous, sir,' but he seemed strangely cheerful about it.

'Still cramping up, is it?'

'Yes, sir. But the nurses give me a massage when it's bad.' Ruth wasn't sure, but that might have been a wink.

'No doubt they do. And no doubt it's worst when the nearest nurse is pretty, eh? And not so bad when he's a big gruff orderly? You don't fool me, my lad. Nor anyone else. This is Sister Taylor, who'll have charge of this corridor from tomorrow. I'd put her wise to the worst of your tricks, only I won't need to. She's as sharp as they come, she'll see straight through you. And your cronies, too.'

While he talked, those fat nimble fingers of his were touching, assessing graft and skin and stitches: like a blind man reading Braille, she thought, learning everything he needed from his fingertips.

'Sister,' the young man said, 'I've been meaning to bring this up, you're obviously the person I should complain to. On behalf of us all, it's not just me: but they have a barrel of beer in the corridor upstairs, and we don't. That's just so transparently unfair, I don't even need to argue it, do I? There'd be no better way for you to start your new regime, than to fight our corner on this. You'd have the whole corridor behind you.'

There was mischief in his eyes, but no malice. He didn't expect to win; she wasn't even sure that he wanted to. It was the game they were all engaged in, playing up to the colonel's expectations, the naughty boy and the indulgent master, with her the strict nanny caught between.

Well, she could do that. She wasn't above obliging with a stern touch now and then. Especially now, when she needed to prove to herself at least that all young men were not the same young man, not hers, not Peter.

'Oh, and do you imagine that my nurses have nothing better to do than chase up and down the corridor all day to fetch you jugs of ale? You can have your beer when you're fit to go and fetch it – which means when the colonel gives you leave to leave your bed, and not before. No sneaking out to join your friends on the floor above, and no inviting them down to party in

86

here so long as they bring a jug. Do you understand me?'

'Yes, Sister.'

He seemed not at all subdued. Colonel Treadgold whiffled into his moustache, and seemed
content. Honour satisfied all round, she thought.
Parts played, territories established. Move on.

Next bed, a man who would absolutely not be
sneaking out of bed, because his legs were
bound together, the skin of one calf being encouraged to grow over the raw flesh of the
other.

Introduction, examination, banter; the mixture
as before. She must be careful to learn their
names and histories, these indistinguishable
boys. It mattered, she knew, to the patients, that
their nurses remember who they were.

Next bed. A man whose face was being rebuilt,
feature by feature. His nose sculpted from a
shard of his own shin bone, his jaw a jigsaw with
nothing yet to cover it. Cheeks to come.

Next bed...

And so on and on, all the length of the corridor.
Men with no faces, with no voices, with no
hands. Other injuries too, but faces, voices,
hands seemed to predominate. Perhaps because
those were a pilot's most vulnerable features,
least well defended, quickest and easiest to burn.
Or because they were how he met the world and
how the world best knew him, what Ruth or anyone first noticed, so the harm done there seemed
that much greater, it lingered in her mind and
drove out all hurts else.

Or else there was another reason, why patients

predominantly hurt in face and hands should be sent here. To Colonel Treadgold, or else to Major Black.

'You think I've given you a hard row to hoe,' the colonel said, as perceptive as he could be gentle, 'the surgical ward, men in their extremity. Well, it's true – but only because all rows are hard work here. You're better off with the surgical cases than the convalescents. At least you know that they'll stay where you put them, by and large. And you don't have to deal so much with the Galloping Majors, trying to hurry your patients away from you before anyone's ready for it. And you have the best of the nursing staff and the orderlies to help you. Come with me now, and I'll introduce you.'

That wasn't fair, to put her through the wringer first and then expect her to do the polite, shake hands and remember names, faces, duties.

No doubt it was deliberate, though. He would have his reasons. Or else they would be Major Dorian's reasons, some devious plot on his part to make some oblique point, to chivvy her obscurely into some desired response. She did think the shadow of Aesculapius hung over all the hospital, much as her own loss hung so precipitately over her. It was only hope and a kind of determined professional wartime optimism that let her assume that his was a more benevolent watchfulness, that something good underlay all his machinations.

She smiled and shook every hand, repeated every name, struggled through minimal conversations until she could seize the first blessed cue that offered, make a sleepless night into an excuse, apologize, retreat.

Not back through Major Black's terrain this time. She found her own way, alone at last and utterly thankful for it, across the courtyard in the dark. Wasn't country dark supposed to be impenetrable? She'd grown up under city lights, with rarely a glimpse of stars. In recent months even the blackout hadn't helped, with the East End aflame night after night. Here in this remoteness, where she might have looked for night like a blanket, the Milky Way slashed across the sky like a myth realized, a canyon inverted, a rip in the heavens, needing small help from the tardy moon to spill light enough to see by. It was almost bright enough to throw shadows before her feet.

It was plenty bright enough to distract her, to let her dizzy mind focus on this alien cast of light and how it guided her feet across an alien ground

She was already stepping up, reaching out to its solidity, before she remembered about the door.

Peter's face rising out of the wood, himself falling into it.

Herself, falling and falling.

It's just a door.

That was in her head somewhere. Not even a thought, it was something more realized than that, more certain. Almost a voice. Her absolute understanding of the world, that doors were things of wood and craft, man-made, nothing to be afraid of.

She wasn't afraid, no. Only hesitant, now that she'd remembered. Barely hesitant, still reaching. A casual watcher probably wouldn't even have seen that falter in her fingers. And besides, there was no one here. No one watching. It was only in her head that she was so constantly observed. Studied. Colonel Treadgold and Aesculapius: one bluff, the other an incisor. Both with their reasons, good reasons to be watching the newcomer. Matron too, no doubt, it wasn't all men.

It wasn't all Peter.

Here, now, it was none of them.

Blessedly alone, she reached again and couldn't find a handle.

Remembered that there wasn't one, decided not to kick it the way the young men did.

Set the flat of her hand to the wood of the door, and pushed.

Just in that little moment between touch and effort – when information flowed one way and not the other, *I can feel the door* before *the door can feel me* – she thought she heard a voice call her name.

Distantly, shrieking, in a dying fall.

Too late to jerk her hand away. She was already pushing, leaning into it, moving forward as the door opened.

Moving into darkness, real darkness, stepping into it because there was no choice, she was committed. She had momentum. That was what had carried her through all her life so far, except for the sudden block of Peter's death, that teetering halt on the edge of something terrible.

90

She had got herself moving again, with tremendous effort – praiseworthy effort, she thought, except that no one had seemed to notice – and never mind what she'd been moving towards.

Then Aesculapius had changed the points ahead of her, shifted her on to a new track. Complicated her metaphor and her life. It was still her own relentless pursuit that actually kept her moving, brought her here.

Momentum.

It carried her forward now, into the dark, and let the door swing shut behind her.

This, now. This was the true dark, utter dark, what she'd fancied to find in a country night.

And there behind her was the doorway that she'd fainted through. She stood in a space she'd never seen, and had no idea where the light switch was.

There was no window, or else it was masked by better blackout than she'd noticed anywhere else in the house. There did have to be a light switch. Didn't there?

She groped behind her and was almost surprised to find the door still there, rough timbers smoothed by age, by centuries of hands. Hands that groped in the dark. She couldn't be the first who tried to find a knob, a latch, some way to pull it open, to let that vivid starlight in.

There didn't seem to be one.

Which was nonsense, surely. With no handle on the outside, there must be one within.

There was a keyhole, she remembered. On the outside.

In here, too, Her fumbling fingers found it, deep recessed. Inaccessible. No key.

It couldn't be locked, it was not locked; she had just pushed it open and walked through.

It ought just to pull, then, but she couldn't find anything to grip. It seemed as smooth on the inside as it was out there. There needed to be crosspieces, didn't there, braces holding the planks together...?

Still. She couldn't open the door.

She reached to one side of it and then the other, running her fingers over roughcast wall, feeling for that light switch.

Not finding it.

An old house electrified late, not built for it: the switch might have gone in anywhere. Very well, then. This was some kind of hallway, a lobby, a servants' route in and out of the house. Flagstones underfoot, a chill in the air – and another door somewhere, access to the house. Closed against her, shutting out light and sound for now, but certainly there must be another door. With a knob, a handle, a way to open it. Of course. All she had to do was find it.

The alternative was to crouch in a corner, huddle in on herself, wait to be rescued. No. She had spent one long, uncomfortable night dwelling in her own memories, under the stars. She wouldn't do the same again, in this pitch black. That would be unbearable. Besides, what should she say in the morning, discovered: 'I couldn't find my way out'?

Pathetic.

Unbearable.

Well, then.

Plasterwork under her hands, from the door frame towards what must be a corner. She could feel her way all around the walls, until she found that other door. At least she wasn't susceptible to night fears, whatever curious tricks her mind might have been playing in her exhaustion, under the long burden of her sorrow. She didn't believe that uncanny creatures lurked in any darkness. This was just a room that lacked a light, and she was a mature sensible woman and would find her own way out of it, and—

And now that she was standing still, utterly frozen by the shock of it, yes, she could hear his breathing in the dark, but actually it wasn't that which had seized her first, made her understand so instantly and utterly that he was here in the room with her.

It was the smell of him, immediate and unmistakable: bay rum and wet wool and warm living flesh, the way he had come home to her time and time again, the way she had met him in their small hallway and unbuttoned his overcoat for him because his own hands were too stiff and unwieldy in the cold, still fumbling to peel off his driving gloves. Oh, she used to scold him for not stopping the ancient Austin, not putting up the hood against the weather, driving home so stupidly in the rain. But in her private treasury of moments these were precious to her, almost beyond measure. They had been precious even then, when she thought they were only a stopgap, moments of mothering him that would satisfy until they had children.

Now she reached in the dark there and found him, physical beneath her questing hands; the damp wool of his overcoat and himself inside it, standing, breathing.

Nearly, nearly she spoke his name.

FOUR

Instead, it seemed, she screamed.

At any rate, that elusive other door flew open and a light clicked on, and there was a shadow that resolved itself into a woman, a nurse, another sister striding in. And here was Ruth standing trembling in a cloakroom, her fists buried in a man's overcoat where it hung from a hook on the wall, just one among a dozen others.

'Oh,' she gasped. 'Oh, how stupid of me. I'm sorry, I'm not—'

I'm not making any sense today. Or *I'm not coping,* or *I'm not up to this after all.*

She was not, apparently, letting go of the overcoat. The weight of it, the smell of it, the way the thick fabric bunched between her fingers – of course it wasn't Peter's, it wasn't even Air Force blue but still she stood here, still she gripped it, she must look half mad, but even so.

Even so, the newcomer had to walk across the flags and unpeel her fingers for her, because she simply couldn't do it for herself.

'You're Sister Taylor, aren't you? My name's Judith, Judith Trease. You look quite done up. Come along, I'll fix you a mug of cocoa in my room before bed.'

'I'm sorry,' again, 'I'm making such a fool of myself.' Fainting first and now this, some kind of hysterical reaction. 'What you must think of me...'

'Sister ... what is your name, anyway? For I'm not calling you Sister Taylor all the time, unless the men are listening.'

'Ruth.'

'Ruth, good. Now listen to me. You were there for the unpleasantness, weren't you, that flock of dead birds? And then the colonel took you down his surgical corridor, I know. He will do that, he believes in baptisms of fire, though it's an unfortunate phrase in this place, and I'm sorry you heard me use it. Listen, no one comes through that unshaken. You cling to anything you can reach, girl, so long as you do it where the men can't see you. We all have something, one way or another. Me, I shut myself away and crochet mittens for my cousin's children. It gives me something to hope for; they're too young for this war, and with luck they'll never have to face one of their own...'

Somehow, passages and stairs had passed beneath their feet while the older woman talked. Here was Ruth's own corridor, here her own room. Here she was still walking, going by.

Two doors down, here was her new friend's room, much like her own. Judith's room. She must remember that.

Some things it would be better to forget.

Not this: sitting on Judith's bed, just waiting. Waiting while the cocoa boiled, waiting for the cold to ebb from her body, the bitter dread from her mind. By the time there was a warm mug to fold her fingers round, her hands had almost stopped shaking.

Her voice, too. She could shape an English sentence without choking, without shrilling, without breaking out in hysterics. She said, 'I worry that I'm going mad, you see.' There. It was out. What she dreaded, what this day was trying its utmost to confirm.

'That hardly seems likely. Sanity is a pre-requisite in nursing sisters. Having two feet on the ground is one of the qualities we look for here.' Judith's voice was quiet, and mildly amused. At least she wasn't being robust about it. If Ruth looked up, she thought she might see the twitch of a smile.

She kept her eyes on the steam of the cocoa, on the dark skin slowly forming in the mug. She said, 'It's just, I keep seeing my husband. My dead husband. Since I came here.' That wasn't entirely true, nor entirely honest – it wasn't all seeing, and there was the falling too, that sense of being drawn down in chase of him – but it seemed to cover the ground. If she didn't mention what predated her arrival here, the wanting to die and the almost-resolve to put herself in situations where she might, where a bomb or a shell or a bullet could find her out. No need to mention that. That wasn't a madness, it was a perfectly rational response to an intolerable life.

'Lord, girl, you turn up here with no sleep and an empty belly, you faint across our doorway–' she'd always known that word of that would get

97

around – 'and come round to find yourself in a fair imitation of hell – and if you haven't read Dante, then I really don't recommend him, not for the duration – and you're surprised to find your own private sorrow rising up to meet you? I'd only be surprised if it didn't. We're all widows and orphans here, it's policy, and I think we're all haunted.'

'Why would—?'

'I didn't say it was a wise policy, did I? They do it because they think we'll be as tough as they are, with the men. Nothing sentimental. They think because we've had it rough, they can depend on us to be rough ourselves. That doesn't always follow, but they seem to have got it right, more or less, with us. We cope, at least.'

Judith, what is it that we cope with? What do they do here, that demands so much more than professional nursing?

It was on the tip of her tongue to ask. Perhaps she actually meant to. Her mouth was open, and she had the air. But then she listened to herself, and what she was saying was not that, no. It was confession still, again: 'Only in the dark there, I thought I was holding him, I could *smell* him, exactly...'

After a moment, Judith said, 'Did he use bay rum?'

'Yes, yes, he did.' Fresh from shaving, impossibly smooth and soft of cheek, and the lingering scent of his lotion clinging to his skin, clinging to hers after she had kissed him.

'My dear, they all do, all these men. It's a part of their uniform, they all need to smell the same.

98

Which is why they all wear overcoats which all smell the same when they're wet. That was Major Dorian's I found you cuddling up to, in the cloakroom there.'

Oh, dear God. Was it? She'd seen him wearing it, of course, earlier. At the sing-song. And, yes, of course he used bay rum. She'd smelled it on him at their first encounter – but she smelled it on everyone these days. Every man, as Judith said. And accused them all, silently, for not being Peter.

No surprise, that it had been that particular man's overcoat that ensnared her. Of course she was going to blame him, even if he wasn't actually occupying it at the time. It was his fault that she was here, after all. So everything that happened to her here, that must be his fault too. By definition. Yes.

Whatever she made happen, though, now that she had come here, that would be her own responsibility. She didn't need to be feeble, always pushed about by men. She could make her own decisions. Chase her own bullet.

Yes.

Choose her own friends, that too.

She sat with Judith on her bed there and sipped cocoa so hot it burned her lips, and talked a little about Morwood – shop talk, the house and how it worked as a hospital, Matron and how she kept it working – and a lot about childhood, friendship, discovery. Not at all about Peter, nor whatever secret adult sorrow Judith cherished, that had laid a path to draw her here. There would be time enough for that. Six months. That was time enough for anything.

And so goodnight, the slightly foolish formalities of parting with a near stranger when you're only going two doors down; and one last gift as she was leaving.

'You'll need this until you learn your way around, learn where the switches are and how to find your way in the dark, this place is a maze.'

A heavy torch that Ruth took under protest and with gratitude. She peeled off her clothes and sank into a bed that only seemed this soft because she was this tired, and so to sleep.

And so to wake, sometime in the dark. She couldn't remember where she had put her watch and wouldn't be able to read it anyway, it wasn't luminous, and it didn't really matter anyway, what the time might be. What mattered was that she wasn't sleepy, not at all. Of course not, after that long nap last afternoon. Her inner clock was out of all kilter.

Well, she was used to that. The regular sleeping patterns of her young life had been broken long ago. Night shifts and raids and anxiety and grief had all contributed in their turn. She had strategies for dealing with wakefulness, but they all depended on her being at home or else at work, where there was always something that needed doing.

Here, well. One thing she knew, that there was no point lying in bed and hoping to sleep again. Up, then. A robe across her shoulders, because the days might be warm but the nights apparently were chilly this far north, this far into the year. Last night she had shivered on Darlington station and blamed the cold stare of the stars. Tonight she shivered in her own room under a strange roof, and went to stare out of the window.

Something monstrous crawled across the sky, a great foreboding. More like spiderweb than smoke, she could still glimpse stars through the strands of it and it had purpose, she thought, there was a will behind it somewhere.

And of course it was only cloud-shadow, wisps of cloud on the wind, utterly meaningless. Meaningless and gone now. She could look down into the courtyard and see quite clearly, by brilliant starlight quite uninterrupted in its fall.

She could see men moving, shadows themselves, figures of darkness drifting silently towards this wing of the house. She might have seen something mystical in them too, her mind was so uncertain and they seemed so unearthly – except that they moved like broken ghosts, hints of damage that was all too physical and real. It was almost comforting that she could read their hurts at distance, in this ethereal light.

She was still shivering, despite the robe. And utterly wakeful, so she might as well dress. Might as well turn on a light to do that, though not until she had seen the last of the men vanish through the door, not until she had heard it slam. There was a comfort in that too, a guarantee of solid actual men, who needed doors to open and caused them to close again.

Never mind that that same door had defeated her. She needed to learn the way of it, that was all. In the dark, that especially. And find where the light switch was, that too.

Before she reached for her own light switch, there was still one thing to do. Virtue transplanted, a city habit that might actually be unnecessary here: she adjusted the blackout curtain, so that not a glimmer could be seen from outside. From above or below.

Dressed, she had no notion what she ought to do now. Not linger without purpose in her room, emphatically not that. She might go looking for a staffroom, perhaps. Or a library, anything that would offer a distraction. Or there must be a kitchen in this wing somewhere, she might hope for a gas ring and a kettle, there was nothing so distracting as a cup of tea...

And if all of that was only making excuses to herself, at least she didn't have to admit it, even to herself. She held it ready in her mind, ready on her tongue in case of meeting anyone, and slipped out of the room. Left the light on and the door ajar, so that she could find her way back; took Judith's torch, so that she could find her way through the rest of the house. Or at least see where she was going, which wasn't quite the same thing.

Stole downstairs as quietly as she might, wishing for carpets on these bare treads or else for lighter shoes. Down one flight and another, using the torch in flashes and no more, mostly trusting for guidance to her hand on the wall and the sounds that drew her. Men's voices, footsteps, the creaks and scrapes of furniture in use.

The chink of crockery, the tap of silver against china. *Sugar in your tea, Major Black?*

Here was the hallway, and she didn't need the torch; the light was on. The voices lay on the further side of that tall door that led through to the ballroom, Major Black's domain. She had always known that, there had never been any question of it in her head. In daylight she had met the other face of Morwood; in darkness, of course it would be his. Even his name was an omen.

Even so, she was determined. She walked up to the door, and as her hand reached to the handle it swung open, and here came Flying Officer Tolchard, awkward with his one good hand working the door and an empty milk-jug cradled in the other elbow. Doubly awkward as his eyes met hers, as he made a sudden hushing gesture, *don't give yourself away.*

She had done nothing wrong, she was clad decently in dressing gown and virtue. And yet she stood entirely still, saying nothing, letting him close that difficult door behind him, allowing him to shut her out. Again.

Himself, he was clad in black, as all those men below had been. It was some kind of exercise, and *haven't you done enough?* but the question was impossible so long as he was young and breathing, so long as the war went on. What in the world he would do afterwards, she couldn't imagine. She imagined that he gave it no thought at all. The war it was that kept him going, him and his brothers in arms.

He pulled a knit cap from his hair, which might

103

mean anything or nothing but she chose to read it as an atavistic gesture, a charming little schoolboy moment, taking his cap off to a lady. The sideways duck of his head was incontrovertible: a message, an invitation, an instruction. *Come with me. Quietly, now.* She allowed that too after only a moment's hesitation, only just long enough to pluck the jug from his elbow and carry it herself.

Across the hall and down another flight of stairs, she hadn't been this way before, and here was the kitchen. Subterranean, in the tradition of great houses, with a mean run of windows high along one wall. Probably they looked out into a railed area of brick, sunk down behind the house. She hadn't seen it, because she had always been falling or fumbling or staring skyward. Besides, those windows were all dutifully masked. No hint of light could have slipped out to nudge at her attention.

There was a lot of light, even at this time of night. This time of morning, she supposed, and of course the kitchen would be awake. Country house or hospital or barracks, whatever this was it would make an early start on the day, which required the kitchen to make an earlier one. Night manoeuvres might mean the kitchen never got to bed at all.

The kitchen, or the cook. He couldn't actually be sole proprietor, she didn't know how the military organized their kitchens but there must be a squad of cooks and undercooks and orderlies. Still, he was here alone for now, and Tolchard called him Cook as though he were the

104

only one, or the only one who counted. Aesculapius had done the same thing, she remembered. So had Colonel Treadgold. The colonel had called him a genius, indeed.

She had herself blessed his spirit, the unknown essence of the man, absorbing soup.

Now here he was, kneading great ramparts of dough on a table that might have served for a ship's deck. He was thinner than she might have looked for, a man in his middle years but somehow not in uniform, no hint of khaki beneath his whites.

Thin but strong in that stubborn enduring way, the kind who would work and work. He looked like he could knead his dough all day, and she knew how much work that was. Tolchard at her side was saying, 'Cook, could you find a wet and a wad for one soul who's been up too long and another who's up too early?'

'Your tea's waiting for you upstairs.' It was meant to be repressive, perhaps, to chase them out of his domain, but she wasn't convinced. His voice had a hint of indulgence in it already.

Which Tolchard had clearly spotted too, or else simply expected, depended on, taken for granted as he had done all his life. Unintimidated, he was drawing out a chair for her at the other end of the table, out of the cook's way, a grandstand view of the heart of the matter; he was saying, 'I can't take Sister Taylor among the men, she'd be appalled.'

'Young man,' it was her turn to be repressive, 'I am quite able to go among the men without your escort. It is, in fact, my job. And I've been

105

doing it long enough–' and under conditions appalling enough, though she wasn't going to say so – 'that nothing you men could say or do is likely to appal me.'

'Well, no,' he confessed, disarming as ever, 'what I meant of course is that they'd be appalled to find a woman suddenly among them when they want to be all coarse and expletive, like proper soldiers. The major gave us a hard time out there tonight, and they need to let off steam. You'd make them swallow it instead. It doesn't do any good, swallowing steam.'

He would know, he and his cohorts. Even if he meant it metaphorically, the actual image rose up, in her head and she thought his own. He blinked, at least, that awkward conscious gesture that ought simply to be self-conscious; and carried on regardless, because that was what he did. 'Be an angel, Cook, let us squat down here with you for half an hour. Then Sister will be on duty and I'll be off, and we'll both be out of your hair before your people come in for the day.'

In honesty, they were already squatting. Her traitorous legs had sat her in that chair, and he had perched himself cheerfully on the table edge beside.

In honesty, the cook was already making allowance and more, pulling off a couple of handfuls of dough and working them into neat little twists. Setting those on a baking tray and brushing them with egg – real egg! – and scattering sugar over, snatching up a dish towel and releasing a furnace-blast of superheated air as he opened a door on the vast range and slid the tray inside.

Everything was out of scale down here, Ruth thought. Or else it was their own fault, they weren't big enough to match their surroundings. The cook played within his kitchen like a child. It should have been a pastiche, like a one-man orchestra, where the joke is the only achievement. But he filled a tiny-seeming pot from an enormous kettle that steamed perpetually on the stove top, and it poured out good thick army tea. There was fresh milk and sugar, and ten minutes later there were those twists, finger-scorching hot and steamily delicious, with butter and plum jam if the bread itself wasn't enough. For her, it was. For Tolchard, of course, not. He expected miracles, and would always want to add sweetness.

Sweetness and wisdom, in that odd combination beloved of the young. They ate, they drank, he talked. He took her silence for the interrogation that it was, the open invitation to explain. Why he had been sidling through the dark on night exercises, he and his companions; why Major Black could seem to outrank the colonel in his calls upon the house and its facilities, its men.

Why everyone had been leaving it to everyone else to explain this to her, until here, now, a not-quite-private conversation in a kitchen corner, at the end of his day and the start of hers.

'It's hard,' he said, and she was astonished that he might find anything hard, except the need to admit it that he did. 'Heroism isn't meant to happen this way. It's supposed to be spontaneous

and, and individual, that lone impulse to courage. Not calculated, worked for, trained in.'

'And is that what the major's doing, training
you to be heroes?'

'Yes, that's right. He is.'

*We thought you were already, you young pilots.
How much more is he asking of you, how much
more do you have to give?*

She did have to say that in the end, as it happened, just to get him moving again when he
seemed to have stalled. 'To us, you know, you
are heroes. You saved the country. Churchill
himself said so.'

He shook his head. 'It ... doesn't seem enough,
you know? To us. A few weeks, a few months
maybe for the lucky ones if that's what you call
luck. Watching our friends die, not quite dying
ourselves but coming close, near as damn it,
leaving ourselves like this–' a gesture of his
good hand at everything that was not good, his
other hand, his face – 'and what now, we just sit
back and wear our courage on our faces – that's
a quotation, I think, I can't remember who but
it's all too horribly apt – and let others go off to
fight the rest of the war?'

'Yes,' she said, vainly, hopelessly. *'Yes.'*

'No,' he said. 'Not that. We can't. We don't ...
we don't know how to live with ourselves.'

And if not now – she thought, and he knew –
they never would. If not in this world, then
where? What would they do, when the war was
taken from them?

Apparently they didn't want to think about
that. Or else they had thought about it, and had

108

turned convulsively away from the prospect.

Had turned back to the war. To Major Black.

Which meant running around doing exercises in the dark, apparently. Airmen who couldn't fly, they'd need a new objective. But if they couldn't fly, neither could they fight. Surely? One-handed or claw-handed, twisted all out of shape, they couldn't fit the military machine any more, they weren't apt parts.

There was something they could do, and he didn't want to say it. She didn't want to hear it. She was trembling already on the brink of understanding, one step short.

There were German uniforms upstairs. Luftwaffe uniforms, she realized suddenly, a dawning light that only added to the fog of mystery. They were training like soldiers and dressing up like the airmen they could no longer be, the enemy airmen they never were, and...

And whether this was confession or interrogation or neither quite of those, it was interrupted. Not by the cook, who was busy weighing his dough-mountain into slabs, working those one in each hand into perfect coherent ovoids, tossing them into loaf tins and lining them up along the back of the range. She wanted to watch him at work, such useful work; there was something infinitely restful about it, seeing raw stuff made into meals.

Better that than watch Tolchard writhe on the hook of his great secret.

Far better that than hear footsteps on the stairs behind her, lift her head and turn around and see another figure dressed as the boy was beside her, only that this was a man in every way that mattered: brisk and neat and confident, quietly compelling.

Compelling Tolchard to his feet just with a glance.

Extending that to take in her too, the two of them together.

Cocking an eyebrow and smiling without humour and saying, 'Excuse me, Sister, I rather need my man back. And you, lad, silent exercise, for the rest of the day. You know you need the practice.'

Tolchard opened his mouth, perhaps just to acknowledge the order, *yes sir* – and swallowed it like a good soldier, saluted without a word, glanced sideways at her with no more than the hint of a rueful shrug.

Well, but Ruth was not subject to this discipline. She had her own place here, and she meant to assert it. She wasn't to be cowed by military manners.

She said, 'Excuse *me*, but – Major Black, is it?'

'It is.'

I do not like thee, Major Black. She had known that already. It was almost inherent. Whatever there was that she didn't understand yet, this much was clear, that he took broken boys – her patients, barely mended – and flung them back into the hurly of war, and no, she would never be inclined to like that in a man. Even where she might acknowledge its necessity. Which was, she thought, not here.

She seemed to be standing up, though she

hadn't quite meant to do that. No matter.

She said, 'Is that ... meant for a punishment, your putting him under silence? A punishment for speaking to me?'

'No, Sister, not at all. Not even a discouragement. I train men to kill, not to exhibit nice manners. Except where nice manners will bring them closer to their targets, that is. No, but men like Tolchard, with a voice that works and a habit of using it? They need to learn not to do that, or they'll give themselves away. So: they all have silent days, you'll find. And it's nothing to do with you. Cook, he seems to have forgotten it, but I sent Tolchard down for more milk and half a stone of sugar...'

A minute later he was leaving, with his jug and his sugar and his errant boy in tow. Ruth found herself still on her feet, almost put under silence herself by the sheer impact of the man. She subsided slowly into her chair, chased breadcrumbs around her plate with a mute forefinger, felt her head reeling with ideas that she really didn't want to consider.

She had it all now, she thought, more or less. German uniforms, and wounded men – visibly, extravagantly wounded men, badged with their honour – and learning to kill in their new conformations, hand to hand, the ways they never had. Exercising in the dark, acquiring what new skills they could in what time they were allowed. Learning not to speak, not to give themselves away.

There must be as many ruined airmen in Germany as there were here. There too they would be heroes, giving their youth and health and beauty to the Reich. A brutally scarred face and a Luftwaffe uniform would almost be a pass in themselves; no official would look too closely or ask too many questions. A scarred voice-box would be excuse enough for a lack of fluency in the language, or indeed the absence of any language at all.

There was a deliberate little noise at her elbow: the cook, bringing her another cup of tea. She nodded her thanks, then frowned, remembered that she was not herself under a burden of silence, and said, 'What does he want all that sugar for?' Half a stone was too much, a nonsense too far. And sugar was rationed, precious, not to be used lightly even here, where there were real eggs and butter for the asking.

'Improvised hand grenades,' the cook said softly. 'He takes all the bottles in the house and fills them with petrol and sugar and soap flakes, stuffs their mouths with rags for a wick and sends the men out into the woods to see how far they can lob one. The colonel won't have them in the courtyard.'

'The colonel lets them shoot off rifles in the house.'

'Yes. It's one of the compromises they came to.'

It probably didn't seem so much, she thought, a little wildly, after that first great compromise. *I'll patch these boys together and do what I can to make them presentable, give them new faces and hands that almost work; then you can send them off to Germany as saboteurs, assassins,*

112

what you will. After that, what did it matter if there were a few bullet holes in the plasterwork?

'Doesn't the owner mind?'

'Mind? No, he says he doesn't mind. So long as they can find a use for the place. I ... don't believe he loves D'Espérance, but he would like to see it useful.'

She didn't see how anyone could love it. Too big, too ugly, all manner of wrong. But still: a house, and a history. A story to be told. This latest chapter she thought another kind of wrong. Done to the house, not by it.

Still. A house ill made, ill treated; it made a fit breeding ground for something more wrong yet, or she thought so.

'It's a suicide mission,' she said bluntly. *Heroism isn't meant to happen this way*, but of course Tolchard would snatch at it, he and all his kind. Nature or nurture, young men will be snatching. Offer them a glimpse of glory, they will always want a handful.

'Many suicide missions,' the cook said, topping up his own great tin mug of tea. 'But yes, largely. Without the name, perhaps, but very few of them expect to make it home again when once they're sent away. They've all lived with that same expectation, of course. For months now, for years some of them. Every time they took off, they felt the hand of death on their shoulder.'

'They didn't seek it out. Shake hands with death, make a friend of him.'

'Perhaps not, but can you blame them? Now?'

Of course not. Young and strong and healthy, in love with life, they had nevertheless hurled

113

themselves into the air day after day in machines of wood and wire, in the frenzy of war, in the teeth of terror. Hurt and broken, marked for life and all their beauties ruined, why on earth would they hesitate now?

It was like asking *what do they have to live for?* And there ought to be many answers to that, and she could list them all and believe none of them, just as the boys most likely could and did themselves, on their own accounts.

She was afraid that they would have understood Peter better than she did herself.

And still, still it was a wrongness, just one more, and she was here to perpetuate it. To make them better soldiers, fitter sooner.

Perhaps that was just war, in its inevitable wrongness. But the tea tasted foul suddenly, all mud on her tongue. A soldier's brew, not for her. She said, 'Were you in the last lot?'

'No,' he said, 'I was just too young.' She heard *just too late*, and a world of regret. Perhaps that was her imagination. But he was a man, he had been young, no doubt he would have been snatching.

Tired of them all, she stood and carried her plate and cup to join a pile of crockery by the sink. 'Thank you, Cook. I'll take myself out from under your feet now.'

It was an opportunity, the opening to a game of platitudes and manners, and he let it by. Just a smile and a nod, and he had turned away already.

Too young for the last lot, she thought, *he must still be young enough for this lot. Barely forty yet.* And yet, not in uniform beneath his proper whites; no kind of soldier, with his hair that long on his neck. Probably that would be another question better left unasked.

With time on her hands and the sun just rising, another dawn reluctantly seen in, Ruth swapped her shoes and went walking in the grounds. Not far and not fast, purposeless, adrift: only cherishing the little things, immediacy. The crunch of gravel beneath her heels and the bite of chill against her skin, these last minutes of solitude before the house woke and her day began again. One day and then one more, and more in brisk succession. Terminable days, endurable, with an end in sight. She could do this.

She must do this. She had no choices now, or none that she was prepared to countenance.

Six months.

Horse noises, horse smells from the stable block couldn't distract her yet. She was saving that for a time of greater need. It was sure to come, some day when she was desperate to lose herself; when she would relish nothing more than the chance to overlay recent cruel history with older memories, old pleasures resurgent. An earlier edition, Ruth Elverson.

Ruthie Elverson. They used to call her Ruthie. No one did that any more. When did that stop, when did it change?

When she married, of course. When everything stopped and started again, all new; before...

Before. Yes. When I had a life, a husband that

115

I loved. Before I lost him.

She shook her head, she raised her head and stepped out determinedly, suddenly weary of this self-reproach. She had had a life, a good life, and had lost it; it was not her fault. These things happen, especially in wartime. There were many in her situation. Most of them blamed Hitler. Some would bring it closer to home, to the generals and politicians of their own side, the men who made the bad choices that saw other men get killed. Not many brought it closer yet, to their own men, *that idiot, standing right in the way of a bullet, when his mates on either side of him were fine...*

Ruth could blame Peter, very easily, if she weren't so entirely busy blaming herself. Perhaps that was why she did it, not to allow herself the room to blame him instead. It was better to be guilty than accusing. She could live with it; he didn't have to.

Still. Accusing herself was morbid, dwelling in the accusation was worse. Unhealthy, self-defeating, inutile. Making herself useful was her last resort; making herself ill would be a last betrayal. This place was tailor-made for Sister Taylor, in her extremity: good food, country air, all the work she could wish for. Someone else to accuse. *I do not like thee, Major Black.*

So. Head up, step out. Step away from misery. Not to leave it behind, but not to wrap herself in it either. Not to allow herself so much indulgence. Brisk and brutal sister, as impatient with herself as with her patients. She could do that. Yes.

A paved terrace ran all the length of the house, behind a low stone balustrade. Steps led down into the layered gardens, all the way down to the lake. She might go that far, she had the time. There was an unappealing mist above the water, but the sun would see to that soon enough, and her other choice was to patrol the rows of vegetables on the terraces between, where lawns and flower beds had been virtuously dug under. She could pass the cabbages in review, practise her strictness on the radishes, inspect the leeks for grubbiness...

She could, apparently, make an idiot of herself, but only in her head. Blessedly she hadn't paraded any of that nonsense aloud. There was nothing for a rising stranger to catch hold of as he loomed up from the soil at her side.

Just for a moment, she believed that literally, absolutely. She thought he was a spirit of earth, compounded of root and rock and tilth together.

Then she saw the mud in the creases of his face, or rather his face beneath its mud. Dark curling hair, too long, and brown fatigues without insignia. Mud on his hands, mud on his boots.

'In this light,' he said, 'it's easier to hoe with my fingers. The little lettuces have a better chance.' And then, 'Good morning.' He said that too, belatedly. 'I hope I did not startle you too badly?'

'No, no,' she said, lying absolutely. Recovering herself, finding just how much there was to recover, how far she'd startled, how clearly he must have seen. No matter. *Brisk and brutal.*

117

'Wouldn't it be easier yet to wait for better light?'

'It would, but I have other duties all the day. I give German lessons to the gentlemen.'

His English was almost perfect, but strongly marked. Could he be a prisoner of war? Luftwaffe, perhaps, shot down and lucky, parachute and capture. There had been small opportunity else for prisoners on this side of the Channel, this side of the war. But it would be a breach of the conventions, she was almost certain, to make a prisoner work this way. And why would he aid the enemy?

Besides, this man's face was all too classically Jewish. He might have modelled for a cartoon, or for Disraeli. He must be a refugee, a civilian, a volunteer.

'My name is Lothar Braun,' he said. 'I apologize, I am too dirty to shake your hand; but perhaps you would not like that anyway.'

'Oh, nonsense. Why in the world should I dislike it? Good manners are not the exclusive preserve of the English.'

'Perhaps. But I am German, and you are at war with my people.'

'Not with yours, I think, Mr Braun.'

'Well. I am Jewish, true, and some people dislike that also. But I am still a German, and that makes trouble enough over here. I am an intern, obliged to this place. For my own protection, they said; and for my safety, I am forbidden the town. My accent makes too much discomfort, they said. They mean that people will attack me, they think. For being smart, perhaps, for running away in time. So, I must plant cabbages for you, and teach your young mute men the German they will never speak. Two jobs, so I must start this early. And you?'

'Oh, I'm just new here. Not sleeping well, my first day. I'm so sorry, I didn't introduce myself. Ruth Elverson – I'm sorry, I mean Sister Taylor. But not all our young men are mute. Some of them must be learning to speak German, not just to understand it?'

'Some, yes. Have you met Flying Officer Tolchard? That one never stops speaking, in any language he can achieve. Unhappily, his achievement is marked by more enthusiasm than aptitude. His accent is atrocious, and his grasp of grammar is slapdash. Slapdash at the best. I might say harum-scarum,' and he frowned, all stern teacher despite the dirt he stood up in.

'Somehow that doesn't surprise me.' They were both smiling somewhere, she thought, internally. She might be the more transparent. Relief bubbled up inside her like spring water through grass, all unexpected. 'So may I take it that young Tolchard is not a prime candidate to be sent away on secret missions?'

A shrug was the best of her answer, the most that he could apparently give her. 'If it were up to me, he would not be a candidate at all. I would keep him here, for the greater morale of all. From the colonel to the cook. But–' another shrug, another kind of shrug – 'up to me it is not. I have no voice in this. I am the opposite of voice; I am a prisoner here.'

'Oh, not a prisoner, surely?'

119

'In all but name. I stay because they say I must. What else would you call this? In fact I would stay of my own will, but they make sure of it. There are guards on every road. Volunteers can walk away; I am too useful to be allowed to do so. And I may be an exile, a refugee, but I am still a German. Not trusted, and not safe.'

Ruth didn't want either part of that to be true, but of course they both were. She wanted to apologize for her country, for its people, but couldn't quite find the words. 'My enemy's enemy may indeed be my friend,' she said instead, 'but it's hard sometimes to be certain.'

Even her voice sounded uncertain, even to herself.

For herself, she abruptly wanted Tolchard to fail and fail, every test they gave him. She wanted to salvage, to preserve. To *keep*. Something of what she valued in men, in mankind, in England, she wanted to see it kept, not all flung into the furnace of war, and Tolchard seemed suddenly to have become a symbol of it all.

FIVE

The sun rose finally, decisively, striking down the valley like a weapon against fog. Ruth went in search of breakfast and her daily task, feeling obscurely as though everyone at Morwood could be measured for their degrees of ruthlessness and found excessive. She herself was ruthless at need, *professionally* ruthless; it had been a school-years' joke that carried through her training and into her years of practice. Now no one joked about it, some people valued it, she only took it for what it was, a useful attribute.

Here, though: here she was almost an amateur. Between Colonel Treadgold and Matron, patching broken men; Major Black training them to kill again and Herr Braun teaching them to infiltrate; Aesculapius doing whatever it was that he did to keep them willing to kill and die ... It was a conspiracy, and she was a part of it now. And, yes, ruthless. She would do what she did, and not protest. She could lose herself in it, create almost an absence of herself, be truly Ruthless.

Yes.

* * *

She could be lulled by work; she could be lulled by learning. Exercise for the body, exercise for the mind. Either was good, when she wanted to lose herself and her sorrows and her doubts. Both together were prime. Here and now, Morwood was sovereign. Never mind that it was the place and its activities that had stirred her up so; the place and its activities could do the opposite too, drain her and stretch her, give her everything she needed, long weary days and a constant chain of discovery, doors that opened onto revelation with more doors beyond, more and more.

She had nursed before her marriage, she had nursed all through the war. Nursing had become almost her notion of adulthood. It was what she did, now that she was grown up. Single or widowed, in peace or war, south and north and night and day. Here she was senior, she had a corridor to manage, nurses and orderlies beneath her. It made no difference. If a patient needed a bedpan, she would fetch it. And fetch it away again beneath a napkin, empty it and scrub it out. This was what she did. What she had always done. It helped her feel settled, secure, a part of the machinery of war. A useful, proper part.

Here, though, she could be more than that. More than she was before. Since the Blitz began, half the wards she worked on had filled with burns and blast injuries, she was used to those; but they seemed crude and clumsy now, rough copies of these airmen's hurts.

If the damage she saw here was more refined, more focused, the agony more intense, then so too was the treatment. Sulfa drugs were commonplace, but Colonel Treadgold was the opposite of that.

All they had really known, all they had had in London for the treating of burns was tannic acid. When the hospital pharmacy was hit in a raid and they didn't even have that, they'd brewed and cooled strong tea to use as a substitute. Privately, Ruth thought that all the tea did was dye the skin, while all the acid did was tan it into leather. Dry, to be sure, no longer seeping, but curiously orange in colour, tough as boots. *Soled and heeled*, the girls used to say in the canteen, joking for their own comfort when they could do nothing more for the patient's.

Colonel Treadgold's regime was inventive, drastic, meticulous. Ruth had never seen, never heard of anything like it. Saline baths and surgery, skin grafts and more radical rebuilding, clamped hands cut apart and remade to work again.

'Eyes are the first thing,' the colonel grunted, taking her into the operating theatre, one more door. 'Faces and hands these fly boys lose, it's their speciality. They're supposed to wear gloves and goggles, but of course they won't. So, faces and hands. Given time and practice we can make them presentable again, even if they'll never be pretty; given time and practice we can give them hands that work, more or less. But they all lose their eyelids, and we can't take time over those or they'll lose their eyes too, and there's nothing we can do about that. My list of failures is a list of blind men. They haunt me, every one.'

The patient on the table would haunt Ruth, she thought. Tough as she was, inured as she thought herself. *Face and hands*, yes. She had helped prepare him for surgery, and the rest of his body was more or less unmarked. Nineteen years old, fit and healthy from the neck down and the wrists up – and his hands were a blackened ruin, cooked flesh, and his face was gone. No nose, no eyelids, no lips. Unconscious, he glared up at them like madness showing its teeth.

I am like Webster, she thought, *I see the skull beneath the skin.*

And much obsessed by death, yes. That too.

Unperturbed, the colonel lectured as he cut, as he sewed.

'We use skin from the underarm, where there's no hair. Wouldn't want hairy eyelids. For all sorts of reasons, and you girls are the least of them. Ideally, of course, we'd want to find clean skin and then a line of hair that could double up for lashes. Too much to ask, the human body isn't so obliging. Lashes are unique. My boys just have to get along without 'em.'

It had been a while since Ruth had served as a theatre nurse, but she hadn't forgotten the knack. Listen to his voice but pay attention to his hands, watch them at their work, think ahead. Think what she would want if she were him, doing that. Be ready with scalpels and clamps, with sutures, with dressings. Be ready to wipe blood from the patient, sweat from him. Don't let your mind wander, don't let him pull ahead or you'll be forever running to catch up.

Don't let yourself be distracted by the gruesome things he's up to. You've seen worse.

Think ahead, get ahead if you can. Wait till he steps back and then dive in there yourself, wipe the patient's dreadful exposed eyeballs with gelatin to keep them moist, don't wait to be told. It's hot under the surgery lamps, they'll be drying out swiftly now that the dressing's off.

Take his wordless grunt for approbation and get out of his way.

Above all don't reply, don't distract him. Don't speak at all unless you have to. He's as aware of you as he wants to be, he's giving you as much attention as he chooses; work with that.

If he's a talker, he's probably only talking to himself in any case.

If he doesn't notice you at all from beginning to end, then you've done a good job. If you're lucky, he'll notice that.

One more soiled dressing in the bin for laundry. Ruth washed her hands, fetched another pile of clean, stood ready.

This might have been a still room or a pantry, she thought, or perhaps a larder for hanging game: a cool square room tiled in white, floor and walls together, with a working counter and a butler's sink along one side. It wasn't quite right for an operating theatre, perhaps, but it wasn't quite wrong either. Easy to clean, at least superficially, though many of the tiles were cracked and would need hard scrubbing.

The equipment was probably standard field issue. Lamps on stands, steel tables. Cables fetching in the electricity, through a high win-

dow unhygienically ajar. She was a little surprised that it was all so temporary-seeming; but
then, she supposed this whole operation must be
temporary. A few hopeful strikes, and the Germans would catch on soon enough. Missions
would fail, visible ruin would no longer be a
passport into trust. The colonel would return no
doubt to a regular hospital, and take his patients
with him. What had been hush-hush would
become celebrated, the surgeon's magic fingers
restoring health and function if not quite youthful beauty to a devastated generation. Major
Black would stay, perhaps, to train fitter men for
other purposes, and not need an operating
theatre. Aesculapius would do whatever Aesculapius did, but he'd do it somewhere else.

She was drifting; it really had been too long.
Fortunately her hands were keeping up, where
her head was wandering off. Colonel Treadgold
reached out, palm up, and she slapped the handle
of a scalpel into it without thought, without
needing to think.

It would be all too easy – no, it *was* all too easy
to look for glimpses of Peter in all this polished
reflective steel. Distorted figures twisted in and
out of view at every movement. Was that her
own face caught in the scalpel's blade, or was
it another's? Was he screaming, was he falling
forever into the endless distance of that flat
surface? Or was this him on the table, come to
ground at last and cruelly disguised, his face
ripped quite away?

Nonsense. The patient's name was Jones,
Brendan Jones. He was a navigator, caught in an

explosion when his Wellington crashed on landing. Most patients here, she was learning, had met their catastrophes on British airfields, either taking off or landing or caught by German raiders on the ground. Few fitted the picture in her head, the lone ace baling out of his blazing Spit, tumbling to earth with his parachute aflame. Those days were gone, perhaps. Not Tolchard – of course! – but most of these boys came from bombers. If too many of them were pilots, that was because the damn fools ordered their crews to jump and then tried to land a burning or broken plane single-handed, made a mess of it and half incinerated themselves in the wreckage.

'He'll do, for now. Wheel him back to the ward, lads. Nurse, you tidy up in here; this is my last for the day. Harry, will you come?'

He had, she thought, forgotten her name entirely. Name and rank both, washed out by blood and weariness. This work honed him like a blade till there was nothing left but skill and focus, a fine concentration and a delicate touch. He slouched off now, heads together with the anaesthetist, both confident in what they'd done, shedding care like a coat as they went. They would hole up in some den and be men together, drink whisky, smoke a cigar or a pipe perhaps and talk not at all about the day. By the time anyone saw them again it would be cider for the colonel, his beloved eccentricity, and his eyes would sparkle with bonhomie above the spruce restoration of his moustache, wilting now after a day's confinement behind a surgical mask. She knew. Peter had been just the same. Even in peacetime he would wear himself to exhaustion, hurling some new crate about the sky and then debriefing after, spending hours longer in discussion with designers and engineers, how to make the thing fly faster, higher, further than before. Then he'd go to the pub with a few chosen friends, sooner than come home to her. By the time she saw him he'd be cheerfully soused and ready for bed, ready to do it all again next day.

War had shattered many things, ultimately everything, but still she saw that same pattern repeat again and again, wherever men clustered together with purpose.

Orderlies took Flying Officer Jones away. One would have stayed to help her with the clean-up, but she chased him off. No better way to learn the layout of a theatre – and the preferences of its master – than by cleaning it. A thorough disinfection must wait till the morning, and hopefully other hands than hers, but she'd leave the room sparkling if she could. One last effort and then her bed and blessed sleep. Dreamless, if she had any luck at all.

She mopped and sponged, she filled and emptied buckets, tipping them into the sink for lack of a drain in the floor. Wet white walls were a satisfaction; water was grey-pink as it swirled and gurgled against cracked off-white earthenware, the broad oblong of the butler's sink. If there was a word for that colour, she didn't know it. She knew the colour itself, though, all too well. It was the colour that people went, people like herself, at their absolute ends. The end of their tethers, the end of their lives. Exhaustion could turn a healthy English rose complexion to this sick and chalky wash. So could imminent death.

Water swirled and sank and tried to carry her tired head with it, down and down. Down into the clouds, falling and falling, with nothing but a further fall beyond...

No.

No. She wouldn't do this, she wouldn't let it happen. Wouldn't let it *be*. She was stronger than this, *better* than this.

She gripped the thick glazed rim of the sink with both hands, and held on grimly. Stared down into the dizzying water and clung just as avidly to what she knew, what was inarguably so.

Her name was Ruth Taylor – by her own choice, that! – and she was not plunging through clouds, not caught in a desperate and catastrophic fall. No. That had been her husband's doom, not hers. Her husband's *choice*, not to pull his ripcord, not to live. Which was something she had to live with, yes, but she didn't need to relive it. Not in her head, and certainly not in this house. That was only water, washing water. If she felt dizzy it was only from the heat of these lamps beating down at her. She needed to finish up here and switch them off, leave the room, breathe cool air awhile. A walk in the gardens, that would be the thing. No doubt there would be another curious encounter, one more ambiguous individual to be somehow wrestled

129

into place. She could deal with that when it happened. Just as she could deal with this, she was dealing with it, here and now. Standing on the floor she had just washed, gripping the sink, gazing down the plughole as it cleared.

Lifting her head as it cleared.

Seeing the operating theatre all about her, tables and trolleys, bright metal and white walls, white linens, fierce lights. Nothing else.

Of course, nothing else. Anything else was only in her head. Perhaps she should see Aesculapius.

Perhaps not.

She wheeled the basket of bloodied dressings down the corridor to the laundry room. Before the war, they might have gone to the furnace for incineration; these days all but the most soiled would be boiled clean, soaked in carbolic acid and reused. Scrupulous hoarding. It suited the national character, perhaps, but it was a weary way of life.

She had learned something similar for herself, a way to manage work and war and grief all together. Short on sleep and chased by nightmare, at the end of a long day's work she still had reserves of energy, hoarded against need. Enough at least to smile and chat to the orderlies in the laundry room; enough to turn away from the enticing kitchen stairs and head determinedly for the dining hall. She wanted nothing more than a bite to eat in a quiet corner, and then her bed. Instead she would sit at a table with a dozen others and do the dutiful Sister Taylor, a figure of new authority making a place for herself in the hospital and the house and the hierarchy all three, linked but distinct. An hour, one more hour before she could be alone. A meal and a cup of tea, both eminently needful; that was not too much to ask of herself.

Just one hour. It was almost a promise. Cool sheets and solitude were more than a dream, achievable. Almost there. This was how you managed the war and the grief together, how you survived it: one hour at a time, one survivable thing after another. It was the whole span that was just too much to ask, the endlessness, the forever of loss and defeat and sorrow.

She crossed the courtyard, came into the high hallway and was met as ever by a blast of noise. No piano tonight, but too many voices. Far too many faces. Patients and staff, officers and men and women too, and all of them apparently staring at her.

It made her head spin once again. But if she hadn't fainted before, on her own, unobserved, she was certainly not going to faint now. Not again. She was quite in control of her body now. Her legs brought her to a table, and, 'Is this seat taken? No? May I...?'

In fact, she already had. She was sitting down, drawing in her chair; someone was reaching for her cup and pouring tea from a vast collective pot.

Here were more names to learn, more faces to memorize. Extraordinary faces, some of them: faces without noses, faces with noses like elephants' trunks, faces so wrapped in bandages it was impossible to see what kind of nose they wore.

'Well,' she said, 'this is like Darwin's finches in reverse.'

Blank looks, puzzlement, curiosity. A man whose nose resembled a walrus more than an elephant, or perhaps a fat sheep's tail more than that, said, 'Sister?'

'Every island he went to, Darwin found that birds' beaks had developed differently, according to the local conditions and the food supply. It was as though they were deliberately isolationist, birds of a feather flocking together. Birds of a beak. And yet here you are, with all your ... wonderful variety of noses, all clustered at the same table.' She beamed around at them, took charge of the teapot and went on because she could really do nothing else now. 'So tell me, is this fellow feeling, or are you talking shop in the mess?'

'Oh lord, no, Sister, never that. Perhaps it's fellow feeling, but honestly, you'll find most of the chaps here short of a nose or so. It's why the colonel is such a particularly dab hand at fixing them up, he gets such a lot of practice.'

It was hard to be quite sure whether he was being ironic or simply truthful, even grateful. Ruth's doubt must have shown on her face. On her other side, another man – no more nose than lips, eyelids two droops of skin he hadn't learned to blink yet, he had to wipe them with a handkerchief at the ever-ready – said, 'Just take it at face value, Sister, whatever we say. Whatever value you care to give our faces.'

'Ah,' she said, 'I see. A double act. Which of

you is the straight man?'

'Oh, he is,' but they said it both together, as though rehearsed. She laughed, and hefted the pot. 'Who wants a top-up, before I send this to be refilled? Dark and chewy by the feel of it, who likes their tea well stewed?'

By the meal's end this was her table, these were her men. The staff were not so easy to win over; she would need to do that with work, make a reputation that would spread through her own ward and further out. Patients were a breeze by comparison. She need only be interested, amused, impressed. All of which she actually was. Let them think her clever but won over, charmed despite their faces and despite their futures. Here and now, that was enough.

By the meal's end she had in honesty had enough. She wanted her privacy and her bed in short order. And was halfway there, heading for the door with goodnights still smiling on her lips, when a hand arrested her elbow. She stopped, by force of necessity; and turned round expecting Aesculapius but hoping for anyone else, anyone at all; and was relieved and frustrated both at once to find Judith Trease standing there saying, 'Oh no, you can't sneak away on your own. Not now, not tonight.'

'Why not?' *Whyever not?* was closer to the surface of her thoughts, close to her tongue but could still be swallowed back, not to be too sharp with her new friend. She could still – just – manage a question rather than a snarl. 'I'm off duty now, I think. What's so special about tonight?'

'My dear, we are never off duty here. And Friday night is dancing, of course. Who doesn't want to go dancing on a Friday night? And you're new, everyone will want a turn with you. I'm sorry, but that's the way it is.' She didn't seem sorry at all, there was laughter in her eyes, in her voice. It might have been sympathetic, perhaps. 'Did no one think to warn you? It's a brutal exposition, but we do all have to go through it.' And then, tugging Ruth out of the general way and going on more quietly, 'What it is, other hospitals with patients like ours, they've found that it helps the men no end to go out of an evening now and then. To learn that girls will still dance with them, despite ... despite everything. East Grinstead, elsewhere, the townsfolk have been extraordinary, by what we hear. But here of course the men can't mix so readily, they're more than patients and who knows what they'd say if they were drunk, if they were seduced into it? So the colonel wants them to dance, and Major Black won't let them run away to town, so we have dancing of our own. And there aren't enough of us girls, there never could be. So we're all obliged. I am sorry–' and perhaps she was after all, seeing how absolutely Ruth wanted to escape – 'but you do not get to skip this. If you utterly hate it, trip over someone's feet and make a fool of yourself. They'll let you be after that, they have nice manners bred in their bone; but you honestly can't refuse.'

Well, she wouldn't, then. Nor would she fake a clumsiness she didn't own. But Ruth hadn't danced with anyone since Peter – well, since Peter. She didn't want, she hadn't ever wanted to feel another man's hands that way, to follow another man's rhythms, to learn again – and again, and again – that the world was very full of men and none of them was Peter.

She could do this, she would do this. She really didn't want to.

She stood with Judith against the wall and watched while patients and orderlies together cleared all the tables to the side of the hall.

Of course young Tolchard was by the piano; of course he couldn't play dances one-handed and the duets were a party trick, apparently, not standard issue. Someone else took the stool and left him standing, stranded almost. He had a pint, he could look busy enough with that. For a while, Ruth wondered – worried, almost – if it might fall to her to be the one who had to ask him to dance.

She needn't have worried. It would probably always prove a waste of effort, by definition, worrying about Tolchard. She had looked away for a minute, distracted by the first figures starting to turn and sway in a cheerful polka. Strauss, she rather thought, though she wouldn't have liked to say which Strauss. Peter would have frowned at her for that: *you either know*, he would say, *or you don't know. There are facts, and then there's guesswork.*

She still thought it was possible to know, absolutely, and to be wrong. It had been one of the arguments between them, in the days when they could still argue.

At least she wouldn't have to argue Tolchard out of his brown study. One of his friends had nudged him, or else his own good training had done the job. Another couple took the floor and that was him, she recognized his tow head from behind, so surely that she didn't need to glance at the piano top to confirm his abandoned pint. He was dancing with one of the nurses. Local girls they were, by and large, while the senior staff was like her, fetched in from far away. No doubt Aesculapius had his reasons.

If it was witchcraft she didn't know whether it was his or hers, whether he read her mind or she summoned him with a thought; but his voice was suddenly in her ear, warm and soft as old worn leather. 'Sister Taylor, will you dance?'

It was, clearly, her duty. What she was here for. Not with Aesculapius, necessarily, his ego didn't stand in need. But perhaps he held a *droit de seigneur*, perhaps all the men else were politely waiting. If she had to get over this before she could do that, give time to him before she could give it to those who needed her, before she could slip away at last, too long delayed – very well, then. Let it be now.

'Of course,' she said. 'Shall we?'

His hands, his body were slightly and so entirely wrong. He was a little too tall, a little too heavy. A little too dominant, that too. Peter used to lead with a charming hesitation, as though all he ever did was to suggest, perhaps, a move this way or that. The major was no less subtle, but much more assertive. He guided, she followed, that was that.

Still. The man could dance. They slipped into the music like a hand into a glove, contained but not restrained. There was a little skip in her tired feet, to say that it had been too long. This night might be duty, this dance might be professional courtesy or hierarchical responsibility or any one of a dozen other complicated things she had not unravelled yet, but there was a lesson here too, something of a revelation.

She might, perhaps, go dancing again. For herself, for her pleasure. She might be able to do that.

Soon, perhaps.

Before six months were up. There must be dancing in the town, even if the men didn't go there. She'd ask the girls, the nurses...

Young men count beats, watch where they're going, worry about the girl in their arms and the people around them: what she's thinking, what everyone else is thinking, what he dare risk now or later. What she'll think if he does, what she'll say.

Older men, experienced men, seem not to worry at all. Their tongues not bound up by all those strings of anxiety, they like to talk as they dance.

He said, 'Settling in, then?'

'Not in the least.' As he well knew, he must know. Any reasonable woman would take weeks to find her feet in an establishment like this. She'd give herself months, if she could afford it. 'I wish you'd warned me.'

'Do you?'

'Yes, actually.' She did like to be treated as a

grown-up, given the facts and allowed to make a true decision.

'Would you still have come?'

'Yes, actually.' She did think that was true. However unlikely.

'I couldn't have told you about Major Black and his ... doings. Only that it was a hospital full of burned airmen. I thought that might cut a little close to the bone for you.'

'It does. Regardless of Major Black.' *Major Black and you*, she didn't absolve him of anything that happened here. 'Even so, I think I would have come. For six months.' It wasn't hope, exactly, she didn't allow that; but a postponement of despair, a chance to think beyond the cloying grey hopelessness, a time and a place where she needn't be yearning constantly for that bullet, waiting for the bomb to fall. She thought she might have come for that.

Or for the pain of it, perhaps. All these hopeful, determined young men who had pulled their ripcords and fought their way through fire and hurt and despair to find some value in life restored. Even if it was temporary, a pint of beer and a dance with a pretty girl before they went off to death and glory, trained and prepared and almost eager. Perhaps she was a masochist, seeking out the pain determinedly, more and more, unsatisfied.

They reminded her of herself, where they ought surely to remind her of her husband.

Oh, Peter...

Sometimes she blamed herself, of course she did. How not? She was apparently not enough to live for. That had to be her own fault, surely.

She said, 'Where is Major Black? Does he not dance?' He was lean enough, fit enough, from what she'd seen of him. He had that killer grace that cats exhibit, movement under absolute control. Self-aware, self-satisfied. Sufficient. Dancing with him, she thought, would be an exercise in concealment, beauty without revelation. The opposite of art. But still, very likely beautiful.

'Not he. He'll be out with some of the men, not wanting to waste a moonlit night. Making them miss their dancing – well, that's probably an element of his training. The importance of sacrifice, teaching them to give up what's unnecessary. Keeping them focused. Major Black is very strong on focus.'

'Yes. I had rather gathered that. And you? Where do you stand?'

'Oh, I'm with him all the way. Except on a night like this, obviously. He's out there in the moonlight with a squadron of cold and disgruntled young men, and I'm in here dancing by lamplight with a warm and pretty girl. I believe I know who has the better of the night.'

Ruth wasn't sure which of them had the better of the conversation. That was the trouble with clever men – clever men in general, and this one in absolute particular – that you could never be quite certain that they weren't actually that little bit more clever than you allowed for, that they weren't dancing you into a corner. Unfolding all your secrets and privacies like envelopes, learning too much from the twitch of your eye and the touch of your guilty body beneath their firm,

139

manipulative, analytical fingers.

She might think that she had pumped him, but she shouldn't be so sure.

Blessedly, the tune wound to an end, their feet lost the thread of rhythm and they fell apart into two separate unrevealing people, politely smattering applause at the pianist. And before she could even think of fumbling for an excuse, an alibi, a lie, she didn't need one after all.

Because here was Tolchard, Bed Thirty-Four in high fig, rampant in his youth and insolence: looking spruce in a clean uniform, his hair brushed as vigorously as the serge and so glossy it looked almost lacquered.

'Beg pardon, sir, but I believe you've had your ration. My turn with Sister Taylor now.'

'Importunate puppy.' His superior officer growled at him but only because that was expected, part of the show, masculinity on display. In fact, Major Dorian had already stepped away, ceding possession. Neither of them troubled to consult Ruth. It didn't matter; this was what she was here for, after all. She was a bone to be wrangled over, by young men much in need of wrangling. It hurt her heart to watch them at it, all around the floor. She could distract herself easily enough, though. There was the pleasure of dancing rediscovered, the pleasure of so much male company, the soft rub of flattery – *a warm and pretty girl*, Major Dorian had called her – like velvet on bare skin, to soften the scratch of uniform wool.

And, more immediately, seeing these two face off like two grouse sparring at a lek, she could

140

wonder about men and their hierarchies, where Major Dorian stood in the chain of command, whether he actually was Tolchard's superior in any way that mattered. Likely not; he might have a voice in the younger man's future – he might have the ultimate voice, indeed – but a psychiatrist was surely a step to the side, not in the direct line. This was Colonel Treadgold's command, and Tolchard was his guinea pig. If by his own will or by military doctrine the boy belonged to anyone intermediate, that would surely be Major Black. She thought he had sold his soul at the crossroads, and had no wish or ambition to redeem it.

She didn't think it was healthy, quite – or at all – but she could recognize a fact when it slapped her in the face.

Oddly, she seemed to be blushing as he turned away from Aesculapius, as those eyes of his found hers. It must be the heat in here, though she hadn't thought a hallway with mounting stairs could get so warm. Perhaps it was the exercise. She hadn't danced in so long...

Dancing with Tolchard was an exercise in difference. His ruined hand was set firmly in his pocket, casual as ignorance, not to be seen or thought about. His face couldn't be put away so easily, but they could overcome that. She was professionally used to wearing her own face like a mask, making believe that nothing she saw could affect her. Nurses need to be made of granite, or to seem so. If they crumble, they must do it from within.

Stepping into the dance, though, into the flow

of the music: that should have been easy, and was not. Trying to fit her body into the hold of a single arm unbalanced her. There must be a technique to it, one that she could learn from these girls around her, but watching wildly over his shoulder wasn't enough. She couldn't pick it up by sight, and improvisation had never been her gift. She needed teaching and practice, whatever she did.

So there was that, her awkwardness married to his own graceless falter, that discomfort with his own body that she had seen in him from the start. In his head, she was sure, he was still what he always ought to have been, whole and unharmed, an expression of the human animal in delight. He was unaccustomed to the new demands, the new limits of his bone and muscle. He must be trying, she could see how much he tried. There was sweat on his fine-drawn face wherever it wasn't marred by new skin or scars, and she thought the effort of it actually hurt him, and still they could neither one of them quite get it right.

'Do you want to sit this out?' she murmured. 'Perhaps we should, I'm afraid I'm all left feet tonight...'

He shook his head. He tried perhaps to set his lips in stubbornness, only these new lips of his were stubborn in their own way, disinclined to stiffen.

'It's not you, we both know that. And no, I don't want to drop out. Unless I'm embarrassing you?'

'Not that. No. Of course not.'

'Well then, I'd sooner carry on. If you can bear it. I can learn this, I will learn this...'

And so would she; they could learn at least something together. His legs were fine, and he still had a musician's sense of time. It was only the unbalance, the emptiness of his right hand side where there should have been an arm to lean into and was not. That was difficult for them both, and allowing for it – always a moment late and a sudden lurching recovery, the mind's memory dragging behind the body's knowledge – did keep throwing them constantly out of step with the music and with each other.

Still. They persevered. There were compensations. For Ruth they weren't all about the physical intimacy of a male body pressed close – closer than Aesculapius, because he was a young man and they were both having to try that little bit harder and he overcompensated – but largely, yes. He was a boy and working hard. It was never going to be about the conversation.

Almost, she found herself leading. At least, encouraging him which way to go: a nudge of her hip, a duck of her head, little hints that he was sharp enough to pick up without protest, or else took on board subconsciously. She didn't mind either way, so long as his fragile pride wasn't injured. So long as they had space to move, to learn new ways of moving, to make their little errors and recovers without trampling anyone else's toes.

A quickstep, a foxtrot. A waltz. One after another, and nobody interrupted. Good manners or good politics should have led Ruth to another partner, and then another; but she was working suddenly, this was nursing too. The other men knew it, perhaps, and let them be.

And so, one dance after another, they both grew accustomed to that lack in him, that absent bond between them. They learned to account for it, to discount it, to adjust. If his arm couldn't take her weight, then hers must take his instead. And of course must never let it show. She was a nurse, she was strong; she had been a wife, she understood. She could do this. Good.

He was a boy, he was quick, he could learn. Also good.

They were doing well, better with every passing minute.

Then the bomb went off.

Flat and distant and not far enough. Loud enough to break through everything, the talk and the piano and the high closed doors; not enough to rattle the windows, but.

These men had been in war, all of them. She had been in London through the Blitz. They could all make the calculation. Small and near, not big and far away. Close to the house, but probably not actually inside it.

'The stables,' someone said, into the silence that followed the sound of it. 'Come on.'

They had been in war, she was a nurse. Every woman here was a nurse. Of course they all went, bar those few whom Matron intercepted at the door. 'You, you and you – come with me, please.' Whatever it was, whatever they came back with, she wouldn't be unprepared.

Ruth tried not to be superstitious, but she still had a bad feeling about this. She thought Matron was right, nursing would be needed. Nursing at least. Bombs didn't just go off, not spontaneously. Even in places that stored weaponry and explosives.

Places that *used* weaponry and explosives. There were armed men around her, she noticed, in the general rush. Pushing themselves to the front now, as people spilled out into the courtyard. Either they had been on guard already, or else they'd thought to arm themselves from caches she hadn't placed yet. Either way, that was the male response, the military mind. They weren't thinking about casualties.

There was a fire in the stable block. They could see it clearly through the arch beneath the clock tower, that guttering yellow light that can never mean anything else.

Someone was already calling for water, for buckets, for hoses. The male response, the military mind: something to be grateful for. It meant she could just go on, through the arch to the source of the fire.

Someone seized her elbow, tried to stop her, 'Sister, no...'

The male response, the military mind. Sometimes it just needed to be stamped on.

She said, 'I am a nurse. Do you imagine there is no one hurt through there?' As he hesitated, she shrugged him off and strode on.

Through the shadows, and into the light.

Not the first – and blessedly, someone was

already seeing to the horses. Of course the fire had made them frantic. If others hadn't been ahead of her, she might have felt obliged. As it was, she could do her more proper job: turn into the light, head towards the fire.

Others were ahead of her there too. Doing their more proper job, fighting the flames. She took one glance in through the open stable door to see bales of straw ablaze and wooden partitions catching, men at work with blankets and buckets.

She needn't worry about any of that. There were men enough in there. And one out here, calling, beckoning. 'Sister, if you would...'

Of course she would. This was what she'd come for. Just the one victim, apparently, dragged ruthlessly out of the stable and laid on the bricks of the yard. One man kneeling over him, duty-bound until she got there, helpless to do anything but stay.

It was hard to make assessments in the dark, but this wasn't the first time. There had been bombs and bodies in the London streets, catching her unawares, never quite off duty.

She might have sent for a lamp, but there really was no need. Firelight was good enough. 'Fetch blankets,' she said, 'and a stretcher party. No – send them, don't bring them. When they're on their way, find Matron. Tell her we'll need the theatre, and a surgeon ready. Go.'

There was actually a blanket already, that she'd tossed back to make her inspection. A horse blanket, she rather thought. That didn't matter, but it was sodden with blood, which mattered rather a lot. Her patient had lost a hand, newly and entirely. The heat of the blast that took it had cauterized the stump of his wrist somewhat, but not enough.

'What do you need, Sister?' A voice above her, another man being sensible, seeing a need. She could bless the military mind.

'Your tie,' she said shortly. And then, as she fashioned a swift and ruthless tourniquet, 'And your jacket.' Anything to keep her patient warm, until the stretcher came. In the dark on rough brick she couldn't tell how much blood he'd lost in the yard here, never mind how much before that in the stable. He was deep in shock and deeply, deeply cold. She'd sacrifice her own jacket too, if she were wearing one, if the stretcher party didn't show soon. All she had was the cape of her uniform, short and impractical and suddenly infuriating. What was the point of the wretched thing, if it was no use in an emergency? She might send this accommodating man for more horse blankets, and perhaps a rein or a bridle strap, a length of leather to make a better tourniquet. But she shouldn't need any of that, the house was right there, how long could it take to find a couple of orderlies and a stretcher? In a hospital?

Astonishingly, he was trying to speak, her patient. She had thought him sunk too far, perhaps too far to recover, even, though she would do everything she could in any case. But here he was, half pushing himself up on the one elbow, staring at her with wide, appalled eyes, working his mouth dreadfully.

147

His face had that almost-accustomed hollow where a nose should have, must once have been. She couldn't tell how harmed his voice had been before smoke and shock and pain got into it, but it was a reedy scratch now, barely comprehensible.

And yet he was trying so hard, it seemed so important. She read his lips by firelight as much as heard his words. Perhaps more.

Either way. He said, 'I was falling, falling ... I couldn't stop falling.'

And he seemed so scared at the memory, and it drove a bitter nail through her bones.

Oh, Peter...

SIX

Men came, with a stretcher and blankets and Matron too, organized and decisive. There was nothing now for Ruth to do. Not needed in surgery, not wanted at the stable – where Major Black had arrived to take charge of the fire-fighting, organized and decisive and coldly, blisteringly furious – she walked out slowly through the carriage arch, feeling for every step, her head swimming with smoke and dark and aftershock.

And shock itself, shock too, the true thing. Visions of her own sorrow – which she had thought private, secret, not for sharing – suddenly reaching out to snare others, to bring them to destruction.

To hurt them, worse than ever it had yet hurt her.

She was, apparently, shivering. She only realized that because of the way she was walking, hunched over with her arms wrapped around herself, soft fabric beneath her palms and chill shuddering flesh, her own flesh under that.

'Here.'

A weight on her shoulders, a sense of warmth,

smells of tobacco and, yes, bay rum; a man's jacket, it should have been Peter's and if ever she was to be confused or transported now would be the time and yet she was entirely clear for once, lifting her head and looking around and finding Colonel Treadgold in his shirtsleeves.

'Oh,' she said, 'you shouldn't...'

'Nor should you,' he said, mock-sternly, frowning above that absurd moustache. 'Where's your cape, Sister Taylor?'

She glanced back over her shoulder, perhaps a little wildly. She had apparently slipped it off after all, though she didn't remember. It must be back there in the blood and the smoke and the pumped water, under all those loud men's clumsy feet, unless it had been whisked away on the stretcher, still inadequately trying to cover that poor man in his pain.

'Well, never mind,' the colonel said. 'It was a foolish garment anyway. We don't use them here, you will have noticed that. See the quartermaster in the morning, he'll kit you out with our own togs. Which are designed, so Matron informs me, for comfort and practicality and nothing more. Meanwhile, are you feeling as pointless as I am? Set adrift, nothing to do, neither use nor ornament?'

She had apparently been bereft of the power of speech. All she could do was goggle at him.

'It's one of the privileges of rank,' he confided, 'to stand back and let your juniors take over. Come you in with me, we'll have a noggin and let all this pass by. It'll do them good to run around and shout a lot.'

'Shouldn't you be ... Won't they need you in theatre? Sir?' Ah, there was her voice now. Thick and awkward, full of blood and smoke. And impertinence, that too. She needed to cough, and hoped he might take that for apology.

'No, no. Not for simple butchery. Nothing I can do that Captain Felton can't. Matron's got her eye on him, in any case. She'll see that all's done for the best. My best move right now is to keep out of his way and hers. Your best move, too. It's our solemn duty to be both available and unnecessary. So long as people know where to look for us, we should be safe; and someone's sure to notice. As you told me yourself, this is a hospital. Someone always notices. I couldn't be private if I wanted to, so I don't even try.'

Deliberately or otherwise, he was making it sound quite solitary, this life he led. The loneliness of command. It was a cliché, she supposed, but that didn't make it untrue. That there were other officers – Aesculapius, Major Black – who seemed to take precedence despite their rank, who mattered more here despite the colonel's achievements: that could only underline his isolation. Above them all and a little cut off, not quite able to make the decisions that would matter most. Tonight was emblematic, almost. He was the finest surgeon in the hospital, he was the senior officer, and all of that required him to stand aside and let others do what was needed. What he himself was all too obviously itching to do.

She could feel sorry for him, all too easily. If that wasn't another impertinence.

If it wasn't what he wanted her to do. He might be just as manipulative as Major Dorian, in his different way. A big woofly moustache and an eccentric taste for cider didn't make him a fool outside his own competence. She might do well to remember that.

Still, she didn't mind being manipulated if he was looking for allies. She was on his side in any case. Assuming that there actually were two camps here, his and Major Black's: the ward and the training ground, the home front and the war, recovery and redeployment. Healing and killing. She knew where she stood.

There, at least, she did. On that safe ground. Otherwise she felt wretchedly, sickeningly at sea. Her mind was off-kilter, veering wildly, like a compass in a storm. Except that it kept coming back – like a compass in a storm – to point the same way, to the one thing, *Peter*...

She knew she was unbalanced. She was starting to wonder again if she was sane.

Logically, it should be Aesculapius she turned to. If anyone. She was an Englishwoman in wartime; she ought properly to stiffen her spine, stiffen her upper lip and carry on uncomplainingly. Be her own cliché. That, or talk to the unit psychiatrist who was so conveniently to hand.

But here was Colonel Treadgold, large and avuncular and leading her away, astray, up to his own office. It was as though he knew that she was troubled by something more than tonight's horror in the stables. Or else it was recruitment, inducement, an offer of the colonel's shilling.

Or neither of those, just the simple chance of a

drink and a chat with her new commanding officer, at a time when they were both tired and restless, underemployed, and neither of them could hope to go to bed.

Perhaps she should just take this at face value. But his face was half hidden, and so she thought were his motives. And her own, those too. Nothing was simple or clear; nothing could be honest between them, quite, so long as she saw spies in the shrubbery and ghosts in the water.

Of course, there actually were spies in the shrubbery. Spies in training, at least, their own spies and saboteurs. Assassins. Hiding behind the faces that he made for them, faces that didn't need hiding because they could give nothing away.

As for ghosts, well. The ghosts were her own. One ghost, solitary and private. Except that he seemed to have reached out beyond her to touch another, a stranger, more cruelly than ever he would touch her.

The colonel's office occupied a corner of the first floor, where the staff wing turned back from the frontage of the house. It might have been a charming room in peacetime, in daylight, if one could be charmed by views of moor and woodland. Herself, Ruth thought the moors too bleak and the woods too menacing, but she knew herself to be Home Counties through and through; she liked her landscapes gentle and tended, tamed.

Behind its shutters and blackout curtains, given over to military use – and he was still a soldier as well as a surgeon, *Colonel* Treadgold, she ought not to forget that – what might have been a lady's drawing room had become a haven for a man beset, or so she thought. There were ramparts of paper everywhere, stacked high on desk and dresser and the floor too, laid out in a labyrinth that needed care to step through. If there were any kind of order to it, that could only be in his head. Perhaps it all made sense to him, perhaps he had built these walls as a stronghold sure against chaos, a mighty fortress, *ein feste Burg* as Luther's hymn would have it. Perhaps. She thought it looked more like desperate defences, a city besieged.

'I think you need a batman,' she said mildly. 'Or a secretary.'

'Already got 'em, thank you kindly. One of each. I won't let 'em in here. Sit you down, sit, sit.'

He swept up a pile of official-looking buff folders from a chair, cast about for a moment like a man adrift and then deposited them on another teetering pile that was building resolutely in the fireplace. Ruth sat obediently, pondering on the wisdom of having people in your service and not allowing them to do their jobs.

Still. Within those threatening drifts of paperwork, he had made himself a nest that was comfortable enough. Man-comforts: she could recognize those. Smells of smoke and leather, soft cushions and abandoned books, a disreputable pair of slippers on the cold hearth. Really, she thought, there ought to be a dog. An elderly retired spaniel to look up and thump its docked tail at his entrance, to rest its chin on his slip-

154

pered foot, to sigh heavily and grunt a little in its sleep.

The colonel was behind his desk, bending, grunting himself a little as he straightened. He had a bottle in each hand, retrieved from a crate invisible to her; and could hold both easily in one hand, neck and neck, allowing him to scoop up two tankards with the other as he came across to join her.

One of the tankards was pewter, one glass. He peered at that one suspiciously, gave it a wipe with his handkerchief, said, 'Well. That's as clean as it's going to be. Do you mind?'

'Not in the least,' she assured him. Which was true, entirely. His handkerchief at least was clean, she had seen him shake it from its ironed folds; and Peter had taught her long ago not to be too fussy, just as she had been teaching him to be tidier than his wont.

She didn't think she would try to teach the colonel. She thought he was beyond her measure.

He set everything he carried somehow on the mantelpiece, though it was crammed already with books and tobacco pots, a pipe rack, ashtrays and matches and figurines that must surely be a hangover from the house's proper owner, a residue not packed away.

He had retrieved his jacket from her shoulders as they came indoors. 'No need to give the gossips more to talk about, eh? They'll be busy enough already.' Now he rummaged in a pocket to produce a penknife that he might have carried since he was a boy, the ivory handle was so worn and grubby. The blade looked keen enough, though, and dealt efficiently with the bottle tops.

Amber liquid gurgled and frothed within the dimpled glass. He passed her drink to her, as the room filled with the heady scent of apples in ferment; poured the other and drank himself, and sighed like that absent spaniel, and wiped his moustache with his handkerchief, and leaned against the mantelpiece and waited.

It was the waiting that was wicked. Learned behaviour, she was sure: all Aesculapius.

She capitulated quickly. 'What do you think happened tonight, sir?'

'An accident, of course. Major Black plays his war games with live ammo; of course there must be accidents. The man was careless, or else there was a fault in the device, the grenade or what-ever he was playing with. Mistakes happen. And they cost us dear, every time. They've cost that poor young man his hand, and likely his hopes of going overseas. If he can't work a parachute – or a garrotte–' added with a twist of the lips, an expression of absolute distaste coupled with ruthless recognition of the facts – 'then I don't see how he can be used effectively. Or put in place to be used at all. It's not my decision to make, but this might be a blessing. I don't sup-pose he'd see it that way, they're all mad keen to go. But I might actually get to rebuild a man for civilian life, rather than as a weapon of war.'

Actually she thought any number of his patients would not be useful to Major Black, but of course it wouldn't be those who preyed on his mind. It was a human thing, to dwell on loss and sacrifice; she knew. Who better?

If it took two hands to manage a parachute, and managing a parachute was a prerequisite for being sent on a mission, she thought she could give a name to one more young man doomed to disappointment in the end, however much he practised silence and wore his scars like a hero.

That was a relief to her, much more personal than the colonel's, sharper and more surprising.

Never mind. Not what she was here for. She could think about that later.

She was here at the colonel's invitation. She wasn't quite sure what he'd had in mind, though no doubt he meant to grill her about something. That, or simply to seal her to his own camp, not realizing that she was there already by conviction and temperament and experience too. It seemed a brutal thing to her, that men who had given so much already should be expected or allowed to hurl their lives away like grenades flung in the teeth of the enemy. Never mind that they were all volunteers. No doubt they thought they would go out in one bright, eternal, glorious flame, that ending they had somehow not quite achieved in their crashed planes, tragic heroes, romantic to the last.

Never mind that they were all of them desperate, damaged beyond bearing, however glib they seemed.

Never mind that she understood them so exactly, that she herself had been seeking a posting overseas and a swift eclipsing death.

None of that mattered. Even the war's need couldn't matter, against the cold reality of what was happening here.

She could say all of that to him, and it was very likely what he had hoped to hear, what he had fetched her for. They could be campaigners in some way, working together to mitigate the worst of Major Black, to save one patient and then another. Find ways to keep them or ways to transfer them, anything to keep them out of the major's hands, not given to his project.

Still not what she was here for. Whatever the colonel thought.

She took a breath, took a sip – cool and crisp like an apple from the cellar, tangy and sharp like an apple kept too long, gone too far – and took the plunge. Said, 'Colonel, do you believe in ghosts?'

That stymied him. It sat exactly between him and his purpose, unexpected and unavoidable. He stood quite still for a moment, then reached for tobacco and a pipe. Just for something to do with his hands, she thought. While he thought, while he tried to fit her question to his understanding.

He said, 'No. No, I don't believe I do. If you asked Major Dorian, I expect he would say that he believed in the power of faith or some such, but I'm not that clever. I've spent a lot of years with my fingers inside men's bodies, and I've never found any sign of a soul. Or any other kind of spirit either. I know how bodies work, and I don't see how anything could survive once they stop working.'

So did she, and nor did she; and yet, and yet.

She had thought Peter was all in her head, her

158

own head. The man in the stable, though, he had been falling and falling. Whatever he did that was wrong – snatching at something or dropping something, cutting the wrong wire or letting a tool slip at the wrong moment, striking a spark perhaps where it was most foolish – whatever he did, it wasn't that which haunted him as he lay deep in pain and shock in the yard there, waiting for rescue. He had lost his hand and maybe more, he might have been dying, he might certainly have thought he was dying; and, *I was falling, falling ... I couldn't stop falling.*

It was her nightmare, her waking horror, the vision that had possessed her ever since she came to this house.

It was her husband, watching his death rise up to greet him. Tumbling coldly into its arms.

Carrying her with him, down and down, again and again.

What in the world – or out of it, in the afterworld, in no world that made any sense to her – but what was he doing in another man's mind?

Falling and falling, yes, she knew that. He would have said that, for the smile of it, when he was alive. In her head, he still could. He could comment wryly on his own death, and her haunting too. But in her head was where all that should stay. Where he should stay. She almost didn't mind, could almost welcome him. This last vestige. But...

But. Not in other people's heads. Not where he could cause them harm.

She thought obscurely that it might be her fault. Must be. Possibly.

How and why? Those were the obvious questions: unasked, impossible. The colonel would send her to Aesculapius. That man would peer interestedly inside her, make a project of her, not allow her to interfere with his other more important scheming.

And meanwhile a man would still be lying in a bed somewhere – here or elsewhere, they might take him away, a failed conspirator, his papers marked as his body was – with new damage, a lifetime of change and difficulty ahead. And Peter still in his mind, perhaps, still falling.

Responsible.

He hated responsibility, always had.

She carried it for him, when she could.

Tonight she wanted to accuse herself, she wanted to scream at him, she wanted to be sane and see that none of this was true. All at once, these things, she wanted them all. And could have none except perhaps the first of them, a bitter madness, *this is all my fault*. And almost opened her mouth to confess it, except that there was cider in her glass and that was easier, gulp and swallow and wrap her fingers around the mug like a man, cherish the thick glass of it and see, not shaking at all, her hands, no. Doing their job, gripping tight. Like her thoughts, tight and strong and secure...

Bless him, the colonel didn't say *why do you ask?* It was the obvious next step, and he avoided it magnificently.

'I think this house would give anyone the vapours, mark you. Even without the black-out and the groans of the wounded and Major

Black's favourites scuttling about in the shadows, practising unspeakable acts. It's why I won't take probationers here. One reason why. I'm not sure the security bods would allow it anyway, but the last thing I need is silly girls shrieking and fainting in coils because they heard a floorboard creak or the draught brought a cobweb down in their hair.'

Was that meant as a warning, *don't get hysterical or you'll be out of here*? She wasn't sure. He seemed too bluff to be indirect, but perhaps he meant it as a compliment, *I don't need to be blunt with you*. Perhaps.

She said, 'The house is very atmospheric, certainly, but I think atmosphere is what you make of it, for good or otherwise.' It was in her head, she was saying. Emphatically. She knew that. And good lord, this house was full of pilots, crashed-out pilots, sky jockeys who had taken a throw. Small wonder if one of them babbled about falling when he was in shock, *in extremis*. She held no lien on that particular nightmare, here or anywhere.

Tight, strong, secure. Yes.

Comfortably in agreement, then, they could move on. Marching in step, and no need for any further confessional. Not from her, at least. He said, 'Does it trouble you, what Major Black gets up to with my men?' But that was his own confession in a thin disguise, *it troubles me*, and an invitation to step inside his tent. Now that she was firmly in his camp.

She said, 'It seems ... a terrible waste, to me. Of your work, and their lives.' Tolchard seemed to be foremost in her mind, as though all the men wore one face, and it was his. That was odd, because she'd gathered that he was almost least likely to be sent, however much he agitated to go.

'War is wasteful, by definition. And doctors like me have always been called on to patch up the wounded and send them back to the front.'

'Yes, but not like this.' He was playing devil's advocate, she recognized that, and not in the least trying to win the argument. Only laying it out, other men's words repeated, to find how she replied. 'Not men who have given so much already. And not to send them on missions they can't hope to survive.' And at last, bluntly, 'We don't encourage suicide. Not in this country.'

He smiled like a man who has lost a chess game to his own bright student, though he'd played as well as he might; and wiped froth from his moustache and said, 'And yet, you know, we do. Of course we do. Men have always gone – been sent – on suicide missions. Just, never on this scale, and never quite this ruthlessly. This is ... industrial. And they've tied me in as more than a conspirator, I'm an *investor*. I hate that.'

It was all about responsibility, she saw. It always was, with men. They did dread it so. Especially where they could sit safe themselves and send others to their distant deaths. It wasn't wastage that upset him, nor senselessness. He did see sense in what they did here, and what it would mean after. He just felt responsible. Rebuilding his patients in order to make them better killers, more efficient suicides, of course he would hate that. Anyone must, if they had the least trace of sensitivity in them. If they had a soul.

She said, 'Not a willing investor, surely. Obedient, as we all are to the occasion, but not willing. That must count for something. If you want to reckon the responsibility–' *though I do think you'd be better off not* – 'then you have to look to Major Black first, surely? To him and Major Dorian.' Because she didn't at all see why Aesculapius should duck it. Sometimes it felt to her as though they were all tools of Aesculapius, pieces that he moved about.

'Perhaps – but without my work, they'd have no raw material. No men to train or send off on missions. Most of these lads would survive, perhaps, but they wouldn't be able to function. They wouldn't be able to throw their lives away–' and suddenly he looked spaniel-sad, a kind man pushed into an unwelcome cruelty – 'be that for king and country or otherwise, without my help to make them fit again. To give them hands, by and large. A face is neither here nor there, but hands, yes. I give hands to saboteurs, assassins. Suicides. I wouldn't mind,' he cried suddenly, though that was blatantly untrue, 'but Dorian catches them at their weakest. It's his stock-in-trade. Of course any young man thinks his life is over, coming round in a hospital bed with his face and hands gone west and all the nice girls flinching when he tries to smile. If he had a gun he'd shoot himself there and then, if he only had fingers that worked. Any man would. Have a plausible fellow loom up at your

163

bedside then and talk about one last service to your country, the chance to strike at the heart of the Nazi machine; of course you'll see it as an honourable way out, hitting back at the enemy and dying in the process, a medal and a hero's grave and no need actually to live with what's been done to you.

'And then he's sent here and I give him back a body he can work with. A face, too. I can't give them back their beauty, but ... Well. Something they can work with. If I only had the time. They do see that, some of them, they see the possibilities. But by then they're committed, of course, and they won't back down. That's what's so devilish clever. It's their sense of honour that gets them, coming and going. Suicide is a disgrace, perhaps, but so is cowardice; and dying in the line of fire, in the course of duty, in time of war, that's another thing altogether. It's the opposite of disgrace, it's nobility. Even where death is certain. *Especially* where death is certain.'

He was a large and florid man, but his voice was quiet when he talked of this, his gestures small and tight to the body. That wasn't discretion, Ruth thought; it was pain. This was the true colonel, stripping himself raw in front of her.

She said, 'Still. What you do here, what you learn, you can put that to use elsewhere, and afterwards.' *On men not doomed already. Yes, and women too, and children.* 'This ... opportunity can't last. The Germans will realize the ruse, and grow more watchful of injured men.'

'Yes. They will distrust their own heroes.

That's a consideration too, of course. Another blow for our side. And as soon as it happens – no, as soon as we *know* it's happening, which will be a little lag of the event – then we'll stop sending these lads. I hope we will. I'll insist on it. And as you say, I will have learned more, and can put it into practice. Somewhere else, I won't stay here,' he added with a glance around his quarters, the hint of a shudder. 'I won't ask for a posting, I'll move my whole hospital. Somewhere closer to the airfields. The ministry will oblige me, I make no doubt. I've earned credit enough, these last months. But still. Between now and then...'

Yes. There would be more months to endure, before that day. Men to heal, men to train, men to send away.

Not Tolchard. She felt suddenly, oddly determined on that. One way or another, she would make sure that boy stayed here. Despite his own best efforts. And as many others as she could keep. She tipped her glass towards the colonel in a mute toast, and saw his rise in response. It was a pact, then, all unspoken. They would do everything possible between them to frustrate Major Black. Yes, and Major Dorian.

Did that make them traitors, working against their own country's interests?

Perhaps it did. She felt she could live with it, if so. There would be no wilful sabotage, no treasonous acts. Just a quiet determination that the life of a man was worth more than a bullet, more than a bomb. Their patients here were not mere ammunition for the war's pursuit. Some, no doubt, must be eaten by the machine of it, already set up and running. But not all of them, no.

Not Tolchard.

There seemed to be nothing more to say. She finished her cider and handed back her glass, wondered for a moment if she ought to salute. Or shake hands on the deal, or...

Or neither of those, apparently. He nodded and turned his shoulder to her, fussing silently with his pipe. Embarrassed, perhaps, or anxious, or overweeningly discreet.

She bade him a swift, soft goodnight and let herself out. Closed the door behind her, took a slightly tremulous breath and didn't quite know what to do with herself now.

Looked up and down the corridor – and, like a summoned ghost, like a figure caught by light and drawn by light, drawn out of light, there was a silhouette that moved strangely, that woke strange feelings in her.

Her mouth opened, of its own accord. She almost said, 'Peter?'

In fact, what she said was, 'Michael?'

SEVEN

And blushed, almost stammered before she caught herself; didn't want to give him that much leeway but corrected herself anyway, said, 'Flying Officer Tolchard, I mean. Bed Thirty-Four. Why aren't you in it?'

'What,' he said, 'in all this excitement?'

'The excitement's over.' And he was dressed for bed: pyjamas and dressing gown, a pair of Turkish slippers on his feet. He must have made that same calculation for himself, and then – what? Something happened. It was too soon to plead *I couldn't sleep.* Even for a child, this would be too soon. He did have that air of little-boy-lost, and at another time she thought he would know that, and use it shamelessly. If he was acting now, he was doing it the other way around, trying to convince her there was really nothing wrong. Reaching for his charm, and not quite finding it; falling back on his wicked reputation, and falling short. No need to tell him that. He looked wretched enough already.

Her turn to act, then. Clipping down the corridor at a rate of knots, tucking her arm through his and turning him for all the world as though

167

she meant to herd him back to his room and tuck him into bed like the nanny she was not with the wilful boy that he was striving to seem.

'And what are you doing up here, in any case?' This was the wrong floor, in the wrong wing. He wouldn't have come the staff's way, across the yard. He must have come all through Major Black's domain in this state. He'd know where the light switches were, but even so that would be a long walk, a solitary shuffle in those unlikely slippers. He might take it on an impulse, but not pointlessly. Not on his own, on such a night.

'I was ... looking for someone.'

'Colonel Treadgold? He's in his office, I've just—'

'No. Not the colonel.' *Not at all the colonel*, his tone said, *absolutely not*.

Which might mean he had an illicit liaison with a nurse or an orderly – but no, not a liaison, or she wouldn't have found him so adrift. If he was only hoping for kindred spirits, he would have found them closer, in the patients' wing. Major Black would still be out in the stables, trying to diagnose what had gone so badly amiss with his exercise.

She made a reasoned guess, then. 'Major Dorian.'

'Yes.' It came out like a confession of shame, all reluctance. 'He's not downstairs, and I, I don't know where his bedroom is...'

Neither did Ruth. She knew his office, but presumably the man didn't sleep on his couch.

'Well. Failing him, you'll have to make do

168

with me.' The nurse instead of the psychiatrist, the ward sister in lieu of the major, the woman and not the man. She didn't know which substitution it was that made him falter, but she was having none of that. A firm hand on his elbow – on his good elbow, the arm that worked – and he had no choice.

At this point, neither did she. She couldn't frogmarch him all the way back to his proper corridor, to the certain noise and curiosity of a dozen other wakeful men. She couldn't try doors at random until she found one that would open into somewhere appropriate.

She took him up to her own room.

It was almost certainly against regulations; but no one had explained what the regulations were in a hospital that was also an assassins' training ground, where patients spent half the night out of their beds conducting exercises with live ammunition. And he might not be ill exactly but he was still a patient, and he clearly needed something, and this was the best she had to offer.

Justifying wildly, secretly in her head, she sat him on her bed and slipped out again. Tapped on a panel two doors down, heard no answer, deduced that Judith was either on night duty or else helping out in surgery – and opened the door, slipped through, stole all the makings for cocoa. Pan and electric ring, mugs and milk and all, she loaded a convenient tray and carried it back to her room.

Tolchard startled to his feet, reached to take the tray from her, remembered or discovered anew that he couldn't quite do that and flushed at his failure.

She smiled. 'Dreadful how deep they go, isn't it, common manners? You can't override them, just because they don't make sense any more. You could close the door–' shifting from the general to the particular with a subtle grace that pleased her mightily – 'if you wouldn't mind. I don't believe I can manage,' without a neat little back-heel that she would have used without a second thought if he hadn't been standing there, feeling so obviously and utterly useless. 'Thank you. Now sit yourself down again while I make the cocoa. Oh, and tell me why you so particularly wanted to see Major Dorian in the middle of the night.'

It would be easier, she thought, for him to talk if she wasn't looking at him, if she didn't seem to be paying particular attention.

Even so, he had trouble getting started. Which must be unusual for him, almost unheard of. But here he was, staring down at his hands, his tongue stumbling and falling still. Trying again, when her own patient silence became too much for him to hold out against.

'Dusty ... Dusty was my room-mate. One of.'

'I'm sorry, Michael,' and this time it was deliberate; there would be nobody else in his hospital who used his Christian name. Probably nobody closer than his mother, and where was she? 'Who's Dusty?'

'Dusty Miller. The man on the table just now, having his hand cut off.'

'Well,' she said judiciously, because she didn't want to think about that man at all – falling and

170

falling – but a nurse has to do all manner of things she doesn't particularly want to, 'I can see how that would be unpleasant for all of you, an empty bed and your friend in pain. What did you want to see Major Dorian about?'

That was perhaps a little too direct. His eyes shied away from her, his mind from the swift answer she'd hoped for.

But then, slowly, sideways, he came back to it. 'The major has ... something he gives me, when I can't sleep.'

'The night nurse could give you a sleeping draught. No need to trouble the major.'

But that wasn't it, of course. He shook his head. 'Not valerian. Not what I'm after. I can't, I'm afraid to sleep sometimes. I have dreams...'

So did she, sometimes. Dreadful dreams. That would be no help to him now, to tell him so. She stirred the cocoa, thinking that it too would be of little help after all if sleep was the enemy when it came, not when it kept away; and said, 'What does Major Dorian give you, then?'

'I don't know. It's ... calming. It doesn't stop me sleeping, but it makes me not afraid; and then if I do dream, the dreams are strange and really rather wonderful. Not at all what I'm afraid of. Only now, well, sometimes I'm even more afraid to go to sleep without it, do you see?'

Oh, she did see. She saw all too well. It sounded like tincture of opium to her, some description of laudanum. Michael would surely have needed morphine for his pain when his burns were fresh, and again no doubt after his operations. He would have grown used to it, come to

171

depend on it. Withdrawal would give him bad nights, only made worse by his memories – and Major Dorian was calmly feeding his addiction instead of helping him to overcome it.

Well, why not? If he was going to give his life anyway in a month or two months or half a year – *throw his life away* was how she thought of it, but this was wartime; she was perhaps insufficiently patriotic and not at all male enough – then why not give him what he wanted now? *The tools to do the job* the major would call it, perhaps.

Never mind that it was most uncertain whether Michael would actually be sent on any mission. He wasn't head of any list, except in his own stubborn head. It would be Major Black's call as much as Major Dorian's. Aesculapius was only covering all the possibilities. Playing Boy Scout with a young man's life, making sure he was prepared.

Ruth could hate Major Dorian sometimes. It really was all too easy.

This, now, this would be hard. Except that he was a sensible young man, accustomed to trouble. He wouldn't fuss over what he could not have. He certainly wouldn't expect her to produce Major Dorian out of the air. Nor to sit up all night holding his hand while he sweated through whatever came, his private hell. He was of that class and generation that did turn to women, had likely done it all his life – nanny or housekeeper, she would still guess, rather than mother – but was too well trained to take them for granted. He'd drink his cocoa and be politely

172

grateful, say goodnight as soon as his mug was empty, leave her and go – where? Back to his ward, to his bed? Perhaps, but Dusty's empty bed would hang in the corner of his eye all night, like an accusation. He might have somewhere else, a place of solitude if not safety, some dark hole in this pitiless house where he could crouch and set his teeth and suffer alone.

No. Not while she had any say in the matter. Certainly not so long as she had him here, sitting on her bed. For the moment he was trapped by hot cocoa and good breeding. Later – well. She needed another way to snare him. It would be no use marching him back to bed and tucking him in. An easy, superficial reassurance wouldn't do it either.

Well, then. If nothing easy would avail, she would do what was harder.

And not spare him, either. If he was stubbornly determined to sweat, he could do it under her eye. Under her whip, if that was what it took to keep him here. The lash of her tongue, wielded all unkindly: he wouldn't run away from that. Too stubborn for his own good, this boy.

She said, 'Why has tonight upset you so?'

He would be staring, she thought – deliberately so, to make his point, little boy with his eyes stretched in disbelief – if his eyes would only allow it. The colonel's handiwork was efficient, but not that artful. Those heavy awkward lids – *cut from your underarms, Bed Thirty-Four, I know far too much about how you're put together* – wouldn't open wide enough to give him the expression he was yearning for.

He said, 'Dusty, what happened to him ... He's maimed for life now, not even the colonel could fix that hand. The colonel's not even trying. Of course I'm upset, we all are.'

'Of course. But let me be brutal, Michael. You're all more or less maimed for life, regardless of the colonel's wizardry. Miller's not the only one to lose his hand.' She carefully wasn't looking at his own, useless in his lap there, but it lay between them none the less. An unspoken truth, an artefact of war. 'And' – *being brutal* – 'if Miller is out of the picture, that moves everyone below him one rung up the ladder, doesn't it? Brings you one step closer to what you all seem to want so much, an actual mission overseas?' *Including you, young man. I know how low you stand, on that wretched ladder.*

Hard to be sure if he wanted to flush or turn pale. The patchwork skin on his cheeks was livid only at the seams, along the lines of his scars. 'I–I suppose so, yes.'

'And you've been sleeping well enough recently, you haven't needed Major Dorian's medication or you'd have it to hand, or else the night nurse would. It's not the normal commerce of this hospital, to have patients trudging from one wing to another in search of a lost psychiatrist. So tell me truly, Michael, what's on your mind? What spectre's haunting you so thoroughly that you need a special dose to see you through tonight?'

Empty-handed, he would have fiddled she thought with the tasselled cord of his dressing gown. Two-handed, he might have turned and

174

turned his mug between his restless fingers. As it was, as *he* was, he sat painfully still, gazing down into the steam of it; and then lifted his head and met her eye to eye and said, 'It's the fear, you see. If it can happen to Dusty, it can happen to any of us. We train with live ammo every day, and none of us is as handy as we used to be. We're all awkward sometimes. Things get dropped. Things that go bang, sometimes. It's that easy, that's the message of tonight. One clumsy moment, and all that we're working for is gone. Or just held up, put back, months more in hospital before we can be patched together again. Any of us can do that to ourselves, at any time...'

Now she'd touched the truth of him, she knew. But she still didn't understand it. Not by a distance.

She said, 'Explain this to me. What is it that's so dreadfully urgent, what makes you so mad keen to get over there?'

His turn now, not to be understanding her. 'Well, it's the war.'

'The war's not going to be over, Michael. Not any time soon.'

'Our part in it is. This whole project is, well, not one strike only, but a few rapid punches. Only some of us can go. The Nazis will catch on soon enough. We go now, soon, in the first wave, or we don't go. The chances are there won't be a second.'

'And you're frightened of missing it. I see.' He reminded her suddenly of her father. After a moment's thought, she told him that. 'He joined

175

up in 'fourteen, right at the start. He says he was terrified of its being all over by Christmas, of his not having the time to reach the front. He was in the trenches for four years, he saw all his friends killed and most of his men, he came out of it – well, I won't say ruined, but damaged, yes. Maimed, if you like. In his mind, I mean, from confronting the truth of it, what war was really like, as against what he'd been told.'

He seemed almost to be smiling, though it was hard to be certain. She heard her own voice die away, as she saw what little impact her words were having. He spelled it out, unnecessarily, brutal in his turn. 'Sister Taylor. Really truly, that's not a revelation that I need. I've seen the truth of war, I've seen the worst of it. Seen it and felt it,' his one hand showing her, gesturing dangerously with his half-drunk cup: his face, his other hand. Had she forgotten?

'I hadn't forgotten that,' though in fact she almost had, and she blushed at the lie of it. He might choose to see that as a compliment. He was what he was, more than the sum of his injuries, and she still found him worthwhile. Worth her time, even in the dead dark, the chill hours of the morning. 'I'm sorry, I expressed myself badly. What I mean is, it's not his naivety you remind me of, just his hurry to immolate himself.'

'For his country's good.' That was flung back at her like a flag waved in the face of the enemy. Scorn and defiance, but she was ready for it.

'Who was it who said that patriotism was the last refuge of a scoundrel?'

176

'Samuel Johnson—' of course he'd know that, he was all too well brought-up, this boy – 'but—'

'But nothing, young man. You don't get to flourish me down that way. You said it yourself, you've seen the worst that war can do. Face to face, and altogether too close. You shouldn't expect to go back again for a second look. There's no need.'

'I've done my bit, you mean?'

'Yes. Yes, that is what I mean. You've done more than enough. There will always be other volunteers, new men.'

'No one quite like me,' he asserted.

'Well, no, but enough who are like enough. Enough like you. Again, you've said it yourself. There are plenty here, ahead of you on the ladder. Too many for your comfort, you're afraid they'll squeeze you out. But if the mission's all that matters, let them go. They're ahead of you for a reason, they're better equipped,' *two hands and a less ready tongue, a voice that won't give them away.*

He said nothing. She had pushed him finally to the wall he didn't want to breach. Determinedly, she pushed him over. 'You know this, Michael. You know it all. And you're still desperate to go. Or is that it, truly? Isn't it rather that you're desperately afraid to stay?'

Again he made that stubborn gesture, lifting his head to meet her gaze. Now it was more effortful, and his eyes wanted to flick away but he wouldn't let them. He'd had fire in him before. Now it was ashes, and she was sorry.

177

He said, 'What do I have to stay for? Crippled and disfigured, what kind of life is that? Listen to your own words. *Face to face,* you said, *too close.* Only it won't be wartime, and it won't ever be over. I'll always be too close, and my face will always look like this. Would you want to spend a lifetime watching people stare and shy away?'

So that was it. She supposed it had to be. She'd let him fool her at the start, or at least allowed herself to feel fooled – *please, you mustn't mind my face. I don't, so why should you?* – but at heart he was still a boy, still utterly exposed. Almost literally so, the skull beneath the skin. You couldn't help but see it, looking at the crude mask that covered it.

She wondered if heroic self-sacrifice in wartime always came down to male vanity in the end.

Sometimes it's just cruel to be kind. She tried the other thing. 'Better to die a hero than live a cripple, is that it?'

She put as much contempt into her voice as she could manage, a biting withering scorn for his weakness, but he didn't seem to be withered. He blinked in that slow deliberate learned way of his, still nothing like an instinct, and said, 'Yes. Yes, that's it.'

'And you're terrified you won't get the chance. You'll have an accident like Dusty did tonight, and rule yourself out. Or Major Black will decide against you, and give your place to someone else, someone fitter or less fit; or you'll just run out of time, the Germans will catch on and the project will be closed down before your turn comes round. And then you'll just have to face up to – well, to life with that face, and that hand, and all that they imply. People being shy of you, as you say. Children shrieking and running away, I expect. You probably like children, boys of your kind usually do: the way they gaze up at you with worship in their eyes, and then run off making aeroplane noises with their arms spread wide for wings. Not so much worship now, just the running away. That must be unbearable, I expect. So here you are, still hoping to escape into some glorious immolation, to go down blazing – again – and write your name in letters of fire across the history of the war; and the prospect of losing even that little hope must be terrible to you. Which is why you suddenly can't sleep without drugs, and why you've come all across the hospital in chase of them. I'm still right, am I?'

She was still trying to sound crisp and contemptuous, which was hard when she was so near tears. Little boy lost, in a world more cruel than he could cope with: he did remind her so very much of herself. It was easier for a man in some ways, but far more pitiful. She had to try to swallow down the pity, and simply let the accusation stand.

Something at least seemed to be getting through. He had to touch his tongue to those rubbery approximate lips of his, before he could even whisper 'Yes.'

'Oh, Michael.' She was abruptly sitting on the bed beside him, without consciously having

179

decided to move. Sitting on his good side, taking the half-drunk mug from his hand and setting it safely out of reach before it could tip all over the blankets. 'Other people's rudeness, their ignorance – is that really worth your life? Children can still learn to love you, it'll only take them a day to get over the way you look, and then they'll be fascinated. You're still a hero, you're a war ace; that's your own courage that you wear blazoned on your face. Like a duelling scar, but infinitely more precious. It tells everyone you meet who you are and what you did for us. You should be proud. We will be, after the war. We'll see men like you and we'll know your story before you tell it us, because it'll be the story of England and how we survived...'

'Scoundrel.' He was trying to smile again, making a worse job of it this time, barely a manufactured twitch at the corner of his mouth. She supposed it would take as much effort as blinking, or more. He'd need to be committed.

'Well. It's mostly a lie to plead patriotism, but I think I'm allowed to celebrate it in others. We won't bruit it abroad, but we'll keep it as our dirty little secret. You can call me a patriot and I'll call you a hero, but only when we're alone.'

She gave his arm a little shake, just to underline their pact, because she did appear to be holding it. Both hands curled around his biceps, one above the other. When had that happened? She used to cling to Peter this way, close and warm. No man else, not ever. Not her father, even.

The arm was stiff, because this one elbow was

braced against his knee. She thought he'd be leaning on both, staring down between his feet, only that his other arm wouldn't bend this way and wasn't reliable for leaning on. She wasn't sure she'd be allowed to hug him that side, it might hurt his *amour propre*, that damned vanity again. Or it might more simply hurt him, there might still be pain. She wasn't sure. She ought to be sure; he was her patient, after all.

Not officially, perhaps; not on her corridor. But still. She ought to know.

He'd slipped into a brown study. Best to leave him to it. Not literally, she wasn't moving from his side. She wasn't so much as shifting a finger, now that she seemed to have taken hold. This might be what he needed more than opiates, just someone to be with him. Someone he wasn't in competition with for those few precious places, seats in a plane and a perilous fall beyond. Down and down...

Her own head might have been spinning a little, she might have been falling herself, but he was looking up suddenly, twisting his head to find her, close and awkward as she was.

Now he had the words suddenly, now they were getting there, the truth at last; and yes, poor fool of a hero, it was all about his vanity after all.

She really should have known.

He said, 'Children might get used to me, perhaps – but they'll never be my own, will they? No girl could get used to this.'

'Across the breakfast table, do you mean? Or in bed, is that it?' Yes, of course that was it. He was trying to blush again, his face like a jigsaw,

181

all his scars standing out. 'Do you really think that poorly of us, as a sex?' She gave his arm a shake again, this time in simple admonishment. 'Beauty's not the only thing that matters, you know,' though of course it must seem that way, at that age.

Perhaps she was wrong, perhaps – at that age – beauty really was the only thing that mattered. Odd, that she couldn't remember. Peter had eclipsed his own face in her mind; now when she thought about him – when she could see past his falling – it was the whole man that she thought of, his entire self. Ten years ago, though...?

'Not all, no – but I don't believe I'll get as far as breakfast. I don't believe I'll get as far as bed. What girl will ever come close enough to see past this?' He wanted to make that gesture of his, *see my face, see me for what I am*, but of course she was holding his arm and she wouldn't let him do it. He tossed his head instead, and glowered at her, almost too close to see him at all. As it happened she could see every detail of his grafts, every stitch mark of his scarring – but if her eyes were less acute, if the light were just a little softer...

I'm here. Is this close enough? She wanted to say that, but it was impossible. He needed to see it for himself, and his eyes were blurred by tears. Something deeper than self-pity, a well of clean distress. That sweet voice thickened clumsily as he said, 'I ... I'm afraid that I'll die, and I will never have slept with a girl. I can get it over quickly, if Major Black will only let me; or I can hang on for forty or fifty years, behind this

182

hideous face, and it'll still be the thing that I carry. Do you blame me, truly, for wanting to be quick and clean and gone? And some use to my country in the going? And then not having to do this any more, not having to talk to girls while all the time I'm thinking *you never will, will you? You and all your kind, you never will. Not with me, not now.'*

'Oh, good heavens above,' she said lightly, not to let him see the truth of it, that she didn't actually blame him in the least. 'Is that all? You astonish me. I thought you pilots had these matters all arranged. There are places you can go, you know. In London, and probably closer to home, wherever your home airfield was. Don't your fellow officers take you there to celebrate your wings? Long before your accident, some-one should have done that for you, silly boy. Virginity isn't a blight, any more than it's a trea-sure. It's just something to be attended to. And after that – well. Your future's up to you.' She wanted to say *in your own hands,* but he'd probably take that amiss. In this mood, he'd turn savage if she gave him half a chance. 'I've been a nurse a long time, you know. I've seen men far worse hurt than you, finding themselves wives and having families. And others turning their backs on responsibility altogether, refusing to settle down, keeping girlfriends all their lives.'

He wouldn't be convinced so easily. He had built himself a tower of isolation, and he meant to leap from the top of it in one fabulous gesture of finality. It would take a significant effort of will now for him to step back to earth and soldier on more plainly. She had to give him better reasons, or he'd never choose to live.

Maybe self-contempt was the spur he needed. He had enough of that, she thought, to spare.

'You do actually have to ask a girl, though. First. Unless you honestly think it's better to fling your life away, sooner than hear her say no. Some of them will say no, I'm sure; for some of them, your face may be the reason. For others, not. We're not all that cheap or silly. A girl might still say no, but I think you'll be surprised how many don't. Charm and good company count for more, Michael. You'll learn that. If you let yourself.'

Charm and good company, youth and vulnerability and impulsiveness and hurt.

He lifted his head one more time, looked at her too closely, didn't try to hide the bitter anticipation in his voice as he said, 'Will you, then?'

Somehow, she had really not expected that.

She had every reason in the world to say no, except that he expected it. He was boxing himself in, one last clever move and it was done; her refusal would be his confirmation, that there really was nothing to live for now.

Boxed in herself, she couldn't do that to him. She had no more liberty than he did; they were pieces on a board, moving each other.

She couldn't say yes, either. She hadn't said yes to any man, since Peter. That was ... long ago. She'd only had the word once, and she spent it. She couldn't claim it back.

Virginity wasn't a blight, but fidelity in widowhood? That might be.

184

She worried absurdly that Peter might be watching from the mirror.

The door was closed, and even so she thought he might be standing right outside. Watching, through the wood.

Her only sureness was that he wasn't quite in here, in this little room. In here there was only her and Michael. So long as neither of them looked beyond, so long as they could keep this privacy, so long...

So long and no longer, but for now, well.

She leaned forward and kissed him.

It was what you did, how things began. Always with a kiss.

Kissing Michael was curiously like kissing a book, she thought. A book in a country-house library, perhaps, a hand-sewn binding with high ridged seams. Those lips of his were like much-handled calfskin, butter soft and warm but not responsive.

She didn't know how much that was ignorance and how much it was nerves, how much the stiffness of artifice. Hand-sewn lips would never be as flexible as nature's own. She wasn't sure if their skin too had come from his underarms, or some other part of his body; she half thought she was still on duty here, testing Colonel Treadgold's handiwork. She hoped not to test it to destruction, sprung stitches and leaking seams.

Or she hoped not this either, but perhaps she was doing Aesculapius' work instead, or Major Black's. Cutting him loose, letting him go. Giving him this last gift, the one thing that he wanted. This once behind him, what more could there be, what could she find to keep him, to give him cause to stay?

Well. All that was for afterwards. Whatever the repercussions, whatever the consequences, she was committed now.

She slipped her tongue between those unyielding lips – rubber, she thought, underlying the leather; how had the colonel made them, and with what? – and teased his teeth apart, found his own tongue lurking. Shy and wet and strange, not Peter, not tasting right. No matter. She should follow her own advice, perhaps. *Your future's up to you.*

He wouldn't relax, of course not. It would be foolish to expect that, a young man stretched like wire, so very ready to snap. Still. He was obedient to her hands, not resistant, if not quite yet ready to cooperate. Starting to believe it, perhaps.

She had to undress him, he didn't seem able to manage on his own account. Perhaps he always needed help, what with that awkward hand, but tonight it was more than that. She thought he hardly dared to move, for fear that she would change her mind or shriek with horror or vanish like a djinn. Or that he'd wake up, as simple as that. Any number of ways, a young man could lose his dream from right there in his arms; he was breathless with fear, robbed of purpose, anticipating them all.

Well. She'd undressed men enough. She dealt efficiently with his clothes, all of them, *you won't keep your socks on, young man, not in my bed; but hold still, let me, I can see that you can't*

186

manage...

It was her own clothes that seemed to give her foolish trouble. This was ... not part of the job, no. She did the one thing, or she did the other; she put men to bed or she put herself. Not both together, not any more, no, never again.

And yet here she was, and here was Michael, still not Peter. Very far from Peter. It would be idiotic to lock the door and drape the mirror to keep Peter out. He couldn't be further away already. No, all she had to do was keep this very young man here. In this world, this life. This body. Here, now...

She fumbled the buttons and tore the cuff, but her blouse was gone at last. The skirt was easier, its own weight letting it drop away. Shoes could be kicked off, no need to fuss with laces.

Her underthings demanded fuss, but – *oh, you boy!* – Michael was predictably fascinated. Did he not have sisters? He might have said; she might have guessed; she couldn't remember. It was hard to remember everything, anything, in the dizzy strangeness of the moment. She was trying to be practical, competent, an experienced woman helping a youth through a difficulty; but – oh, she had difficulties of her own, and no one to help her through them.

This was ... not easy, no. It felt artificial, like his lips: a deceptive layer of alien skin laid over something utterly man-made.

Still, though, there was nothing artificial about his body. She was glad she hadn't turned the light off. He had something to look at, something to learn: the intricacies of women's intimate wear, girdle and stocking tops and suspenders. She could look at him. All dispassion spent, she didn't need to see him as a patient now. Indeed, she needed not to. There had to be a better reason. She could be his salvation, perhaps, but not his nurse.

And he, he to her – he could be what? A youth to train, a means to pleasure. Something that was neither patient nor husband. A body lovely to her eyes despite the scarring, despite all his hurts; eager to her touch despite his nervousness and doubts.

Come, then. There were doors to open here, for both of them. No harm in the world.

EIGHT

The second time, she thought the doors were at their backs, and closed behind them. She thought they were moving on.

She hadn't really expected that there would be a second time. Certainly she hadn't intended it, that night or later or ever again. If she'd thought about it at all, if she'd been made to stop and think, she would have said that this was a treatment she could offer, a knowledge she could share. Either one of those, or both together. Once would do. She thought.

She would have thought, if she had stopped to think. If she'd thought she needed to.

After that first time, she held him until he stopped trembling; and then he was all good manners and gratitude, expressed in clumsy whispers. She thought he wanted to go now, to relive this extraordinary night in the privacy of his own head, his own bed, where he might hope to understand it; only that he didn't quite know how to leave. How to say goodnight, in such intimate circumstances.

How to let go, when you were tangled skin on skin.

She could have helped him, of course. It would have been another useful lesson for a boy, how to leave a woman's bed with grace and tact. How to leave her happy.

But just when she thought they were both ready for it, there were crisp heels in the corridor and a soft tap on her door.

Ruth held her breath and his too, her palm laid lightly over his mouth. If they were caught, it would be the making of him and the ruin of her. She wasn't – quite – prepared to sacrifice herself that way, to boost his reputation or his ego.

Suddenly she was shivery in a whole new way, cold and tense and not at all delightful. She hadn't felt this way since her schooldays, when she'd been out of bed and making mischief – nothing like this! – and on the edge of getting caught. There always used to be a pleasure in the risk of it, but not tonight. She supposed she was just too old now to be so perverse, or else things mattered now in ways they couldn't matter to a child.

The tap came again, and this time a low voice calling through the panels of the door: 'Ruth? Are you awake?'

Not pitched loud enough to wake her, unless she were an absurdly light sleeper. Still, pitched loud enough to hear and to recognize. Nurses learn these tricks.

Judith. Her new friend, her near neighbour. Her victim, coming up to bed after a desperate evening, full of that weary energy that wants nothing more than a brew and a conversation before sleep; finding herself cocoa-less, without even the makings of a nightcap.

Without companionship, that too, unless she had another friend elsewhere on the corridor. Ruth tightened her hand over Michael's lips.

Just for a moment there, she had taken the touch of them for granted. It was strange how quickly that could happen, when an hour ago all his body had felt wrong to her, wrongly sized and wrongly trained, not Peter.

A little moment longer, and blessedly Judith didn't open the door to peer in, to check. Matron would have done that, absolutely. Judith was more sisterly. She clipped back to her own room.

Reassured, Ruth turned her head to find Michael's eyes glittering at her in the moonlight, to feel his tongue teasing at her palm. Tickling.

'You're *enjoying* this!' She was almost enraged, hissing at him, didn't he *understand*...?

No, of course he didn't. He was a boy, new-made man; he was almost laughing. She snatched her hand away and he murmured, 'I suppose there must be other nurses on this corridor?'

Indeed there were. These were the women's quarters, set aside. The men probably called it the harem between themselves, or the seraglio. Forbidden temptations. There weren't many of them, not enough: and all senior staff, like Matron and Judith and herself. The local girls arrived in flocks on bicycles and departed the same way, presumably trusted not to talk at home; but most of the nursing, most of the cleaning and cooking was done by orderlies, drafted men who were subject to military discipline and billeted somewhere in the house, somewhere else.

She grunted non-committally. He stretched himself slowly beside her, almost lasciviously against her, relishing all the length of her, head to head and toe to toe in her narrow bed; and said, 'Not safe to leave, then. Not after all that fuss below, they'll be coming and going all night.'

He wanted desperately to be right, she realized. Not to have to leave after all. That little moment of near discovery had changed something in him, or between them. Perhaps he too felt his schooldays resurgent, the thrill of near discovery, the kick of relief.

She wanted him to be wrong, but he wasn't. He couldn't leave now. Not for a while yet.

He said, 'Could we, you know ... do it again?'

And she had somehow not expected that, which was stupid. She should have felt it in him; she could feel it now. He had no arts of disguise, no thought of tempering his desire to the moment.

She sighed, perhaps, a little, and never thought of saying no. So long as they were here, held here and like this, it would be ridiculous.

Instead, sternly, she said, 'Can you be very quiet?'

'As a mouse,' he promised, on a breath. And rolled himself over to lie above her, taking his weight on his one good elbow; and she did briefly think *you'll have to learn other ways than this, my lad. Have you no imagination?*

No, of course he hadn't. Or he had, rather, he had too much, but he'd need to be taught to use

192

it. And not by her. She was resolved on that. This was treatment, like physiotherapy. One session, one night to make it possible. After this, he was on his own. She was not, was *not* going to be his doxy.

His or anyone's. No.

There wasn't much she could do in the way of training or advice, when they had to strive for silence: except in subtle ways, trying to let him know what felt good and what did not. She was surprised how quick he was to pick up on those cues. Less self-involved than she'd expected, now he was past the first raw shock of it. More interested in her. Her pleasure, her satisfaction.

One-handed and mismouthed, sweating breathless and biting his own strange lip when he must otherwise have cried out, inexperienced and distracted and awkward in more ways than one, still he managed to bring her somewhere she had not thought to go, through a door she thought locked and lost and forgotten; and, *oh, Michael...*

And so there was a second time, and then he was asleep. Cradled like a boy in her arms, his head on her shoulder, his maltreated face quite hidden and all his hurts fallen away, for this little time. She could feel not proud but pleased at her own wise remedy, a way to bring him sleep without dreams and without drugs, a way to soothe away his night fears and his needs.

Something woke him, none the less. Before she thought he should have woken, before he was ready for the day or she for him. Another

193

kind of need, or just desire, stirring in his sleeping body. Stirred by her, perhaps. A shift in her, or just the smell of her, the fact of her, the presence. Speaking to something in him below the level of his conscious mind, an awareness, physical, animal...

He stirred and woke, swift and silent, all predator. And looked at her, at her wakefulness. And his hand on her back was all male, enquiring, demanding. Animal.

No words this time: only her own body saying yes, shifting to accommodate. Her leg sliding over his, her hips lifting, sidling, settling.

His eyes, stretching in wonder at finding her on top.

Oh, you – you boy. Had you never even thought...?

Apparently, he hadn't. Apparently he was delighted to discover something else that was new, when he thought already that he knew it all.

She did *like* this boy, she couldn't help it. He had all the gloss and artifice of his class and breeding, but underneath that he was still delightful, in ways that couldn't be so readily manufactured. And he was biddable and complaisant, even when he wanted to take charge; and extraordinarily willing to share beneath all that superficial ego and selfishness, and...

And so there was a third time; and still no sleep after that because now he wasn't sleepy, he only wanted to be awake and stroke her, touch her, find ways that he could hold her and touch her at the same time. With a shyness and a boldness and a doubting and a certainty all at once, all these things. She could marvel, a little, at how he had changed, how grown, how this one night had changed him. She only had room for a little, because mostly the rest of her was marvelling at herself.

This was not what she had come for, nothing that she had sought. Not what she had promisd, to herself or to Peter. Or to his ghost. Not what she felt that life had promised her.

Still, it didn't feel like breach of promise either; more like a step beyond, into a place no former promise could contain. She lay in the crook of Michael's arm – his bad arm, because he could apparently manage this without hurt if they were careful, and that left his good hand free to roam, to his pleasure and to hers – and thought that she betrayed nobody in the doing of it.

And knew that almost nobody would agree with her, or believe her. Worried a little, whether Michael understood that too. He was so delight-ed with himself and with her, so enraptured, she thought it had perhaps slipped his mind that he could never tell anyone else about them. Not brag, not share, not confess. It was very much in his nature, she thought, to do all three, at sundry times in sundry situations. As it might be with his colleagues, with his closest girl-cousin, with his mother.

She did worry, then, but only a little. Only as much as she had room for. She had begun the evening feeling oh, so much older than he was, older by an eternity; now she thought she was acting even younger, kitten-young and absurd with it, unable to hold anything in her head that was not immediate and delightful, not here and now, not him.

This was meant to be treatment for a broken boy, nothing more. It wasn't meant to touch her, change her, move her too.

She had surely known that she was broken too, but she'd meant to stay that way. She'd thought herself irreparable.

Now? Well.

Now his hand was on her breast and her bed was filled with the shape and weight of him, her head with the smell of him; it seemed to be enough.

She took a breath, touched his lips with her own – *in our end is our beginning* – and shaped the word more than said it.

'Enough.'

He blinked, slowly and effortfully. Thought for a moment, thought he understood her, took his hand away. 'I wasn't—'

'No. No, you weren't,' though she had to reach for his wrist, draw his hand back, replace it before he was reassured. Oh, how could he *be* so young? And why was she suddenly having to be the grown-up all over again? 'But we have to get you out of here somehow, and back to your own proper bed; and soon enough–' *too soon* – 'that corridor out there is going to be busy again. Far too busy to smuggle a young man out of a nurse's room unnoticed.' He was, perhaps, beginning to smirk a little at the way she said that, with all its implications; she added, 'It would

196

ruin me.' Quietly, sincerely spoken.

Nice boy: he sobered on the instant, nodded once, tossed back the sheet that covered them. And struggled a little to rise on his bad arm, until she kissed him again and called him an idiot, pointed out that she was lying on it.

She sorted herself out first and then him, helping him quite unnecessarily to his feet. They dressed together in the small space, and now they did have to help each other, finding clothes where they had been dropped or strewn, passing them from one to the other. Mostly she helped Michael, because dressing would be awkward for him even with room enough; and also – if she were honest, which she didn't need to be because there was almost a ukase against talking – because she enjoyed it. These little intimacies seemed to bridge the gulf between the one thing and the other, between lover and nurse; she could be both, it seemed, and also something not quite either.

Together, then – with all the easy physical intimacy of nurse and patient overlaid with something more, a weary wonder that did keep drawing them back into contact even when she thought it should have been exhausted – they stood by her door as she swung it cautiously open.

Realized, as she did so, that she was still expecting to find Peter there. Outside, shut out, rejected.

At her back, Michael huffed with relief at the empty corridor. Relief coloured by a breathless giggle, because, however solemn he tried to be and however dreadful the weight of scandal that he might dimly sense hanging over her, he was still a young man at the latter end of an astonishment, an adventure barely hoped for and surely not foreseen. He wanted to whoop and caper, she knew that, she could feel it in him: all the tension of restraint, the sheer simple effort of adulthood. Perhaps he could learn to love that too, to be pleased with his own maturity, but he might need her help to see it.

She reached behind her to take his hand, simply for ease of guidance.

When she turned right out of her door, though, towards the stairs she knew, he tugged her the other way. The little window here barely let in any light; she frowned monumentally, just to be sure that he could see it.

He nodded, laid a finger on her lips, tugged again. *Trust me, I know what I'm doing.*

If he did, it was the first time tonight. She blessed the dark that hid her smile and followed him down towards the dead end of the corridor. Past one door and another and another, any or all of which might hide colleagues no longer sleeping, blundering about in the half light for dressing gown and sponge bag, hand reaching for the latch.

If she was holding her breath, she wasn't going to admit it. Not to him, and not to herself either.

If she was baffled by him, well. So she should be. She was utterly baffled by herself tonight.

Almost utterly.

Here, now, where he stopped, here was no door at all. A stretch of wainscot wall, no more, opposite another mean little window.

Until he slipped his hand free of hers, reached out and pressed the planking, and she saw it swing back into a greater darkness. A door after all, on hinges hidden in gaps between the boards; and then a light, quite startling, as he pressed a switch.

In, then, in, if that's where we're going; quick, before someone rouses. Her hands chivvied him through, and she followed. Learning to duck as she went because he did, because the door was cut low and the ceiling beyond was lower, the drop of the roof, but here were stairs leading steeply down.

She pushed the door hastily closed behind them, to block in the light. She was more than grateful for it – these stairs were difficult despite it, difficult for her and surely more so for him ahead – but it could betray them as easily as it helped them. She thought that was the nature of the world, that the gifts it offered were always a betrayal of something that had come before.

She followed his shadow down, and around a twisting corner and down again. They passed another door on to another floor, and he ignored it. Down to the ground, then, all the way; and here he did open a door, and here they were coming out behind the grander sweep of the East Staircase.

'Stop, Michael, wait a moment...' He had mis-buttoned his shirt. Before they left the privacy and the light of that hidden stair, she straightened it for him. And tucked it in like a nanny, and took advantage of the moment to kiss him like a sister, on the cheek. 'Now you'll do. Will I do?'

'You'll do grandly,' he assured her. Hand on her hip, until she batted it away.

'Not now. You have to be good now. My reputation is in your hands,' not her body any more. She needed to be sure he understood that. 'But – Michael, what is this? I know every great house needs its secret passages, but still. Stairs behind stairs?'

'Servants' ways,' he said. 'Wouldn't want to meet the housemaid on the family stairs, now would you? There's a whole network of passages like this. Not quite secret, but not much used.'

'Except by you, apparently.' No surprise there. 'And presumably those like you, your brother officers, your brother *patients*, sneaking hither and yon when you're meant to be in your beds?'

'It's known to exist,' he confessed cheerfully. 'We might have explored it, a little,' meaning that they had mapped its extent entirely, and knew far more about it than anyone who worked here. 'I mean, you know. We're not really patients. Not bed-bound, often. Not *sick*. Though I'd like to be bed-bound with you more often. Bound for your bed.' His new face wasn't good at showing subtle emotions – humour, anticipation – but his eyes made up for that. His eyes sparked with them.

That way danger lay. She had to force herself to focus on his features, not to be seduced by youth and yearning and the tumultuous thrill of achievement. That was her, his achievement: her body, her self. She had been achieved. She wasn't quite sure how she felt about that.

This, though, she was quite sure about this. 'Michael, you shouldn't expect that. You must not.' They were walking through the ballroom, Major Black's territory; thank goodness he had opted not to switch on the lights. One swift courtesy, more than nice manners: a delicacy, a degree of tact she wouldn't have expected. She'd have thought him too young. Perhaps he didn't know where the switches were, any more than she did.

Deliberate or otherwise, this darkness meant that she needn't look at his face, watch his eyes, measure his disappointment. The depths of her betrayal.

She had promised him nothing. It wasn't a betrayal. That was absurd. But he would see it so: a door opened, and then slammed shut. In his face. He could hardly do otherwise.

In the dark, her feet stumbled over something, she didn't like to think what. By instinct or training, his or hers, she was the right side of him, his good side; his arm found her elbow, even in the dark.

Apparently he'd lost his tongue, or she had stolen it from him. He didn't even say *careful!* the way she thought he would have done two minutes back, laughing at her, pleased to be able to shield her from little consequences.

One of them had to say something. That would be her, then. 'You must see, we can't make a habit of it. Word would get out, somebody would see. Hospitals are havens for gossip...' *It was therapy, not romance. This isn't a love affair.*

Really, not.

He could still find nothing to say. Somehow he could find his way like a cat in the dark, to the far door of the ballroom; she let him steer her, that firm, unhappy grip on her elbow, out into the main hall with its swooping stairs. The broken skylight had been masked with canvas but not well, not well enough. It must spill light, it must shine like a beacon to any bomber that ever came this far, when the lights were on down here. For now it let light in, enough for her to see where she was walking. Over black and white tiles, watching her feet. Avoiding his face.

'How often would we be lucky enough to do this, to get you safe away? Even now, at this hour, there must be people about. We've been lucky–' and she was whispering as they walked the long corridor of store rooms and lecture rooms, where the major and his cohorts taught their dark arts – 'and we can't count on that again. The cook, the night staff, orderlies on fatigues, we could run into anyone...'

And just as she said that, too loud, a door opened and light spilled out around a silhouette and here was someone and they were apparently not lucky after all.

She had forgotten about Peter.

Until this moment, in the urgency of trying to explain, she had forgotten quite about Peter. It might have been the first time since she lost him; it surely was the first time since she came into this house.

Her first thought now was, *at least it isn't Peter...*

202

And of course it wasn't. Of course not.

He was smaller, this man peering out at them with light at his back. Older and smaller. And bent of back, bent of leg, and balding...

'Herr Braun!' Relief made her shrill, so that she flinched almost from the sound of her own voice as it carried up and down.

She wasn't sure how relieved she ought to be. What could he have heard, how much? And how much deduced, from what he heard? Perhaps it was only the sound of footsteps that brought him out, or the sound of voices. One voice, at least, her voice.

Michael still wasn't saying anything. He had lost his manners, seemingly, along with the power of speech.

His hand was still on her elbow. He showed no signs of letting go; she couldn't think how to detach him, without being even more obvious than she was already. Two people together in hasty dress, in the desperately early hours, without the excuse of duty. Never mind what Herr Braun had overheard, it could make no conceivable difference. Everything he saw amounted to a confession.

Nothing in him amounted to an accusation. He blinked at them, and smiled, and said, 'It's very early. Would you like a cup of tea? I have a kettle.'

And somehow she seemed to have said yes. It must have been her, because Michael still wasn't speaking; and it must have happened, because here they were being ushered through the door by this unlikely man into a tailor's workroom, apparently. Patterns and fabrics, panels cut and laid out on long tables. Uniform serge and plain white cambric, good for men's shirts.

He had pins in the lapel of his tunic, she saw.

'Herr Braun, you're a tailor?'

'Indeed I am.'

'I thought you were a linguist. Or a gardener.'

He shrugged. 'Both of those, at need. But this too, this first. I always was a tailor; the rest came later.'

No doubt his kettle was meant to give him steam for pressing cloth, not water for making tea. It wasn't only people who doubled up in times of crisis.

That explained his bandy legs, she thought. There were no chairs in the room; no doubt he sat cross-legged on his table, traditional to the last.

'It's very early...'

Hadn't he just said exactly that? No matter. If they meant different things by it, no matter for that either. She couldn't stop him drawing conclusions. The only question was what he would do about them. If anything.

'Yes,' he said equably. 'Too early for the garden. I sleep very little, so...'

'Most people would read a book,' she murmured. And then thought that probably wasn't true, most people would just stay in bed; and then she blushed, and hated the light that let these two men see it.

She shouldn't be a conspirator, she shouldn't try to keep secrets if she was going to give them away so blatantly, so soon.

Having discovered them, Herr Braun seemed determined to spare them, or at least to spare their blushes. Hers. He said, 'The good major needed someone who had worked in Berlin, on gentlemen's clothing before the war. Officers' clothing. We do things a little differently, you see. It was important that the stitching be correct, the cut of the lapels and the way we fix our buttons. Any little detail might matter. So he came to the internment camp, and found me. This is my, my...'

For once, he seemed to have lost an English word. He offered the German, but that was no use to any of them.

'Bailiwick.' That was Michael, startling her, finding his voice at last if not his feet. Blurting like a schoolboy, laughing harshly, trying in his turn to blush. Again that patchwork pattern like a web across his face, as ugly as he sounded, as distressed.

'Bailiwick,' Herr Braun repeated blandly. 'Yes. That is the word. Thank you, Mr Tolchard. Now, tea...'

He not only had a kettle, he had a pot too. Not a military tin monster and not hospital issue either, not the chipped enamel of a thousand wards. Not economical earthenware. This was china, good china. Her mother-in-law had taught her something about porcelain: not enough, but a start. Enough to give her an ignorant love. The war interrupted those lessons; the last of them had been spent packing the china into tea chests, putting it away for the duration. And then Peter's posting had come through, and now ... Well.

Now he was put away himself. For the duration.

It was too late to take the pot from Herr Braun and turn it upside down to look for marks, but she thought she would see Meissen if she could. She wanted to cradle it suddenly, to hold in her hands something good that had come from Germany.

There was Herr Braun himself, of course, but she wasn't going to cradle him. Even if she'd been sure of his goodness, which she wasn't, yet.

She wasn't going to cradle Michael, either. Not again. He at least she was sure of, but ... No.

He had to let go of her sleeve, to take the cup that Herr Braun offered.

Proper cups, with saucers. Matching crockery, you didn't see much of that these days: pieces that matched each other and the teapot too. Porcelain so fine it was almost transparent, pearly like the brightening sky.

She could look safely at the bottom of the saucer.

Yes, there it was, the Meissen mark, crossed swords. She could imagine crossing swords with this man, in a fencing match, perhaps, with rules of engagement and simply for the challenge of it. Or in a duel, formal still, a Heidelberg encounter: flashing blades and fierce purpose and someone ends up scarred.

Or the other thing, deadly intent. Fighting to survive. He was a small man, civilized, ruthless, entirely a survivor. He brought his china from Germany, realizable assets that he hadn't realized. She wondered what he'd had to do to keep it. What he'd been prepared to spend instead.

And shivered, not wanting to think about such things, especially not wanting him to read them in her face. And curled her fingers around the warm bowl of the cup – Army tea, really too crude for such fine china, but you take what you can get and where would he find Earl Grey, up here in the north country, in wartime? – and tried not to think at all.

There was suddenly no such thing as safe ground or easy conversation. If she asked about the china, that would be to ask about him, his story, how he had come from there to here with himself intact and his porcelain too. She wasn't sure she wanted to hear that. And one question notoriously leads to another, turn and turn about; and if he should ask, oh, anything about Michael and herself, anything at all...

Civilized, and ruthless. She was, she thought, a little afraid of Herr Braun. Or more than a little.

He smiled at her, as brightly as an early bird, and produced a biscuit barrel. Just a battered old tin thing, no family heirloom this; but there was treasure in it none the less. She peered in, ready to refuse anything before breakfast, and, 'Oh – shortcake!' She couldn't think when she had last seen a slice of shortcake.

It was bad to be greedy, especially in these straitened times, and she hadn't even cleaned her teeth yet; but she seemed to have a mouthful before she knew it, the rest of the slice between her fingers and her other hand cupped beneath her chin to catch the crumbs, not to waste a soft grain of sugary pleasure. No thought of a plate.

Herr Braun was still smiling. 'Cook makes this

only for his favoured few. Me, I use it mostly as a bribe, to make the young gentlemen speak German when they would really rather not.' And he turned to Tolchard with the barrel still in his hands but not held out in offering. Held up as a promise, rather, withheld for now. What he offered instead was a stream of German, softer than Ruth would have anticipated because she had thought it a harsh language until this moment, but she had only ever heard it used in newsreels, at rallies, by Herr Hitler and his cohorts and his chanting multitudes. From Herr Braun's mouth to her ears it was almost liquid.

Still incomprehensible, though. And Michael's reply was fluent enough but sounded nothing like, sounded entirely like an English schoolboy speaking effortfully in a foreign tongue. Ignorant as she was, she would never have been fooled into thinking him a German native. She could be, should be glad of that. Major Black would never send him to imitate a Nazi officer, he had no hope of passing muster with that accent; and Herr Braun simply wouldn't have the time to inculcate a more convincing one, even if Michael had the aptitude.

Listening to it now, though, seeing how he struggled, she was embarrassed for him, and wanting suddenly to be somewhere else. Anywhere else.

And remembering that she hadn't cleaned her teeth, and feeling grimy in yesterday's clothes, pulled on any old how in the dark; and thinking that if she was quick she could take a bath, before the morning rush filled the washrooms.

Watching him now, seeing the strange face distort as he tried to frown over his words but didn't quite have that right either, needing to practice it in front of a mirror, she ached for him and was angry for him and wanted to lead him out of there but couldn't do it. He'd be better now without her, better here and better on his way back to the ward. She had no help to offer him, here or there.

It was like the shortcake, done before she realized she was doing it. She didn't bid good-bye to either man, she only found herself abruptly in the corridor again, the other side of the door and closing it quietly behind her.

NINE

'Sister Taylor!'

'Matron?'

'You'll find your ward depleted this morning, half the beds abandoned. Your lambs haven't gone far astray; only it's their turn, so those who can walk have gone out for their bath.'

'Excuse me, I don't quite...?' All her patients had dressings that needed changing daily. Saline baths were an innovation that the colonel swore by, to help his skin grafts take and heal; burned airmen who ditched in the sea recovered sooner. It made sense to combine the two, to use the baths to soak old dressings away and then let the patients wallow for a while.

But there was a bathroom at the end of the corridor, still within the context of her ward. No need for men to wander off elsewhere and make her chase them down.

'Ah. I was afraid that perhaps no one would have thought to warn you. I blame the colonel–' though she did it smilingly – 'he's far too lax; but the men found a bathhouse in the grounds, and all the ambulatory patients insist on using that, turn and turn about, when the colonel gives them licence. It's a kind of club for them, I warn you. Cigarette smoke and no doubt vulgar conversation–' though clearly not in her presence – 'and nurses tolerated on compulsion. They'll spend half the day there, but don't you let them keep you. And don't let them treat you as a servant, either. They will try; but they have orderlies to run around with towels and drinks and so forth. See to their dressings and keep your distance otherwise, is my advice.'

'Thank you, Matron.' She would most assuredly do that. And be doubly glad that Michael was not on her ward, not her responsibility. Not for her to attend him in his bath like royalty. Not that he currently had any dressings to change – and how strange, to find herself blushing at the thought of a patient's nakedness; she hadn't done that since she was a probationer, when she'd felt as though she spent her first six months flushed beetroot-purple – but that wouldn't keep him from lording it among his fellows. Splashing and steaming himself like a Turk in a hammam. And, yes, taking any advantage he could, of herself and anyone else who came to hand. 'Uh, where...?'

Matron was looking at her a little curiously, as well she might. 'Beyond the lake, just in the shadow of the wood. You'll find it.'

It was all manner of inconvenience, to go traipsing across the estate in pursuit of errant patients, self-indulgent boys. *Indulged* boys, as pampered in their convalescence as they had been in their brief careers, the exalted few, eggs for breakfast and beer at any time, even now, even in hospital...

She didn't really begrudge them the beer. It was hard to begrudge them anything, given what they had faced and what they had faced down, what they had done. She tried to be cynical about heroes as any nurse must be – and any wife too – about any man. But still, there they were. Here she was, here England was and the Nazis weren't, because of them. That was heroism enough, surely, to justify a short walk across the grounds.

On a day like this, crisp and clear, she would not have begrudged a longer walk. She and Peter used to walk sometimes for the pleasure of it, along the canal towpath with the moorhens and the mallards and the great black gates at every lock. Or else they'd motor up into the hills and leave the car at an inn, beg for sandwiches and bottled lemonade, walk all day never knowing quite where they were or how to get back, only that they were with each other and so they'd find a way.

It was different now. She had to find her own way.

Still, there was pleasure, albeit a different pleasure, in walking alone. Independence could prove its own reward, in time. If she had time.

In the meantime, she had this: the stillness of the valley to stand in stark contrast to her memories, her recent life, her London in all its noise and chaos. Here she walked under an empty sky – and was that irony, she wondered, with these downed pilots all about her? Or was it just the brand of their honour, the record of their achievement, the very thing they had fought and fallen for? – and it was the silence that seized her deeply. Her own footsteps were the loudest thing she heard, crunching on gravel paths and skittering on stone-edged steps as she went down from the house, down and further down.

Here was where she had met Herr Braun that first time, in the fog: where she had stalled and turned back. Today she went on, further down, all the way. Past beds of cabbage and beetroot and broccoli, tall bare canes in pyramids and scaffolds for the peas and beans of summer, looking in vain for flowers or fancies. Nothing so frivolous in this bleak landscape, in this bleak time. She'd never seen a garden look so earnest, or so grim.

Here at last was the lake, though it wasn't truly quite that grand. Probably it had been a fish stew once, before some ambitious owner had it incorporated into his formal garden, the corners squared off and the length dug out to balance the house above. Perhaps there were fish in there still, below that dark reflective surface. If not, perhaps there ought to be. If the lawns and flower beds could be dug up and turned over to vegetables, surely the lake could be stocked with fish. Perhaps she should mention it to Cook. Or to the colonel.

Perhaps she shouldn't stand musing above black mirror-water. She hadn't been lucky with mirrors here. She might look down to see a figure grow and grow beneath her feet, a man falling, falling from an empty sky.

Keeping her head up and not at all looking at the water, she walked the stiff straight fringes of the lake, as there was no bridge across. She could already see where she was going. It looked more like an observatory than a bathhouse, a folly of some kind, a stone building with a domed roof standing alone against an encroaching wall of trees. Really, she was surprised that none of these military men had thought to build a bridge. Perhaps she should mention that to Major Black; he could make a night exercise of it. *Build me a miracle, a bridge before morning...*

Perhaps she should just mind her own business, and keep well out of Major Black's way. She thought that was a better idea.

Here at the short side of the rectangular lake was the back road that had brought her in. No traffic on it this morning and no one working in the grounds that she could see, no interns in their overalls bent among the cabbages. With the house behind and above her, out of sight and out of hearing; with the light-swallowing, sound-swallowing woods ahead and above; with nothing moving in the sky or on the road or anywhere about, she might have been utterly alone. How long, since that had been true? Years, long years. Before Peter put his ring on her finger. *You're never alone in a good marriage.* Even in his absence, she'd never felt alone.

And still didn't, if she was afraid to look at the surface of a pond. If what she feared was the sight of him plummeting to find her.

No, that was folly. But she still kept her chin

raised and her eyes averted, looking where she was going, to this wholly other kind of folly, some rich man's extravagance from long ago.

It stood on a bank of grass that lay between the woods and the water. With no formal path laid down, the patients had been their own pathfinders. The constant tread of their feet had laid a clear line along the lake's edge and directly to the bathhouse door, where it faced the water across half a dozen flagstones.

Where that makeshift path met the stone steps of the bathhouse, Ruth paused. She looked across and up at the house, where it lay in a fall of thin sunlight, and felt it staring back at her. Not quite antagonistic – in honesty, she thought it didn't care – but certainly judgemental. *This is what you brought here; this is who you are.* A woman whose sunlight was eclipsed by falling men.

Only the one, she wanted to say in mitigation, *one falling man.* Except that there was another now, wasn't there? Another burning angel streaking from the sky, and never mind that Michael had fallen long before she met him. If she were morbid, she might think he was her punishment. She already felt guilty enough about Peter, and the choice he had made; appallingly guilty sometimes, at her weakest, when it seemed that everyone blamed her and everyone was right, of course it was her fault, it had to be. How else? How could a happy man, a happily married man make such a choice? He could not. What, make a widow of his wife, and a childless widow at that? Not possible, if she had made him happy. Therefore...

Therefore nothing. Ruth had been through that and through that and out the other side of the shadow, long since. That didn't stop it creeping after her. And now, of course, now that she had taken another man to her bed, of course guilt was stalking her again. Whatever her reasons, whatever the circumstances. Guilt was a bully, heed-less of reason, inflated with its own brute importance; it could fill her sky with airmen, all plunging to their doom.

A shadow flicked over her face and she flinched physically, flung an arm halfway up to shield herself against him as he came.

And then looked, looked up and saw a solitary crow, stark black against the pale sky. Relief was absurd and overwhelming. There were voices behind her, loud with echo and high spirits. She had duties to the owners of those voices, but she needed a moment more alone.

Stood still to watch as the crow came in to land on the bathhouse portico. Such a mess it made of that, awkward and cack-winged, any self-respecting instructor would have sent it around to try again. She thought, *birds should be more graceful.* And was answered by a single raucous call, ill-throated and ill-willed, and had to remind herself that birds, even corvids did not read minds nor understand even simple English, and were not omens of any kind, no.

It was hard to be rational when she did keep seeing Peter everywhere, when he was dead.

But she didn't believe that the crow meant anything. Truly not.

She bit her lip, straightened her spine, heaved the high door open and positively marched into the bathhouse.

She hadn't expected steam.

In honesty she hadn't thought about it much, if at all. Men with burns couldn't take heat, that was understood. On the ward her saline baths were all cool, cool to cold.

She had forgotten: these were not men with burns but men with grafts, their seared skin all cut away and the seams starting to heal.

Also, they were men, young men unsupervised. Of course they would want their baths too hot, and who would tell them otherwise? Not the orderlies who stoked the boiler, that for sure.

So she walked into steam, clouds of steam that billowed seemingly in rhythm with the voices, as though mere shouts could push the vapour to and fro.

Just a few paces in she went, just far enough for that steam to engulf her. Then she stopped, taking a minute to let her eyes adjust, her mind take stock, the men catch on to her presence.

If not an observatory and not a folly, this place might look like a temple from the outside, squat and heavy and manifest. Nothing on the inside wanted to disabuse her. The walls enclosed a space higher than it was wide, drawing that steam up and up into the hollow of the dome. It was all too easy to imagine the smoke of incense and a priest's voice rising, a congregation murmuring, perhaps a sacrifice, burnt offerings.

For a moment she thought she saw some low bulky shape shoulder through the fog, something animal and mean.

That was just imagination. Instead of strange exotic perfumes, frankincense and spikenard, what she smelled was carbolic, with perhaps a hint of drains. What she heard was no prayer to pagan gods, but rather a complaint. 'I say, has someone left the door open? Again? There's a positive gale howling around here.'

And the steam swirled and lifted like a curtain, like a veil of scrim whisked away in a theatre, to reveal...

Well, to reveal her.

Silence fell. A lone late voice cried, 'Cave!' and someone laughed.

She said, 'I'm afraid that was me. I'm sorry, I wasn't sure how dark it would be in here.'

That would do. In fact it was gloomy, and the open door at her back did help to fetch daylight in as well as clearing the air. There was another line of light up high, a clerestory below the dome, but that was narrow and diffused by the clouds of steam. Lower down there were soft yellow glows that she took to be paraffin lamps – indeed, she could smell those too, another acrid texture in the air – but they drew the eye more than they pierced the fog.

'No matter, Sister. But truly, the draught is a little chilly on bare wet skin.'

On grafted skin, he might have said, to make his point the stronger. No need; she was already turning back to drag the door closed against its difficult hinges. A little loss of light would make little difference, and she had her bearings now. She knew the source of those silenced voices, and could put names to them all.

She'd been warned that the men treated this as a clubhouse. She hadn't realized till now that it had been built with that in mind, but surely so. This was such a male space, high and formal and overdone, with Victorian tiling everywhere and an ironwork gallery that could have no real purpose except to allow gentlemen to stand and smoke cigars and call down pithy comments to the bathers below.

The baths were arranged in a circle, seven or eight of them, around a central drain. She supposed she might have mistaken one of those tubs for some massive creature looming, a great pig perhaps, the mirage of movement conjured by the movement of steam, confusing her mind as much as her eyes. She supposed so.

Here by the door was a table laid out with steel trays and everything she would need, forceps and dishes, scissors and fresh dressings. On the other side, another table held clean towels in heaps.

'What do we do, then, lads? Soak off the dressings while you're in the water there, then apply new ones once you're out and dried off?' Meaning, *I'll help with the first but you can dry yourselves, I'm not your nanny.*

'Something like that, Sister, yes. Only, the colonel usually comes to look at how we're healing, so we mostly stay in the water until then.'

'Just as well,' she said, 'there'd be small point in a saline bath if you only splashed and rinsed and came out of it again.' There were blocks of

219

salt stacked up beneath the table, gleaming faintly in the moist atmosphere. She thought she could smell that too, as though the distant sea had reached a tendril of itself this far; and wondered if it was actually possible to dissolve salt into wet air, and whether it would be beneficial if you could.

And took what she needed in a kidney dish and stepped forward to the first bath. 'Now, Johnson, let me see those hands of yours. Have you been soaking them long enough for us to try peeling that dressing off? Shout out if this is too uncomfortable – though if you can take the water that hot, I think you can take a little tugging.'

'I like the heat, Sister,' Johnson said mildly. 'We all do. It does sting, but it's a good stinging, if you know what I mean. It feels cleansing.'

'And so it is, I'm sure, as long as you don't overdo it. This'll be easy for you, then. Lift that hand up to make it easy for me too, and we'll go at it nice and gently...'

Around the circle she went, from one bath to another, one man to the next and the one after that. Perhaps she ought not to be doing this alone – or at all: it might be properly beneath her dignity as a ward sister – but she was glad of the chance, glad of the time she could spend here. Her corridor in the house, her ward, that was her territory; this was theirs, and it made a difference. Here there were ashtrays between the baths, and benches where a man might sit to cool down, draped in a towel or a dressing gown or nothing at all. Here a woman had to take them as she found them, at their ease, doing man things.

Arguing about the war perhaps but more likely the crossword puzzle or whatever cricket scores they could discover, games in far-off Madras or Mandalay or Melbourne. Or doing boy things, perhaps, playing catch in the gallery with a bar of soap, hurling it fully across the width of the bathhouse and demanding forfeits of whoever let it fall. Or doing nothing at all, only lying and soaking and letting the time slip by as patients ought, convalescent, being no trouble to their nurses.

In fairness, they were no trouble to her today. They submitted to her ministrations and talked nicely to her and hardly at all to each other. At last, with the last dressing eased away from her last patient's red-raw back, she took pity on them and removed herself. Not from the bathhouse altogether, she wasn't finished here yet, but a tray of sodden soiled dressings made a fine excuse to explore below, down a tight and turning stair to where the ancient boiler banged and hissed in its cellar.

There was a man here too, an orderly. A stoker, she supposed they would call him overhead, if naval parlance were allowed among all their own proper jargon. Stripped to the waist and black with dust, he shovelled coal into the boiler's gape, sweated himself clean and shovelled more.

'When these have dried off,' she said, laying the tray of dressings down in a corner, already starting to sweat herself in the fierce heat, 'toss them into the fire, would you?' They reused what they could, but these were beyond salvage.

221

'No need to wait, miss. A little wet'll do no harm in that there fire.' And he scooped up the dressings on the blade of his shovel – neatly done, practised – and hurled them into the orange glow. She barely heard a hiss come back, barely saw a puff of steam erupt.

She thanked him, then, and lingered a little to learn his name and rank and other duties. She wanted to know everything about everybody. Also she wanted to give the men above some time without her. Let them relax in her absence, and perhaps they could stay that way when she went up again. When they bantered despite her presence rather than behind her back, then she'd feel that she had won her place.

She stayed longer than she should have done, longer surely than the stoker wanted her to. He'd have been far happier heaving coal alone, than holding conversation with an officer. *Peter, I'm an officer now, we could salute each other* – the thought could make her smile, almost, sometimes.

But at last she did leave that searing basement and make her way slowly up the stairs again. She was thinking that if the men had settled down to chaff each other as they were used to do, perhaps she'd slip up into the gallery until the colonel came and they were ready for their new dressings. Keep out of their way, out of sight and hopefully out of mind, let them get on in their own way without giving her a thought.

But as she came up into the light, she heard voices that were not her patients', and not in the echo chamber of the bathhouse.

It was the anger she heard in them which made her pause. The stairway came up just by the door; that stood open again, or half open, held by one man's arm. She could see his figure silhouetted against the light. Not see his face, and she'd never heard him so transformed by fury, but even so. She knew the colonel by his bulk, and by his voice.

She wasn't so sure who he was speaking to, because they were standing on the steps outside. She had no view of the other man and only an oblique shadow of his voice, muffled by the colonel.

Still, from context, it had to be Major Black.

Surely, it had to be. She couldn't imagine the phlegmatic colonel being this angry at anyone else.

'You'll be telling me next that you want to use the men while they still have a pedicle, before they begin to be finished with surgery.'

'Absolutely I'll use them with their pedicles, if they can only handle a parachute. Who's going to challenge a man whose nose is a tube sewn into his shoulder? That's ideal for my purposes.'

'Oh, for God's sake, man! Have you no thought for the men at all, beyond their usefulness as an artefact of war?'

'No, I don't. This *is* a war, Colonel, and they are all officers. Volunteers. Injury does not excuse them. In the last war, they would have been patched up and sent back to the front, scars and all. No one would have thought twice about their damn scars. In this war, if we can use the scars to our advantage, that's all to the good. The more damaged they are the better as far as I'm concerned, if they can only function.'

'Would you have me dress up healthy men with surgical damage, just to distract the enemy? Disguise them with operations, cut their faces apart so that no one will look them in the eye, amputate the first joint of every finger so their prints can't be used against them?'

'Do you know, that's really rather a good idea. I'll take that up with SOE at our next meeting. Colonel, thank you. I believe you're beginning to get the hang of this at last.'

'Good God, man! You disgust me. Do you have no limits, no moral standards at all?'

'No, none. Morals are a luxury we can't afford. Backs to the wall, Treadgold. These are desperate times...'

There was more, of course. There was always more. Ruth couldn't hope to slip out of the stairwell without being spotted, so long as he was holding the door open that way. She stayed where she was, trapped and trying not to listen. All her sympathies were with the colonel – except that some cold, distant part of her, perhaps the bitter heart of her did acknowledge the major's argument – but he was losing all down the line, losing and losing. Rhetorical questions were always a mistake, she thought. Always a weakness. She'd learned that in debates at school, so long ago. Marriage had only underlined the lesson. Those times that she and Peter fought, he would fall into that same trap, always asking questions. Which left the initiative with her, to startle him with answers and so

224

drive home her point.

Which Major Black understood too well, and Colonel Treadgold not at all. He knew he was losing, but he didn't know why. So he blustered and spluttered – she could imagine his moustache, all fluffed out with indignation, a distempered walrus – and it did him no good at all, in the major's eyes or his own.

Or in hers, hidden down here, wanting not to hear his defeat spelled out so boldly. She might do better for him, perhaps, if she only had the opportunity. She could argue that the men were not ready, not functional enough – but the men themselves would do their best to disprove her, so keen they were to get back to the front. Or behind the front, these lads. Madly keen to throw their lives away in desperate heroics that would see them shot as spies if they lived that long, if they didn't blow themselves up with their targets or die in a hail of bullets or...

'I say!' A voice shrill with discontent. 'Whoever's out there, will you close that damned door, please? The draught's like a tornado in here.'

There was a great booming sound as the door slammed shut, with both the arguing men still on the outside. She didn't think the interruption would stop their arguing, but at least it meant that she could scurry up in safety, unseen, into the shadow of the narrow hallway and then through to the bathhouse proper.

The steam seemed thicker than ever. If the colonel wasn't coming in, she would have to chivvy the men out of the water and get them dry. Honestly, they were like schoolboys clinging to their beds of a morning, the way they lingered in these baths. The salt water might be doing them good, but she didn't have all day, even if they did.

There was an odd silence all about her, as though the weight of fog had finally subdued even young men's spirits, or the heat exhausted them. She ought to be glad of that, perhaps, it might make them more complaisant. But it felt ominous to her, as this thick heavy air did, this blanket of blindness.

Oh, nonsense. Again, nonsense. She was fey this morning, off-balance and disturbed.

She took a breath to call out, to order all the men out of the water; but she never made that call. Another voice cut across her own and stole all her breath away.

A scream, rather, no words in it and barely a voice at all, an animal cry. Brute pain and terror.

And as though one throat could shift an atmosphere, one butterfly flap its wings to raise a storm, the steam stirred and shifted, rose and gathered like low cloud in the dome above, like a soft repulsive ceiling so that paraffin light could show her just exactly what had happened here. What had been done, what there was to scream about.

At least she wasn't screaming.

At least he wasn't either, not now. Not after that first wrenching horror, a cry dragged deep from the bone of him, irresistible, rising appalled in outrage at the insult to his flesh.

All around her other men were surging from their baths, naked and distressed and heedless of their own half-healed hurts. Unlike her, their first impulse was to move, to act; like her, once they were up, they could find nothing to do but stare.

Just the one man lay still in his bath, half submerged.

He too had nothing to do but stare.

At himself, at what had been done to himself, to his body while he lay there lost in fog, sodden with heat and water.

All of Colonel Treadgold's surgeries and interventions lay exposed on his bare skin and deeper, where they had cut through fat and muscle and sinew to the bone beneath. All the grafts and reconstructions, all the work to save his fingers and his face. It should have shown as patchwork, seams and scars, the stamp of former hurts and fresh recovery. Not this. Never, never should he have looked like this.

When Michael was upset, his own scars showed through his skin like a jigsaw. This, though – this was like a jigsaw broken up, thrown back to pieces.

All his operations had come undone, all at once: every one of his wounds was gaping wide, all his grafts peeling off, his face disintegrating as she watched with nothing now to hold the jaw together or the rebuilt nose to the skull.

Lips fell away like obscene petals.

It was as though all the colonel's stitches had dissolved, and all the healed tissues too. She couldn't remember the man's name, that was lost too in the horror of it; but he was starting to bleed now from all those gaping injuries, and that was almost a blessing, as blood clouded the water and hid the worst of him from her sight and his own.

Almost a blessing, almost. Until she remembered, until it reminded her: open bleeding wounds and salt water, how cruel that could be.

In the long run it might help him, if anything could; but right now he was drawing a shuddering, gasping breath, ready to scream again as the pain of it pierced the shock that had gripped him till this.

That was something else to be thankful for, perversely. It broke her out of her own shocked trance, gave her something to do. Something she could achieve.

'You, and you.' Pointing, picking, snapping orders. This at least was manageable. Somewhere to stand. 'Help him out of there. Gently! He needs ... he needs not to be sitting in hot salt water.' In honesty she didn't know what he needed, except that he needed this not to have happened; but that was a beginning. 'You and you, fetch cold fresh water and wash him down. You, run him another bath. Nothing but cold. That'll stop the bleeding.' Well, it might. If anything could, if he didn't bleed out entirely. And again they wouldn't have to stare at his body so roughly engineered, so brutally exposed.

That was all the men busy for the moment.

That freed her to do the one other thing she could think of.

She ran back to the door and hauled it open, stepped out into the chill air and screamed at last herself, screamed for the colonel.

TEN

He was still in sight, storming along the lake-side. No sign of Major Black.

Her shrill cry reached him, better than any man's bellow would have done. He stopped, he turned; she waved wildly to draw him back. Kept on waving until he broke into a lumbering run.

Then she went back inside, to do what she could. To be a nurse in crisis. Not to think.

Thinking came later, as it had to. When that poor disintegrating man – Flight Lieutenant Barker, his name had come back to her at last; his room-mates called him Bunky – had been pieced together as best as they were able; when he'd been carried away to theatre by a stretcher party accompanied by the bewildered, anxious colonel; when they'd been followed by a chain of half-dressed patients no less bewildered and no less anxious, worrying inevitably about their own grafts and surgeries, wondering when or whether they might suddenly fall apart themselves. When she found herself abruptly and un-expectedly alone in that overbearing bathhouse

230

and didn't break, didn't flee the building. Went up instead: climbed the winding iron spiral that stood like an inverse to the cellar stairs, like a mirror image in every dimension that there was.

Up to the gallery, though the steam still hung there like a cloud caught napping. She wanted to stand in that loss of fog, not see her feet let alone the world beneath her. It seemed too thick for bathroom mist, even – or especially – a bathroom on this scale, eight steaming baths could never fill such a dome and the open space beneath it. And yet, here it was and here she stood, with her own feet lost to her, gripping the gallery rail because she had nothing else to fix her and she might otherwise have been falling. Falling and falling, and—

Oh, Peter.

He would not have done this. Surely, he would not? Neither the man she knew nor the ghost she kept seeing, the presence that she felt. She was beginning, reluctantly, to believe in him. So perhaps he could have done this – but he would not. No.

Even if he could, he would never want to. Not harm a stranger, for whatever strange point he might want to be making. His message, his mission was to her. If he were here at all, in any form at all.

So. She needn't feel guilty, nor responsible. Not for this.

Puzzled, then, and frightened, and more than a little desperate, she found the fog no use to her; and went in search of something better.

The mind of Aesculapius, she might have fled

to that. Or the cold brute logic of Herr Braun the tailor, the survivor.

In fact she found herself in the subterranean kitchen, begging time and tea from Cook.

Wanting to.

It was the first time she'd been down here in the middle of the day. Of course it was busy, with lunches to dish up for the whole hospital, patients and medicos and administration too. And the men on guard duty at the gates, and very likely others she hadn't seen yet. Any large organization runs on its back-room people, every big house depends on its staff, maids and janitors and stable boys.

And yet she'd come down here in chase of a memory, the peace of the very early morning, a quiet corner to sit in and one man to watch at work.

She was an idiot.

She stood in the doorway and barely watched the frenzy, didn't even try to pick out the man at the heart of it, Cook in his kingdom, in his time. She might have closed her eyes and still known everything she needed to: from the smells of it, from the dense hot heavy air, above all from the sounds that battered at her, all the noise of a working kitchen at its climax. Metal on metal in a hundred variations, the hiss of gas and the rush of bodies and the voices, voices over all, each pitched louder than the last as every man struggled to be heard.

There was nothing for her here. She turned to go. Almost had gone, indeed; it was only that the stairs back up seemed suddenly so steep, her legs so tired and her mind more tired still.

In her hesitation, the touch on her arm was a startlement but not exactly a surprise. Like the touch of a man's hand in bed – yesterday that thought would have been *Peter's hand* but things were different now, she had known more than one – which was never a surprise but could always raise that unexpected shiver.

'Sister? May I help you?'

And there he was, Cook himself, come from nowhere or from everywhere, knowing everything. Knowing her need and confident to meet it, *may I?* and not *can I?* – and perhaps she was building too much on such a small acquaintance and such a little word, but his voice was more refined than his role and she thought he knew exactly what he was saying.

And she was trembling now, and that wasn't only her knees faced with a climb of stairs. Trembling all through, and his hand beneath her elbow was the only solidity offered. She leaned on that and he led her away from the stairs, through the steam and sweat of the kitchen, through the scents of frying onions and boiling potatoes, past the seethe of vast pans over roaring flame and the press of urgent bodies turning this way and that. She was aware of them all, but only distantly; detached almost from her own body, focused just on that point where her arm met his, reliability amid the flux.

It was how she thought of him, she realized: a fixed point, security. Why she had come to him, from the bathhouse fog.

From one fog to another, but this was different.

No one was falling here, she didn't need to hold on; someone was holding on to her.

He brought her through an arch of brick and down another flight of steps. Today seemed to be all about going down, when she wasn't going up.

The last cellar had been a claustrophobic inferno, the furnace raging through an open iron door. This was just the opposite: broad and dim and cool, reaching away and away, wooden racks and whitewashed walls and just light enough to find your way. You'd need a torch to read the labels on the bins and bottles.

'Really, it all needs drinking,' Cook murmured at her side. 'A lot of the lighter wines are too far gone already. The port's all good, and some of it is excellent, but port's not always what you want.'

'No.' There was a quip ready on her tongue, *any port in a storm*, but that felt tired before she said it and it wasn't true anyway. Apparently she was more particular. She'd come to him and he'd been ready for her, and that was – well, not quite startling, but certainly a surprise.

He led her past a run of racks and bins and through a door of panel and glass, into an office unexpectedly walled off from the wine.

'I don't know what to call this, quite. It's where they kept the cellar books, when the cellar was an active consideration. They can't have had a man just in charge of that, though; I suppose it was the butler's prerogative. I'm just not sure why he needed a separate cubbyhole down here. His pantry was upstairs, of course, convenient to the family. Still...'

Still, there was a table, there were two chairs. There was a clean glass in front of her, the pop of a cork as he reached a bottle down from a shelf where it had stood dusty between ledgers. She didn't want wine; this wasn't wine.

A gurgle from the neck of the bottle as he tipped it, and the aroma hit her hard before ever the first dribble of pale gold liquor hit the glass.

'Oh!' Apple-crisp and honey-mellow and neither of those, the sharp volatility of brandy underlying all. 'Should we...?'

'You should.' He had only produced the one glass. 'Drink that off, you've had a shock. Look sharp, now.'

Sharp, like the brandy. Like his voice. She seemed to have no resistance. The glass was in her hand, the weight of it, the touch against her lips; the brandy in her mouth like a fire coal, a source, heat and light in suffusion through all her cells.

'Good. Now, sip this,' another gurgle, another measure in her glass. 'Don't rush it again, this is too good to rush. Take your time, let it work through you.'

It was all through her already. She could feel it in her fingers, in her feet. She spread her hands on the table and settled back in her chair and felt rooted, through wood and stone to the earth beneath and the rock that underlay it, the whole planet in its turning.

She thought about that for a moment and said, 'I ought to eat something.'

'Yes,' he said equably, 'but not yet. This first. Then I'll have someone feed you in here, you don't want to face the scrum upstairs.'

No. No, she didn't. But, 'Oh, you shouldn't worry about me. You can't keep making me a special case,' in need of special treatment, soup or brandy or whatever he had in mind today.

He just shrugged, seeming curiously content with it. He wasn't joining her in the drink, but he did sit down across the table from her, apparently endlessly patient, not at all like a cook with a meal to serve. *This first*: apparently he meant more than a glass of brandy. This place, his company, his time.

She said, 'You've been here a while, Cook. Longer than most, I'm guessing.'

'Longer than any,' he said easily.

Of course they'd want the domestic services in place before the hospital staff could come, before the patients. Doctors need feeding, and their beds making and their laundry done.

'Yes. I don't suppose anyone knows the house better than you do.'

'No.' He'd have its geography at his fingers' ends, to know when and where and how to deliver urns of tea and cauldrons of stew still piping hot. And, yes, a bowl of soup at need.

'No.' She hesitated, one last little moment; and then said it. 'There's something here, isn't there? Some presence in the house.' *Something evil* she wanted to say and would not, not quite, not yet.

'Oh, no,' he said in flat denial, bluntly confusing her, not at all what she had expected. 'No, the house is empty.' And then, smiling thinly as a man might in the face of something difficult and deeply loved, he went on, 'Of itself, it has nothing to offer. What you find in D'Espérance is only what you bring.' And then, his lips tightening around that smile as though to hold it in the face of her defiance, her disbelief: 'It can seem ... heavy. I do know. I came here myself, with luggage enough of my own and no one but me to carry all the weight of it. I barely made it through the door.'

'I ... I don't think I understand,' though in honesty she thought she did. She only didn't want to. Not this, not now.

'It's not the house that's haunted, Sister. It's you, always. You fetch your own ghosts with you. All D'Espérance will do is show them to you. Think of it as a lens, to make the unseen clear.'

She was glad then that she hadn't said a moment ago just what she'd been thinking. *Not evil. Not Peter. No.* But a man had ... come apart; and another had lost a hand, and she couldn't just screw her fingers into her ears and shut her eyes and turn her head away. Nor deny that she had come here haunted, with her ghost in tow. He had greeted her on the very doorstep, rising from the woodwork like Marley in the door knocker. That made her his first victim, she supposed, fainting across the threshold as she had. And since then he'd escalated, striking again and again, finding other targets, random men...

No. She did not, would not believe that. Not Peter. Not evil. No.

She cupped her hands around the bowl of the glass, bent her head above it and inhaled, wanting to draw the fumes in deeply, wanting to feel

237

the astringency of them like a purge all through her mind, searing out such ideas.

In vino veritas. If there was truth in brandy, it was a harsher kind. But welcome none the less, as the man across the table said, 'Everyone brings something. Show me a man who isn't haunted, I'll show you a man who's never lived. Or a man who's lying to himself, but that cuts no ice here. D'Espérance will show him the truth of it.'

What he was saying – surely, what he was saying? – was, *not Peter*. Not Peter, and not her; she wasn't responsible, she hadn't brought this down on that poor man in his bath. Other people's ghosts were at work here. The sense of relief was bitter and welcome and almost overwhelming.

Even so, she said, 'But, but surely, he can't have done that to himself. Whatever burden he carries, whatever guilt or loss or...'

Her voice died away in a gesture. She couldn't encompass the thought of so much disturbance in a man's mind.

'No, I'm sure not. That would be beyond enduring. But D'Espérance is not a kindly house, it won't spare the innocent. A lens focuses the light, and people can get burned. Other people, if someone's ... passions ... are violent or uncontrolled, or wilful. There would be ways to use it as a weapon.'

'No, but why? Surely not...'

He said nothing; he didn't need to. A man had bled half to death in his bath. That couldn't be incidental. It wasn't an incident, it was an act. Actual.

This was a hospital. More, he ran the kitchen of a hospital; more yet, an army kitchen in an army hospital. Gossip would be the fuel here, more even than tea. Of course he knew exactly what had happened in the bathhouse. He probably knew exactly how the patient was doing in theatre right now. One of the nurses would be relieved, and talk to her special friend when she came out; and her friend would talk to the orderly who swept the corridor, who would talk to the orderly who fetched the lunch, who would bring it all back to Cook. No need to be discreet, then. No point in it.

She said slowly, 'It was as though someone had undone all the colonel's work. Unstitched him. Not put him back the way he was, but worse. Left him with his own wounds and the colonel's depredations too, everything the colonel has to do – or undo – before he can patch a man together. How——?'

'Never ask how. That's not a question here. These things happen, that's all there is to say about the how. About the house. It's much more useful to ask why. If it was deliberately done, then why would anyone see that as a thing to do? Who hates the colonel or his work so very much?'

She wanted to say *Major Black, and I heard them fighting just before it happened; if passion is the trigger we should look for, there it is* – but that made no sense. The major used the colonel's work to his own ends, to support his strategies. He even wanted the colonel to do more, he wanted to fake it, to give healthy men such surgeries

239

before the advantage of surprise was lost. She couldn't in fairness accuse him of this. He didn't actually hate the colonel, he only wanted to govern him. There must be something else, someone else. A saboteur, finding a strange eldritch course against the war effort? Or a personal grudge, against the colonel or maybe against the man himself, poor Barker...?

She shook her head, fidgeted with her glass – her empty glass, and when had that happened? – and shook her head again when Cook reached towards the bottle. 'No, no more. And no lunch either, just give me a slice of bread and let me go. I have a wardful of men in shock. Half of them were actually there to see it, and they must all be wondering now how strong their own stitches are. The colonel has been a miracle worker up till this. Now he has feet of clay. Fingers of clay. And he made their faces for them, and – well, faces of clay. They can be pulled apart.' So could that image; her English mistress would have been appalled. No matter. 'But – Cook, you hear all the whispers in the house.' The soldiers' gossip and the nurses', the patients' too, it would all trickle back here like water finding its level. And that wasn't all she meant, and he must know it. He heard what the house was telling him. She didn't quite under-stand how, but that was a lesson she'd take on board, not to ask how in this house. He had his story, that was obvious. Perhaps he'd tell her another time. Perhaps not. She wasn't plan-ning to tell him about Peter, but she could imagine its happening, regardless of purpose or desire.

He nodded, non-committally. There was what he heard, and what he was prepared to share, and they were different. As no doubt they ought to be.

Still. 'Will you tell me? What you hear about this, what it means?' *Tell me what to do* was what she was really saying, though she only realized it herself once the words were out. She was perhaps too ready to provide herself with heroes, especially since Peter's fall from grace. He had left a void she had a need to fill, a voicelessness, a silence where she went to hear wisdom. She would install anyone if they gave her half a reason. Aesculapius, nearly: if he had made any move to win her trust, if he hadn't kept himself so neutral in his distance. Colonel Treadgold, of course, though he seemed ... damaged now, not the rock she looked for.

Michael? No. Even the thought of that could make her smile, even now. Bed Thirty-Four was not a throne, and she did tend to enthrone men.

Cook, though: so far he'd shown himself to be a source of what she needed, just when most she needed it. Soup, pastries. Brandy.

Knowledge too, it wasn't just the inner woman that he catered to. He seemed embedded here, deeply rooted. Perhaps it was the other way around, that every institution taps into its cooks. Perhaps he was the source, rather than the messenger.

He nodded again, non-committal again. Ruth took that as it was meant, she thought: as a promise to consider what she'd asked. No more.

She left him then in his little glassed-in cubby, closed the door behind her, went up to work. Up and up.

ELEVEN

If there was war in the house, it was a strange and disproportionate kind of warfare, with only the one side fighting. Fighting and losing.

Colonel Treadgold spent all afternoon in surgery, trying to patch Flight Lieutenant Barker together again. Crudely, swiftly, trying to save his life. Not his face, not his hands, not any of the colonel's careful early work. All that had been expunged, leaving the man worse off than before, teetering on death's edge, dragged there by simple pain and shock and loss of blood.

Still living when they got him into theatre, he was still living when the last of the stitches went in; still living when they installed him in a room of his own, with a nurse of his own and a guard quite useless at the door. Unconscious, but that was probably a blessing; still living, which quite possibly was not.

Weary beyond measure and strained beyond exhaustion, probably the colonel should have retired to his room, to his cider and his solitude. Instead he came down to join staff and patients at tea.

Tonight there was no sing-song at the piano, no

queue for beer. Even young men can be sensitive, even en masse.

They wanted to talk, of course, but quietly and among themselves. Ruth supposed that the beer barrels upstairs might be seeing some custom, but that would be for comfort. Nobody would be rowdy tonight, and for once no one wanted to sit among the staff. They'd rather whisper in corners and hear nothing and not ask the professionals, not know. *Is my face going to fall apart, like Barker's...?*

No one knew. But here was the colonel, and he wanted to talk: and not about Barker and not about the surgery, the calamity, what could have gone wrong with the treatment, no.

He wanted to talk about Major Black and how wrong he was to be sending men off on one-way missions, to die for the war effort. Encouraging them to volunteer, snaring vulnerable minds when they were weakest, when they were in despair.

'He trains them to kill themselves, you know, in the last resort, if that's the only way to reach their target. Blow themselves up with their man. It's an inculcated hopelessness, when everything I do is about hope for the future, it's the very opposite...'

It was; and Ruth sympathized with him all down the line, and so she thought did half the staff or more. Many more, perhaps. This was the argument she'd overheard, played out in public now. Nobody could want to see their patients off to an inevitable end after so long spent rebuilding them, body and soul.

And yet, and yet. There was a war, and the major didn't become wrong because his methods were wrong, because young men would die in the pursuit of them. Young men always did die in war, that was how the thing happened. And if they could die with purpose, striking deep into the heart of the Nazi command, there had to be a value in that; and if they had been persuaded that their lives had no value else, well, that was very wrong, but it was surely their privilege to believe it. It was a privilege that Ruth claimed for herself, with far less reason.

And it would do him no good anyway, agitating amongst the staff. They could all line up behind him and change nothing, achieve nothing. All they had was what they did, which was to make the patients comfortable and help them heal faster; and all that did was send them sooner into Major Black's hands.

Major Black's and Major Dorian's. She didn't forget Aesculapius, even when he wasn't much in evidence. The trick couldn't be worked, she was already sure, without his active participation. Health and vigour could restore hope in young bodies, never mind what their faces looked like. He must be working to counteract that, or to redirect it: to teach them that hope lay in their enemy's defeat, before or more than in themselves. That some things mattered more than life itself.

It was a hard case to argue against, subtle and insidious. Subtle and insidious and true, that too. She knew.

So, yes, the staff might side with the colonel,

but even they could see the merits of the major's project. No one wanted to send their sons off to fight, but everybody did it in the end.

The colonel could argue and agitate as much as he cared to. It was an argument he lost and lost and lost again, and Major Black wasn't even arguing. He didn't need to. The men had given their word, and that would have been argument enough; none was going to back down under his comrades' eyes. Besides, if the hope that Colonel Treadgold peddled was liable to come apart without warning, if their new faces couldn't be depended on, then what in the world did they have to live for, beyond the chance to strike back at the war machine that had done this to them in the first place?

A blaze of glory and a sweet release. It was all the more seductive, in the light of Barker's collapse. That was so clear in the days that followed, Ruth began to wonder if Major Black hadn't initiated the disaster after all, it worked so well on his behalf. He had lost one man he might have used, but cemented all the others in his service. He was ruthless enough to do that, she had no doubt.

But he was practical enough, surely, to know that it wasn't necessary. It never had been, never would have been. His volunteers were committed already; they didn't need horror to whip them on. Even if Major Black could conceivably have sat down thinking that he might, thinking that he could use the spirit of this house to such savage effect. If he could have understood a way to do that...

246

Oh, it was all too strange and terrible. Like everyone else, she wanted not to think about it. Like everyone else, she was finding that too hard.

Like, perhaps, everyone else – like others, certainly – she couldn't sleep any more easily than she could forget, or turn her mind aside, or...

This house never had been safe for a nocturnal wanderer, with Major Black's black-clad trainees likely to emerge from the shadows at any moment. These days – these nights – with so many of the staff too restless to sleep and so up and about when they should have been abed, the creak of foot on floorboard was almost constant in the corridors.

Ruth lay wide awake in the little privacy of her little room, listening to all the sounds of the house and trying to reconstruct all the movements of its people. And then realized what she was doing, deemed it futile and flung back her blankets, sat upright and thrust her feet almost angrily into her ready slippers.

There was no point pretending that she might sleep if she only lingered long enough in bed. No point either lurking in here, in hopes of evading a random encounter outside. She didn't want water; a trip to the bathroom would just prove another way to hide. She didn't really know what she did want, only that it involved being somewhere other than here, doing something other than this.

If Judith happened to hear her go and wanted company, if she put her head outside her door and asked Ruth in – well, cocoa and a chat wasn't what she was looking for herself, but she could endure it. Perhaps better than that: it might even prove to be what she needed, all unknowing. Stranger things had happened, than that a milky drink and a quiet conversation with a friend should prove the answer to a sleepless night.

Even so, Ruth opened and closed her door with a palm across the latch to silence it, and stepped down the corridor as lightly as she could manage, and it was nothing but relief when she reached the stairs uninterrupted.

Down below was dangerous territory in darkness, Major Black's. The kitchen was further, deeper down; and in this dead of night, not even Cook could be expected or sensibly looked for.

No. Her eyes turned the other way, upward. A mean, steep flight of stairs led to the attic floor: unused, she had gathered, except for storage now. In another house up there would have been the servants' quarters, but not here, where the house had been built on too grand a scale and the servants had this whole wing to themselves. Used to have, in the days before wars came home to England to gut her great houses and their families too. Ruth couldn't conceive of this wing ever filling itself with staff again, once this latest war was over. She couldn't imagine how the house might live after this.

Nor, if she were honest, how it had lived before this. Too grand, yes, and too remote. Not famous and not beautiful, not worth travelling to. What family had lived here, in former times? She didn't know. D'Espérance, she had never

248

heard of it: which said a lot in itself, because Peter had grown up on the country-house circuit and dropped names as he dropped cuff links and collar studs, which meant at random times in sundry directions but thoroughly, comprehensively. If the house had been known among his friends, she would have heard of it. As she had not, therefore it was not; and therefore – as it wasn't a house that one came to, a gathering place for the Beautiful People – she had trouble picturing what life it had known, what purpose it had served. Who had come here and why, how it had grown so large and so ugly, what impulses had driven and shaped it in the shadows of these woods and hills?

What creature, what spirit, what power had invested it with madness? But she wasn't going to think about that.

Besides, she thought it wasn't madness. Insight, perhaps.

But she wasn't going to think about that.

She was going to climb these stairs and find herself some dark space with some privacy, where nobody else would be. Where nobody else would come. Where nobody would be pacing up and down in the room next door, or tiptoeing down the passage, or...

Yes.

Up.

She should have brought the torch that Judith gave her. Never mind. There might be lights above. If not, if the wiring didn't reach so far or else there were no bulbs, she could possibly find her way by moon and starlight. If not she could always retreat again, defeated. Defeat was sometimes no disgrace. And she could always come back, with the torch. Tonight, or another night.

Or of course she could come back in daylight. Why not that?

In the meantime, up she went. Smiling at herself, a little; surprised, a little, that she still had that capacity. *Keep smiling through.* In wartime, of course; in widowhood, the same. That was what you did, and never mind how false it was, how you longed for it all just to be over. How you sought the bullet or the bomb. Men weren't the only ones who could find honour in that kind of ending.

Perhaps she should just laugh at herself, laugh aloud and come back up in the morning.

Instead she went on up, of course she did, and it wasn't only her own resilience that could surprise her tonight. The house could do it too.

Tonight and any night, again and again, D'Espérance could and did surprise her.

Rooms on the floor below were small and mean-windowed, presumably because servants deserved no better and should not be encouraged to linger or to socialize. Beds were for sleeping in, long days were for work. Ruth had been tacitly assuming that whatever rooms she found up here would be smaller yet. That was the scale she was used to, the way big houses worked. The higher you went, the more the walls cramped in about you, the less light and space you were allowed. Perhaps senior servants slept below and skivvies were squeezed in above, three or four to a room, even two to a bed...?

She came up expecting pinched bare corridors and grim cubbyholes, box rooms with perhaps no windows at all. It might be that all those dormers were on the corridors, to light the poor maids and bootboys their way to work and back.

But she stepped up into a sense of unexpected space and openness. There was light from both sides: not enough for glamour but plenty to show her a switch on the wall, right by her hand here.

She pressed the switch, and bulbs flickered into life. Even that was at least a little unexpected. She was probably still looking to be disappointed or turned back.

Instead, yes, she was surprised.

Storerooms, she'd been told, and there were indeed great clutters on either side, rising islands of crates and tea chests and heavy family furniture stacked up beneath the sloping ceilings and between the window bays. But under and between those stacks were beds, plain iron-framed narrow bedsteads with wooden boards and mattresses in rolls, institutional ticking stuffed with straw or horsehair. Far too many for even a houseful of servants, enough to sleep a barracks. Perhaps that had been the plan, to billet a regiment here, before they'd found another use for the house?

It still seemed odd to find the attics so broad and light and roomy, after the strict confines of the floor below. Walls and ceilings had been whitewashed, not recently but recently enough. There were curtains at every window, a bright patterned fabric only a little faded by the sun.

Curtains, but not drawn; and not proper blackout anyway. She must be blazing the house's presence to the night. She really ought to have brought the torch. She ought to go back for it now. Or just go back, come again in daylight if she had to come at all.

And yet she wasn't shifting, neither to kill the lights nor to retreat. For a while she only stood and looked; and when she did at last start to move, she seemed to be going forward, down the centre aisle between all those beds and all the other things.

There was a strip of carpet beneath her feet, something dark and woven and hard-wearing, fraying at the edges, meant for the kind of use it had all too clearly seen. It felt like a path laid down for her exactly, drawing her irresistibly on.

Along to the end, to a door. She really should not be spilling all this light. Light was precious, it seemed sometimes, and rationed, and in need of saving.

And yet. Her fingers reached and closed around the handle, almost without volition on her part. She turned her wrist and tugged, pulling the door open.

Beyond was just such another long dormitory, with her own long shadow stretching down the aisle. Dark shapes of beds on either side, heaped up with stuff. She couldn't quite see what, only that it seemed softer in outline and less angular, bundles rather than boxes. Furnishings, perhaps, rather than furniture.

If there was a light switch here, she couldn't find it. Perhaps there would be another flight of stairs at the further end, and the switch there where it would be most use. She had light enough to walk on and see – or grope, at least, walk on and grope – although she really oughtn't. She ought to be turning back, redeeming herself, turning lights off rather than making things worse, laying down this bright beacon for Hitler's bombers to cluster to.

Was she still hoping for that bomb to seek her out? Still praying for that bullet?

Oddly, she didn't think so, quite. Not here, at least, not now. She had never been callous enough to want to take others with her. Not even Major Black. Or Major Dorian. He might be worse. Black at least was a professional soldier. Aesculapius was a professional mind-muddler, playing chess with people's lives. Twisting their emotions and laying their bodies in the way of danger. Worse, sending them off with certainty to uncertain but probably cruel endings. Sometimes she despised the man, but she still would not willingly call down a bomb on his head.

She really ought to turn off those revealing lights.

The odds were remote, though, that a bomber would ever find its way to this remotest setting. Let alone tonight, this hour tonight, when she happened to be letting light leak out. This wasn't London, or anything like it. She ought to be safe, and so ought everyone.

Her own motives were still mysterious to her, but she did seem to want to go all the way. To walk step by step into her own shadow, as if that silhouette were a pathfinder, a beacon in reverse, a guide into darkness.

She hadn't stepped beyond the light yet, her shadow still fell framed entirely within the outline of the doorway; but she felt less sure of her footing suddenly, and looked down.

And oddly couldn't see her feet, they seemed lost within a rising fog, a cloud that swirled about her, grey in the shadows and white where the light fell upon it.

She might have screamed, but that she had no breath to do it with.

No breath and no bearings, as the fog engulfed her utterly. She couldn't feel the floor any more beneath her, that convenient textured carpet seemed to have melted away; she wasn't sure which way was up, she seemed just to be falling and falling, *oh, Peter...*

He could find her anywhere, at any time. Of course he would find her here. Or she would reach to him, or the house would do its best to bring the two of them together.

Well. That could work. She could just fall and fall. She could let herself do that, sooner than wait for that problematic bomb or go on to seek a bullet.

Eventually, someone was sure to notice the lights up here. They'd come to investigate, and most likely find her dead, she thought. Fallen to the floor, and never mind if her ghost just went on falling.

They could go hand in hand, she thought, herself and Peter. Fall forever, together forever.

She could sense him, she thought, in the fog beside her. In this cloud. Perhaps they'd fall through into sunlight, sooner or later.

Perhaps she needed to reach out, to find his hand.

Perhaps he needed her to do that.

And yet, she wasn't doing it. Not reaching.

Drawing her arms in, rather, as if she wanted to fall faster. Making fists of her fingers. *Stubborn as all-get-out*, her old nanny used to say.

Really she only wanted to feel the bite of her nails against her palms. Something to focus on in the fog, the touch of something real – and an absolute guarantee that no one and nothing could take her hand.

Sorry, Peter.

She wouldn't do it. Not like this. She would choose her own future. If death was her choice – and she did still insist on her right to choose it, coldly and rationally – then she would chase after it when and where she chose to. And doing something useful, that too. Mending what was broken, until such time as she broke in her turn.

Not like this, just falling and falling. Even with Peter, she would not. That was a choice he had made, that she ... detested, actually.

Yes.

So. The bite of her fingernails into her own skin, and her teeth chewing on her lip, that too. Another sharp pain to hold her attention, to keep her fixed within her body here, and not falling after all.

Not falling for it, not being sucked into the illusion. This was a game the house played, she thought, and the weak would tumble headlong into it and make it real. Allow it to be real, let it happen. Let it swallow them.

255

Not her. She was nobody's mouthful.

Her eyes were closed; that made things easier. She reached out inside her body, to the limits of her skin, and of course she wasn't falling. No. Where was the rushing, where was the wind? She was quite still, and standing upright. There would be floor beneath her feet. There must be. The slight give, the slight springiness of that tough carpeting; she could almost feel it.

She *could* feel it.

She could open her eyes at any moment, and find herself standing just where she had been, just in the doorway between light and darkness, between one dormitory and the next.

She could, she could do that. She could open her eyes.

Yes.

And did, eventually, though it seemed to take forever. She was, perhaps, more afraid than she'd admit. Afraid of herself, not of the house, and certainly not of Peter. If she fell into catastrophe here, it would be the strength of her own will that dragged her down, neither the hand of her dead lover nor the creaking floorboards and malign intent of a house that harboured mystery at its core.

Actually, she thought the house was neutral, and Peter might all too easily miss her in the fog.

Even so, it took her a long time to open her eyes. Shamefully long.

Still. At last, she looked.

No fog before her eyes; only the long stretch of the dormitory, as it ought to be, awkward with shadow in the difficult light.

Good, then.

She looked down at her feet.

No fog. Just her own feet in her own slippers, standing in her own shadow on the carpet.

She lifted her head, in surging wordless relief—

And saw two shadows within the bright frame of the doorway, where it stretched away across the floor.

Two.

One, she knew, was hers. One was larger, broader. Masculine.

Oh. Peter...?

It had taken her forever to open her eyes. She would take longer to turn round, to find his face.

She couldn't actually move at all, it seemed. Nor speak.

The long peril of that moment hung suspended, timeless and undecided. *If I never move, he never can. It needs me to confirm him, a gesture of belief to make him real. And I can't. This is like the fog, the two of us forever pent on the crux of movement, in the perfect moment of its stillness.*

Only that it was worse than the fog, because it needed her to do something either way, to save them or to damn them both, and she could not. Not even dig her nails into her palms, not even that.

Only then she didn't need to, because he spoke to her.

She knew his voice intimately, and had never expected to hear it like this, in such a moment; and he said,

'I suppose I ought to boom something sepul-chral at this point, and scare you out of your girlish wits, but – well, I don't believe you scare that easily, and I don't really have the voice for booming, not any more. Besides, I think that kind of practical joke is just plain bad manners, when you come right down to it.'

She still took an age to turn around. He didn't think she scared that easily, so absolutely she did not want him to see – or feel! – the tremble he had left in her fingers. Nor hear it in her own voice, that same tremor. So she stood staring at his silhouette for that extra time, until she wasn't physically shaking any more; until she could turn safely, and take a step forward, and come up hard against his waiting willing body, and speak his name.

'Michael...'

Her hands seemed to clench themselves in the thick stuff of his dressing gown. He was smiling, pleased with her and delighted with himself. His good arm had wrapped itself already around her waist, and she rather thought he was sniffing her hair as if he had a right to.

She ought to puncture that self-satisfied mood of his. Truly, she ought to. She tried for a frown and couldn't quite achieve it, but did manage to say, 'What in the world are you doing here?' *Sneaking up on a girl that way* she might have said, and didn't.

'Looking for you,' he said, triumphant, *found you.* 'I couldn't sleep–' well, nobody could – 'so I thought I'd come and see if you were, you know. Awake.' *If I could slip in with you again* he seemed to mean, as though he had entirely misunderstood all the things she said before. Perhaps he had. Or she had. She wasn't exactly fending him off. 'So I sneaked up to your room – oh, don't worry, nobody saw me! I came like I was on a mission, through the back ways, silent as the grave – and you weren't there. So I went in hunt of you, and saw the light was on upstairs, and tried up here, and found you.'

And was so burstingly proud of himself and his skills and his reasoning, she couldn't burst his bubble if she'd wanted to, and actually it was the furthest thing from her mind. Or at least from her body, which was leaning quite outrageously into his. That tremble seemed to be coming back into her voice again, or into her pattern of thought, because in fact she was really, really glad that he had, and then she said so.

Or mumbled it, rather, into his woolly lapel; and felt his hand stroke her shoulder, and shivered at the touch of him, and heard him say, 'Here, are you all right? You look like you've seen a ghost. It's a spooky old place, this, but—'

'Michael, do you believe in ghosts?

'Oh, what? No, silly. No, I don't.' And now he could relax because he had a place in his mind that he could put this, *girlish fancies* or some such, he would have been taught all his life that the female of the species was more credulous than the male. 'No. I've been up in the best place God made, close enough to touch His face if I only leaned out of the cockpit, and I didn't see Him there. I've been down in the worst hell you can imagine, and I never saw the Devil either.'

'That wasn't what I asked, I didn't ask if you were religious.'

'No, but it's the same thing, isn't it? It's all about faith and susceptibility, and I don't think you can have degrees of it, you're either a believer or you're not. If I don't believe in the big stories, God and the Devil and eternal life, how can I believe in something as piddlin' small as a human ghost?'

Sometimes she was so busy remembering how young he was, she forgot to remember how bright he was. His mind would be something else to lean on. She could do that easily, the cold clear reassurance of an English education giving shape and structure to a habit of rational thought.

Especially, he would be good to lean on here. His young, savage life could hardly have left him short of ghosts, and she knew – none better! – that he was not short of passion either. And yet here he was, resolutely unhaunted. Patronizing her a little. Managing not to mock, but she could tell that was an effort. It would be another less welcome residue of his time at school, that he would have two common forms of address: respect one way, mockery the other. Everything hierarchical, his life would always have been that way, and the RAF wouldn't teach him differently, and nor would the hospital here.

Well, but she might try.

'Besides,' he was going on, arguing from the general to the specific, as no doubt he had been taught to do, 'I grew up in a haunted house and never met the ghost. Not for lack of looking. The kitchen boy and I, we searched that place from attic to cellar, by day and night and candlelight, we were desperate to scare ourselves stupid; and the only times Harry got spooked it wasn't actually Old Boney, it was me lending a hand, laying traps with cobwebs and bits of string. So no, no ghosts. Have you been scaring yourself up here, in all this dust and shadow? I know a good cure for that, you taught it to me...'

And there he was being utterly young again, utterly self-involved. Wanting what he had come looking for in hopes; what she had been so determined to deny him.

Something had melted that determination like wax, like a candle left heedlessly on the hearth. She wasn't quite sure what had done it. The immediacy of his body, the heat in him: that was something but not enough, surely, she wasn't that susceptible. She hoped she wasn't. She knew women in London, at the hospital, who went from one man to the next, predatory or inconsolable, vampire or victim. She had a sudden vision of herself among that sisterhood, waving successive lovers away to the front and instantly turning to find another, in utter opposition to everything she believed and everything she used to be. War could do that, she knew, it could change a person radically; and perhaps a person ought to seek such a change. Perhaps it was her duty to the country, or to a generation of doomed lads, or...

She shuddered, and felt it against his solidity like an echo bouncing off a wall.

He felt it too, and of course misunderstood it

261

completely. 'You really have given yourself a fright, haven't you? Poor old girl,' for all the world as though she were an arthritic gun dog. She had to bite hard into the dusty stuff of his dressing gown, just to bite off the giggle that would have deflated him too cruelly when he was being so mature, a friend in need. 'Here, let me see you back to your room, come on now...'

Let me see you back, then let me stay. The subtext was so clear, it needed no spelling out; only a refusal, which she could manage on a quick gasp. 'No, not there. Everyone's still upset and nobody's sleeping, the staff as well as patients. People come and go in the corridor all night. My neighbour's up and about right now. I can't afford to have you seen, coming or going. My reputation...'

He grunted, allowing the point. 'Well, I can't take you back to the ward, can I? I mean, I'd have to chase the other men out, and, you know. They'd swear not to talk, but of course they would, they couldn't help it.'

Happily, there was no danger in the world of her going back to his ward with him. The notion was so fantastic she could lift her head at last and laugh up at him; and lose the laugh all at once as she saw how the angles and planes of his features struck strange shadows in the light. Until this moment she had forgotten that there was anything unusual in his face at all. At some point in the recent past it had just become the face of Michael Tolchard, not a medical experiment or a professional responsibility or an unusual sensual experience. It was the face that meant the man behind it: something to smile at, something to reach for.

Something must be showing in her own face, because he was trying to frown, not making a very good job of it. 'What? What are you thinking?'

Actually, I'm thinking about kissing you – and she seemed to have shed more than her professional detachment and all her good resolutions, she had shed her inhibitions too, because she heard herself repeat the words aloud. 'Actually, I'm thinking about kissing you. But it doesn't seem fair to lead you on, when there's nowhere I can safely take you. Never start anything you're not prepared to finish, my father used to say, and—'

And she was babbling, perhaps, and perhaps it was just as well that he stopped her. By starting something, by kissing her, which wasn't fair at all. And – when he would allow her – she drew a breath to say so, and was sweetly and blessedly forestalled.

'Silly,' he said again. 'We don't have to go anywhere, your room or mine. If we just turn these lights off.' And he suited the action to the word, leading her by the hand to do it and letting go only for the moment, finding her again in the near dark and dropping his voice like a conspirator, like a veil over the event. 'Nobody's going to do what I did, see it from below and wonder, come up to find out what's going on. Safe as houses, we'll be. No one even remembers all this is up here.'

No house was safe in these days. She thought this house unsafe in any way, any meaning of the word. Him too, he was perilously unsafe. He was tugging her back down that strip of carpet, out of the first dormitory and into the second, where the heaps of bundles turned out – unsurprisingly, she supposed – to be blankets and pillows, tied up in sheets.

He unrolled a mattress and laid it on a bed frame, giving himself away entirely, conventional boy with no imagination. The darkness hid her smile. Working by touch, she assembled a nest of bedding. Sheets were too much trouble, but pillows and blankets went more or less where they ought to go, soft enough and formal enough to make them both comfortable.

Then, while she helped him with his clothing, 'Michael, what is all this? So many beds, what for?'

'Oh, the owner turned the place into a school for a while, after the last war. I don't think it lasted. We didn't have to kick the kiddies out, they were long gone before the ministry requisitioned it this time around. I'm not at all sure about these blankets. Can you smell mildew?'

'Certainly not. I'm a nurse; I don't even know what mildew is, just something nasty I heard about. It doesn't dare come anywhere near me or my patients, I wouldn't allow it. Now lie down and be quiet. Be *very* quiet.' They had closed what doors they could, between them and the restless house. Even so, she felt vulnerable in this wide dormitory. Almost like making love in the open, where someone might chance along at

264

any minute.

Vulnerable and excited, young again. And not falling. A hand to hold her, a body to grip, a firm surface beneath them both. Somewhere to begin.

TWELVE

O let me not be mad, not mad, sweet heaven.

She thought she was in danger of it, twice over. Once because she had decided – coolly, rationally, intellectually – that she had to believe this house was haunted, which was a definition of stone-cold raving madness if ever she had heard one. And once again because she was doing the one thing they were most warned against, from the first days of basic training. She rather thought she might be falling in love with a patient. Most certainly, she was having an affair with him.

She'd expected to find herself the strong one, fending him off, sending him away. Bed Thirty-Four, and no nonsense. Instead, their trysts in the attic had become regular, almost commonplace, except that they burned in her heart and mind like a lodestar, the way she turned instinctively for comfort and guidance and security. Their hasty nest was a fixture now, a bed made up.

Perhaps it was greed more than instinct. At times, replete with self-disgust, she tried to think so, but could never manage it, quite. Not even Peter could drive her to that dishonesty.

He did try: picking at her guilt-ridden soul like

266

fingernails picking at a scab, nibbling at confidence and composure, haunting the ill-glimpsed edges of her awareness. Always somewhere close at hand, in the glass of a door or a spill of water on a threshold, lurking in an archway in the dark. Always wanting to suck her down like quicksand, like a whirlpool, a Charybdis in her head.

That was where he truly lurked, though, in her head, not in the house around her. She had the measure of him now. Michael helped, all unwitting – just thinking of Michael helped: he was in her head too, and all elbows when she wanted him to be so – but mostly she could manage Peter by herself. As she always had, really.

And her duties, her patients, she could manage those. On a good day she could even manage to be sociable. There wasn't so much singing now and the beer drinking was more intense, even a little desperate, but these boys had learned already to cloak their fear with a brittle brightness. There was still laughter at her table, still rampant foolery and practical jokes that she was obliged to frown upon. And afterwards she could have a quieter time with Judith in one room or another, with perhaps one or more of the other nurses on her floor. She could remember their names and their situations, talk about family and before-the-war. Nobody wanted to talk about after-the-war, because looking ahead meant looking into that space where Major Black waited, to send their boys away.

More and more, she thought of him as an executioner. A slow hangman, relentless and inevitable, not to be evaded.

Perhaps that was true of any officer in wartime who sent men to their deaths. What choice did he have? She should as readily blame Colonel Treadgold, who patched men up to make the major's missions possible.

She was so torn sometimes, she thought it might just be easier to run mad. In fact, though, she was holding herself together remarkably well. She thought so, at least. Certainly better than some. You did what had to be done, and for a nurse there was always something next to do. It was harder on the patients, who were mostly not too sick and nowhere near busy enough. Young men should be good at being idle, but these had lost the art of it, all unexpectedly. They did their best, and knew the cracks were showing. Too harsh a laugh, a sudden flare of temper, a solitary figure hunched in silence flinging a fives ball against a wall, over and over. Too long spent sitting by Flight Lieutenant Barker's hushed bedside, or else not long enough, blatant avoidance: either one spoke volumes.

Flight Lieutenant Barker ... didn't die. He didn't die, and didn't die. That in itself spoke volumes for his stubbornness and the colonel's skill in surgery, the nurses' care. If there were those who felt that perhaps he ought to die, for all their sakes and his own above all, they weren't saying. They were letting their silence speak for them; that, and the endless bouncing ball.

There was little enough that Ruth could do, beyond watching over her own long corridor of cases. Half of them were still immobile, less troubled because they had not seen. She did her best not to let them listen either, not to let the walking wounded gather around the beds of those not so lucky. Or else they were luckier, but either way. It was a hopeless struggle and she tried anyway, chivvying patients back to their own beds or away to the recreation rooms or physiotherapy or even Major Black's classes, because any distraction just now had to be better than none.

For herself, too. *Any distraction is better than none*, and sometimes she tried to tell herself that was all Michael was. Just a distraction for the night hours, when her body had no work and her mind spun off above the abyss, where it might fall and fall forever. Michael gave her something to cling to, in the crudest possible sense. She should be content with that. She should insist on it, indeed, not let herself imagine that he might be anything more.

Or, of course, she should not do this at all. Not slip out of her room at dead of night in slippers and pyjamas – Peter's pyjamas, these had been, before she adopted them for practicality and warmth and mostly comfort, all manner of comfort since his death, clothes that had shaped themselves to his body, just as she had herself – with Judith's heavy torch in her hand, as much light as she needed.

Not whisper to the end of the corridor and up the stairs, throwing a beam ahead of her like a searchlight. Like a child playing ack-ack, picking out Heinkels for the guns to shoot down.

Except that a child playing ack-ack would be noisy, noisy above all, and she was silent as she could manage. And good, too, trying not to let her light betray her to the skies. A child wouldn't think, but once she was up the stairs Ruth kept her torch trained just before her feet. She could almost turn it off and trust to touch, to the guiding feel of the carpet beneath her slipper soles; but she didn't like that sudden rush of darkness after the light went out, before her eyes adjusted. Especially out here in the middle of the dormitory, with no wall to brush her fingers along to give her balance and assurance, to let her know she wasn't falling.

So no, she kept the torch switched on, its pool of light at her feet as she did all these things she should not do. That was enough. Her body knew where to go and what awaited; she needn't peer ahead. Michael was always there before her, as much undressed and ready as he could manage. After so long as a patient, in others' hands, dependent, he was impatient now: impatient with himself above all, with his own limits and inabilities.

She had some hopes of teaching him better. She was teaching him so much already. She felt like a figure from boarding-school mythology, every adolescent's dream, conjured in whispers after lights out: an older woman but not too old, wise in the ways of the flesh, the tragic widow willing – nay, eager! – to share her body and her experience. She could accuse herself of being a cliché or worse, the classic predatory female, stepping fresh from the pages of many a lurid melodrama. Or she could accuse herself the other way, of being desperate and needy, clutching at whatever passing fancy offered. Taking frenzied advantage of Michael in his vulnerability, pampering his ego to her own weak and selfish ends.

She might not actually believe either accusation, but they'd be hard to evade or defend against, if any word of this leaked out. *This is a hospital* – it was an article of faith with her, that secrets were impossible within this fevered isolation. And yet, she couldn't stop. A dozen times a day she thought she ought to call an end to it, before it brought disaster down on her head. A dozen times a day, she wished that Michael were mature enough to see that and call an end to it himself, because she couldn't.

She might find comfort in that, if she tried. If she tried hard. She could see it as a measure of what mattered, how deeply he was embedded in her heart. How this was more than a cold or a cruel fling, more than a frantic grab for comfort. She saw the dangers and risked them all, because of him: because of who he was, and what he might become. What he was already, a treasure held in cupped hands. Her challenge was not to hold too tight and not too loosely: neither to squeeze the life out of him, nor to let him slip away.

Her torch made a path of light through the darkness, a circle before her feet. That was it, she had to watch her feet. It was like a bubble within the glass, a closer isolation. If she could only keep the two of them within that bubble and let nothing leak into the dark, then perhaps...

Step by step, day by day. Night by night. She did worry that she was walking towards a precipice, but she didn't seem able to stop walking, nor to turn aside.

One step after another. Ruth watched her feet, didn't lift her head. Didn't try to peer forwards, into the dark.

Felt a hand close suddenly over her mouth, heard a grunt of satisfaction by her ear. 'Here's one for the knife. One slash, no more trouble.'

She should perhaps have been more scared than she was. The surge in her blood was more despair than terror. She had dreaded discovery, and here it was. Her mind was bewildered by the man's words. Even so, she knew a threat when she heard it.

Her body was reacting already, before her brain could catch up. Every sense in her revolted at being handled so casually, so contemptuously, by a stranger. There were only two men she had ever licensed to come this close. One of them was somewhere ahead of her in the shadows, in the same danger – *one for the knife* – while the other...

Well, Peter might be dead, but he hadn't gone away. And not everything he'd left her with was sorrow, bruises on her soul. Peter had worried about her walking London streets after dark. Once the war started and the blackout came, he had worried enough to do something about it.

Here, I picked this up in basic training, let me show you. Here's how to break a man's grip, if he grabs you from behind; here's how, if he comes at you from the front...

So Peter had basically trained her. And so, now, she turned not against that grip but unexpectedly into it, twisting around to face her assailant, almost nose to nose.

Lifting her arm as she did so, that heavy torch suddenly a weapon, *use anything you have to hand.*

With room and time to swing, she might have killed him. The torch was that solid, her impulse that ferocious. To save herself or to save Michael, she wasn't entirely clear which.

She was too close to do it handily, though, that long-armed sportsman's swing; and too rushed to step away, once she'd broken free.

Too surprised at herself, in honesty. She had taken Peter's instructions to heart and practised assiduously, but for his sake more than hers, to ease his anxious mind. She'd never expected to need any of these moves, or, if she needed them, never expected to find that she could actually use them, or that they would actually work.

This one seemed to have worked too easily, and so she was too slow. Too slow and too close, and still in a killing mood. She slammed the handle of that long torch upward, clean into her assailant's face.

She couldn't see him clearly, could barely see him at all with the torch beam pointed the other way: just a pale round, moonlike, distorted.

A moon that shrieked and fell away, clattering into piled furniture, all awkwardness and angles. Ruth's breath came hard, with puzzlement riding the triumph. Who was this man, where in the world had he come from, what in the world did he mean...?

She was turning the torch in her hands – blessing it twice over, for the weight of it and the robustness too, that the bulb was still alive and glowing – meaning to look for answers. But the straying beam found the doorway first, and there stood Michael, half naked and bewildered, coming to help in any way he could.

Her torch was his betrayal, and he knew it. He stood exposed, framed in the doorway like a portrait of guilt, like a confession. She understood a moment too late, and snatched the beam away – *too late, too late!* – and felt hands close on her upper arms, hands from behind, because of course that first man hadn't been talking to himself, of course he had a companion.

One at least, and Ruth was seized again, and this time she had no easy escape. She did try, but he was wise to every move she could fling at him in a few brief seconds of struggle. Seconds were all that she had, and she didn't know how to use them. If she called out, if she told Michael – *not by name, don't say his name!* – but if she told him to clear out then that was her confession, crystal and inarguable. This was a tryst discovered, and whoever these men might be, whatever they were about, that was her career they held in their unkindly hands. Gone with a word, herself shamed and broken, Michael desolate and alone. She knew too well what he would do.

Any moment now, he would come flying down the aisle. One-handed and unarmed, he would come anyway. And there was still a knife in the case somewhere, and she would take any last desperate chance to get them both out of this, whatever it cost.

A lens focuses the light ... people can get burned ... There would be ways to use it as a weapon.

She was betraying everyone tonight, it seemed; herself and Michael, now Cook too.

Now Peter.

It was easier here, perhaps, because he had already tripped her here. She couldn't feel this carpet beneath her feet without remembering how it had not been there, how cloud had lofted her out of all touch with the world, how she had been lost entirely in mist and fuddlement.

It felt perverse, but so did all of this. She stood abruptly still, and closed her eyes. Heard her captor's grunt of satisfaction, felt him draw breath for whatever might come next: a word to her or to his companion, a challenge to Michael, a call for the knife. It might have been anything.

She forestalled it.

She summoned Peter, or else just let him slip from where she had held him penned all this time, where she had been constantly fighting him back. That was how it felt, at least: that she released him – *like a weapon, Cook, yes* – from some dark corner.

Not me, him. He's the one, take him...

Peter couldn't know, not really.

It wasn't Peter, even, not really. Not his conscious spirit, self-aware. Something she summoned, rather, some aspect of herself, guilty at being here alive when he was not, at choosing to

275

survive when he had made the other choice. The house, she thought, found her weakness and exploited it mercilessly, driving in and twisting her open to the heart, as the knife does the oyster.

The house did that to her, and she – well. She could use that.

No matter if he was an expression of the house or an expression of herself, given shape by loss and shame. Peter was a weapon to her hand, and she used him shamelessly.

She flung him back, behind her, from her mind to her captor's: *him, take him.*

She felt the startlement in the man who held her; felt his grip tighten momentarily, as if all solid ground had been suddenly snatched away and what else did he have to hold on to?

But she wrenched herself away, she could do that now. There was no conviction in his hold and panic starting to build in his breathing, in his voicelessness.

She could turn the torch on him, and see the black clothes that let him stalk in darkness; above the roll-neck sweater, see his face. See how his eyes stared blindly as though all they saw was a light through fog, bewildering.

There was no fog for her. She saw him clearly, and knew him immediately by his great coarse nose, bulbous and undefined. That was the colonel's work, early work and he wouldn't be happy with it now, only that he wasn't allowed to go back for a second try. Not one of her patients, this. From another corridor, a senior class. One of Major Black's favourites, ready to graduate as soon as they had the go-ahead. Ready to kill, and die in the doing of it.

Except that he was not ready for anything now, he was floundering where he stood, casting about with his hands for something, anything to grip. Moaning softly, unable even to find his voice. She knew exactly, *exactly* how he felt, and couldn't bear to watch him, so she turned her torch to find the other man where he lay slumped against a bare bedstead.

He was another patient, of course. She knew him too, and felt a pang at the damage done, the careful construct of his nose a swollen pulp now, oozing blood. The colonel would have a task to rebuild that again. Only, just a bloody broken nose ought not to leave him slack at her feet like that...

She stooped to peel back a lid, all nurse for a moment. All she saw was white in the torchlight, and for a moment she thought the fog had invaded him all too literally. It was nothing but relief to realize that his eyes had rolled up in his skull. Even so, she thought she hadn't hit him that hard; she thought it was the fog, Peter, reaching out to both of them at once.

So she turned one more time, herself and her attention and her torch. Here was Michael standing over her, pale and confused and a little afraid. No, more than a little.

He said, 'I don't ... I don't understand.'

No more did she, but she thought he ought to. Both men were dressed alike, and she had seen him just the same.

'What would they be doing up here, Michael –

something for Major Black?'

'What? Oh – yes. Yes, of course. He likes to give us exercises inside as well as out: *sneak through the house, break into a nurse's room and bring me her badge of rank. Don't get caught.* That sort of thing. The higher the rank, the more kudos – though I don't think anyone's ever risked Matron. He sets guards on the obvious doorways, so we have to be inventive. And then he sneaks around himself, and tries to catch us. It's fun, in a way. And deathly serious, that too.' Which of course was what made it proper fun. In their heads they were all doing it for real, in occupied France or in Berlin. 'They must have thought he'd enrolled you as a proxy, to patrol the attics. But – Ruth, what's happened to these two, what have you *done*...?'

That of course was the only real question, and the one she couldn't answer, for a boy who didn't believe in ghosts. *I unleashed my dead husband on them, and now they think they're falling.* No. Not that. *The house has a restless spirit, which has them in its grip.* No, not that either. That was like saying, *I gave them over to it. They frightened me, and I gave them over to something monstrous*, and he couldn't encompass either part of that, though it was true entirely.

She said, 'They'll be all right. They're just ... confused,' and hoped that might be true too. She had nothing to offer beyond hope. No true control, no knowledge. 'It's a nurse's trick, that we use on difficult patients in the wards at night. Like hypnosis, only cruder. Men are very sug-

278

gestible by torchlight. I really shouldn't have hit that first one, I didn't need to, only he startled me. If you go now, I don't think they'll remember seeing you here. Tell me their names, and get you gone.'

'They're Dolley and Rawlinson. But I'm not leaving you.'

'Don't be ridiculous. You're the danger to me now, not them. I'll bring them round and march them back to their beds and give Major Black an earful about sending men to terrify innocent sleeping nurses, apologize to Colonel Treadgold in the morning for breaking one of his fine noses, and that'll be that. So long as nobody sees the two of us together. Go on with you, get away and leave me to manage these.'

She was striving to sound competent and in command, manifesting Matron, all the matrons that had ever terrified him at school and since. Poor boy, he had come for a romantic erotic adventure, and had found something utterly other. Even now she had to round on him and drive him off. He went, though, the perfect example of his class and species: cowed and mannerly and anxious, still wanting to stay but with no resources to override her crispness. Another few years would put weight on his shoulders and stiffen his spine, he wouldn't be so easily bullied. If he had another few years, if she could win them for him.

He went. She lit him down the stairs with that admirable torch, and then went back to the befuddled twosome. She said a prayer, nearly, and reached out a hand to each because that felt

279

right, because that was what you did; although in fact she hadn't needed to be touching either of them to make this happen, and she thought she didn't actually need to now. She thought she could feel what she had done, what she called Peter like a rope tangled all about them, and she still had a grip on this end of it. Him. Whatever he was, whatever she had made of him.

A weapon. Yes. Not meant that way, but you used whatever you had to hand, whatever came. Peter himself had taught her that. He wouldn't mind. If it was him, if there was anything of him in it, in this thing, this horror she had constructed.

It was horrible, utterly. She knew. She couldn't bear that she had done this to them, wilfully; but it hadn't felt wilful at the time, only necessary. So long as she could undo it now...

Peter, come back. Release them, let them be. I'm safe now, you can let them back. Bring them home. Please? Don't leave them to fall forever.

She had done this, or else the house had done this: not Peter. She did know that. But whatever had been conjured here, however it had happened, it had the shape of Peter in her head and she could only deal with it as though she dealt with him. As she always had dealt with him: tenderly, intensely, honestly above all.

If there had really been a rope, it would have fallen slack in her hands. She could have hauled it in.

That was, in a way, how it felt. As though she had a fish on the end of a line, a dog on the end of a lead. As though she was, after all, in control here.

Gently, gently. If it was some aspect of her own mind that had assaulted the two men, she eased it back: like drawing the needle from a patient's arm, unhurriedly, not to leave a bruise. If it was in fact something outside herself, she had her touch on it, like a hand laid on the shoulder of a tiger. She could soothe it, persuade it, call it back.

Call it and it would come. Hand over hand, reel it in.

Release them.

She could see it in each of them, that moment when the fog lifted. The slumped one shuddered suddenly, and lifted a hand towards his bleeding nose. The standing one dropped down, to sit hard on the reassuring floor and lay both palms against it, feel its fixity, how it yielded not at all beneath his touch. How he really wasn't falling after all.

She didn't want to shine a light in their faces. She waited, and after a little while she saw the torch's glitter reflected in two pairs of eyes, open and bewildered, turning to her.

'Well,' she said briskly, to both of them impartially. 'Are you feeling better? You've had a nasty turn. I'm not quite sure what made you so dizzy; something in the atmosphere, perhaps, if it wasn't something you ate. I'll have these rooms put out of bounds, for fear there's something noxious stored up here. But let that be a lesson to you, not to go sneaking about in the dark, disturbing honest nurses. I won't have you troubling the staff, whatever mission Major

Black may set you. I'll be seeing him in the morning, you can depend on that. Dolley, I'm afraid your new nose is badly squashed. But what Colonel Treadgold can do once, I'm sure he can do it again. Though I'm equally sure he'll grumble. Come on now, the pair of you, up you get. Lean on each other, that's the way. I'll see you back to your ward, and send your excuses to the major.'

Like that, washing them along on a river of words, which really was an old trick learned in the wards and known to every nurse. They offered her no resistance as she coaxed them out of the dormitory and down the stairs, still by torchlight, letting them see no more than she could help. Not giving them a chance to wonder quite what had happened, let alone remember a face half glimpsed, a body half naked, another figure in the dark.

THIRTEEN

True to her word, true to her temper: Ruth went
in search of Major Black, once she'd handed the
two men on to the night sister to be cleaned up
and coerced or coddled into bed. 'Give them a
draught, if they won't sleep by themselves,' but
she rather thought they would. Shaken and dis-
orientated, they'd find sleep a haven, and be that
little further distanced in the morning, that little
less likely to remember, that little bit more
muddled between what had happened before the
fog and in the fog and in their dreams afterwards.

She hoped.

No more that she could do about them now.
Resolute in pursuit of a fiction, constructing the
story she wanted to tell, she marched down to
the major's domain and found him where she
expected, in the old ballroom with others of his
black-clad troops.

He cocked an eyebrow at her, waited with
apparent interest. She said, 'You'll be two men
short at roll call. Dolley and Rawlinson are on
the sick list, and I've put them to bed.'

'Have you, indeed?' Her bristling aggression

didn't seem to trouble him at all. He made a note on the clipboard in his hand and said, 'May I ask what's the matter with them?'

'Dolley has a broken nose, I think. Rawlinson passed out.' There, let that stand as the official record. No doubt he'd want to debrief them, but not until the morning, and even then she didn't think they'd make much sense. Meanwhile, attack was still and always the best form of defence. 'May *I* ask what you think you're doing, sending men to break into the women's quarters at dead of night?'

'Training. They'll do worse things, if I pass them fit.'

'I'll do worse things, if I catch them at it again.' Which was as good as to say *I disabled your two tough fighting men, I alone, a startled girl.* Which was as good as to guarantee he would not find them fit. *Dolley and Rawlinson, I may just have saved your lives,* although they would not thank her for it. 'I will not stand for this, Major Black. Have them sneak around their own wing as much as you like, but I have better things to do than patrolling ours. I want your word, please: no more missions on the women's corridor. I'm sure it adds a little spice to the occasion, but it's not necessary for them, and it's not fair on us.'

He made a noise of non-committal, which was fuel to her fire. She snapped, 'I'll see you in the morning, then. In the colonel's office. Ten o'clock.' Colonel Treadgold would back her up, he'd do anything now that worked against the major, however petty; and she could play the

284

petty tyrant guarding her girls, and slather one more layer of deceit and hypocrisy over what she had done tonight. And what she had meant to do.

She really wasn't sure that they could do it again, she and Michael. Already that was an ache in her heart, something missing, a new-found treasure lost. But the attics would never feel like safe ground again, and she didn't know where else they could go. It was a big house, there were sure to be other rooms, empty corridors; and there were outhouses, sheds, possibly lodges in the woods. But she hated that sense of hole-in-the-corner conspiracy, and didn't want to seal it in Michael's head that sex, love, romance was something to be conducted in the shadows. There was a legitimate thrill, of course, in the illicit rendezvous, in secrecy and private codes and hidden places. She could feel the surge of it in him with every public glance and every dangerous liaison. He loved what lay between them, the hush of it as well as the rampant. And she loved that, she loved the simple excitement in him as well as she loved his more complex character, as well as she loved his handmade face. Even so, she would so much rather be making love to him with the lights on. Teaching him that there was no disgrace in it, in any of it, not in her nor him nor anything they did together.

And she couldn't have that, and didn't quite see how she could have him at all any more. *I'm afraid I may have to give you up, my beautiful boy*, and she couldn't bear the thought of it but of course would bear the reality, as she had borne so much already. That was what one did. One kept calm and carried on. And tried to save the life of one's beloved, regardless of whatever private vows one made to give him up.

The morning's interview would only be a skirmish, no victory for either side. Really she wasn't pursuing it to disgrace Major Black, only to lend more cover to the night just gone, further to muddy a story that was already far from clear. To keep anyone from placing Michael anywhere near her.

She put herself to bed, and waited for sleep. And waited, and waited, and refused to let her weak and skittish mind dwell on what she was missing: a hot body and male sweat, youthful energy and awkward affection, all his clumsiness and hunger to learn. Hunger to touch. Oh, she did miss being touched. That above all, perhaps, that licence to be familiar with someone else's body.

So she lay there wanting and so not sleeping, although she waited for it. Waited till the sun rose and so did she, weary to the bone of her and so very much not looking forward to the day.

She did her duty, by both staff and patients. She ate a bite of breakfast because that was a duty too – one had to keep healthy for one's work – and scrupulously avoided anywhere she might have seen Michael. And time methodically inched around to her ten o'clock appointment, and that was a duty too, to throw some sand into the machinery of Major Black's project. To support the colonel in his campaign, hopeless though she thought it. To do whatever she could to limit the major's scope, to slow him down, to give him pause for thought.

To save Michael's life, if she could only manage that.

If she could manage only that.

At ten o'clock sharp, she tapped on the colonel's door.

'Come in!'

She had the door open and was halfway through before she realized. That was not the colonel's voice that summoned her, nor the major's either.

It was Aesculapius who sat in an easy chair before the fire, who smiled up at her and gestured her towards the other chair.

A quick glance around confirmed that they were alone in here.

She took the proffered seat cautiously. 'I've been ambushed, haven't I?'

'No, no, not at all. We simply felt that it would be more useful if you talked to me rather than the major.'

You're a major too. But you like people to forget that, don't you? Aloud, she said, 'Actually, I wanted to speak to the major and the colonel together. I suppose you must have told him, unless you make free of his quarters as liberally as he does of yours. But—'

'We *all* felt it would be better for you and I to talk. Of course the colonel had a voice in that decision; this is his facility, after all. And, as you say, his office. Which he has been gracious

287

enough to cede to me for the nonce, so that we can have this little chat in circumstances that don't include the, ah, tools of my profession.'

His couch, he meant. *I don't think you're crazy,* he was saying. *Only misguided.*

And, what, she should let him be her guide?

Sooner than that, she tried to take charge herself. 'Well then, you talk to me, if you speak for the triumvirate. Explain to me why anyone should think it's all right for Major Black to send his men to break into the nurses' bedrooms while they're asleep, and rifle through their things, and—'

'Sister Taylor,' he said, with a smile that was not yet long-suffering but could clearly turn that way, should the occasion demand. 'This isn't really going to be a discussion about exposing innocent nurses to moral danger, is it? I don't believe for a moment that that's actually what's troubling you. Our female staff is as carefully chosen, every one of them, as you were yourself. I should know, I did the choosing. There's not a shrieking Nancy among 'em. Nor a shrinking violet. If men come down their corridor, I'm confident that every one of them would know what to do.'

Goodness. He couldn't truly be saying what she thought she was hearing. Could he? Perhaps he could. She was fairly sure that there were only nurses here at all for the benefit of the men's morale; male orderlies were perfectly able to do all the work of the wards. She could see the colonel and Major Dorian on the same side for once, perhaps uniquely: *the sight of a pretty face* and *a soft voice in their ears, a soft hand where they're most sore,* the two of them nodding in agreement, *it'll do wonders for the men.*

It would be no surprise, if Aesculapius meant more than that. Or if he expected more.

Or if he knew more, that too. She said, 'To be sure, we can look after ourselves. And each other. But we shouldn't need to, that's my point.'

'No, indeed. You're here to look after the men.' He was ... growing harder to misunderstand. She supposed she ought to be shocked. Then he said, 'I'm sure there's not a woman on your corridor who wouldn't behave exactly as you do yourself, should the occasion demand it,' and she was truly shocked, because he might as well have spelled it out.

Had Michael talked? Bragged? Confessed, perhaps, to his psychiatrist as he might have to his priest? No, she didn't believe that. Wouldn't believe it. He couldn't be so careless of her welfare. He might have perfect trust in Major Dorian – or more, he might be desperately eager to satisfy the man who could sign him off as fit for Major Black's enterprises or do the other thing, stand him down, forbid him utterly – and she still thought he would have better care of her.

If anything, she thought he was less eager now. She thought she had taught him to find a value in himself and in his life. Not enough yet to have him stand himself down, but that would come. Nothing worked so well on a young man's self-image than knowing himself beloved. She still wished that she could kiss him in the light, to show him that it wasn't his face they had to hide.

She'd kiss him in the dining hall if she could, under the stare of the whole hospital. She'd told him that, but her words would never have the impact of her lips on his skin.

Presumably something in her or in him, something between the pair of them had too much visible impact, even when they sat at separate tables. Aesculapius had picked up on it, and was obliquely letting her know. Enjoying himself.

Was it a threat? She wasn't sure. Which made it a poor threat, which meant that it was something else, because he wouldn't leave her in any doubt if he meant to threaten her. Mind games were his profession and his stock-in-trade. He wanted her to know that he knew about Michael, and to be sure that he would keep it quiet; which meant that this meeting really was about something other than its ostensible purpose, her ostensible protest.

She might as well just sit back, then, and wait for him to tell her what he wanted.

He said, 'I don't know exactly what happened last night, and I don't propose to put you through the mill to make you tell me.'

She said, 'I've written out a full report.'

'I know,' he said, 'I've read it. You heard a noise upstairs, and quite properly girded your loins, took up your torch and went to investigate. You were assaulted in the dark, defended yourself admirably, and then found that your assailants were Major Black's trainees.'

'Colonel Treadgold's patients,' she corrected him. 'Yes. So I took them back to their ward.'

'Indeed. And then you bearded the major in his

den, and so this. Quite so. Some of the major's trainees – I beg your pardon, some of our patients – are grown quite adept at interrogation, and I have no doubt they could win a different story from you, given time. Or at least a more thorough one, with fewer puzzling lacunae. I know how Dolley got his broken nose, but I'd love to know what happened to Rawlinson.

'Still,' he went on, waving her response aside before she could even begin to form one, while she was still drawing breath without a notion what to do with it, 'you're free, white and twenty-one, and we can hardly give over a British subject to the major's less salubrious methods. Actually, I've half a mind to put your name forward to join Major Black's team in your own right. You're clearly lethal in an enclosed space, and yet you look so naive, no one would ever suspect you of anything worse than gullibility. How is your German, by the way?'

'Non-existent,' she said, determinedly cheerful, while her palms sweated on the arms of her chair.

'Well, Herr Braun could attend to that. You're clearly very bright. Too bright for your own good, I'd suggest – but not too bright for ours. What I'd actually like to propose, Sister Taylor, is that you should help us to train the men for Major Black's adventures. In addition to your regular duties, of course. It'll eat into your free time, I'm afraid' – *you won't be able to slip away so readily with young Tolchard,* he was saying – 'but we all have to make sacrifices in these times, and I do believe that your input would be useful. More than useful.'

'I don't understand,' she said. 'What in the world do I have to offer your assassins?'

She chose the word deliberately – for impact, yes – but he only smiled. She wasn't quite sure if she was being patronized or applauded. Both, probably.

He said, 'Well, you can teach them to rough-house at close quarters. Those were two of the major's finest, and you disabled them both in short order. Sometimes a soldier's not best placed to see what's needed. He looks for the military solution, the big guns. They need to un-learn that, and improvise with whatever comes to hand. As you did last night. Fighting from weakness is an art these men have to acquire, and they might best learn it from a woman.

'More than that, though,' he went on, lifting a hand again to stifle her, 'you can teach them to be confident in themselves. Lamed and twisted as they are, we can only do so much. The colonel can patch their bodies, and the major can train them up. I can work on their minds. Much as it pains me to admit it, though, that's not the last requirement. These boys have souls. I'm sorry for the word, it comes with too much baggage, but it's the best I can manage, the closest to what I need to say. We're asking them to do something tremendous, and they need every possible wea-pon in their armoury if they're to stand any chance of achieving it. I do believe that you can help. I've seen what a difference you've made already, and not only to the men on your own corridor.'

He meant Michael again, of course. He wasn't seriously suggesting that she should sleep with a whole platoon of men, of course not – though she'd like to accuse him of it, just to hear his laugh, and then his comeback – but he was asking her to make a commitment to them. For the benefit of their morale indeed: to make them feel better about going off to their deaths, and to help them do it better.

She said, 'You do realize that I'm totally opposed to your whole project here? That I stand with Colonel Treadgold? I want to make these men well and healthy, I want to restore them, not send them off to destroy themselves.'

'Of course,' he said. 'That's what I want from you: that restoration of spirit. You can make them feel like men again, it's a gift you have. You don't see it, perhaps, but I do. Even when you're only passing cake and pouring tea, you lift their souls.'

'Oh,' she said, suddenly confused, 'any woman would do that. Any female company. Men really are that shallow, at that age.'

'I think not. Well, yes, they are, of course – but I'm seeing you do more than others can. Matron doesn't lighten their hearts, other sisters don't send them away feeling as though they could bend iron bars with their teeth. You do it without even realizing the effect you have – and all this even when you were feeling like death yourself. I think your husband must have been a very lucky man.'

He knew about Peter, he knew about Michael. He knew about her. *You know too much, Aescu-*

293

lapius. Knew too much, saw far too much and understood what he was seeing, which wasn't fair at all. He was probably never shallow. He was probably never young.

She could suddenly not bear to sit under the gaze of those knowing eyes any longer. She'd come here on a mission, and felt that she had failed it: or rather, that it had been doomed from the start, a non-runner.

She said, 'I'm sorry, I don't think I—'

She didn't have the words, apparently, for what she didn't think; but she was on her feet already, and that surely should be clear enough.

He said, 'Take your time. Let the idea settle. None of us is in too much hurry here. Think about what we do, think about what you can do. For us, for the war effort. Give me a decision when you're ready.'

She was technically an officer. That meant he was probably technically her superior, and could give her an order. And was not doing that, would not do it; was making it clear that he wanted her as a volunteer or not at all.

And of course she would not, could not volunteer, what was he thinking? She was on the other side, firmly with the colonel against everything the two majors stood for.

Except the war, of course, winning the war. But even so. Not this way. No.

She nodded meaninglessly, and blundered out of there. Even if he'd wanted her only for her prizefighting skills – *oh, Peter*, and was this what his tuition was worth in the end, not to save her life after all but to land her in a maze of her own making? – she would have felt a fraud, because it really wasn't she who reduced the two men, it was the house. Or Peter, or some combination of the two. Not her, not really. She didn't think.

He didn't see everything, then. He hadn't seen that.

It was something to cling to, perhaps.

Not enough, perhaps. If the floor felt a little yielding beneath her feet as she walked away, that wasn't Peter up to his old vertiginous tricks, trying to trip her into falling with him. Nor the house, trying to hurl her after him. Only her own dazed state, startled and confused and uncertain on her feet.

Ruth set her back decidedly to Aesculapius and all that he implied. Marched away down the corridor, or tried to. What he had said came with her, sitting in her head like something dirty, like someone self-consciously dirty, leaning forward as they sat, not to leave their grime on the antimacassar.

The men respond to you. Of course they did, they were men. Young men, boys. She'd been saying no more than the truth, when she said that they would respond that way to any woman.

Well, all right. Any woman except Matron, perhaps. Matron would daunt them. Ruth didn't do that. But nor did Judith, she was sure, nor any of the other women here. There wasn't anything different about her. Nothing genuine, for Major Dorian to be seeing. It wasn't as though boys had flocked about her particularly, wasps to the honeypot, when she was younger. Peter had been her first love, first and only.

Until now. Did that make a difference, was there a difference in her? Well, yes, of course. Michael made her feel ... extraordinarily different. That must show, however discreet she tried to be. Perhaps the men picked up on that, responded to it. Wasps to the honeypot. Yes.

Except that to Aesculapius, at least, Michael was a symptom, not the cause: one more wasp, evidence of attraction. Nothing else in her was new, except...

Except. Yes.

She came to this house, and it haunted her. Whether or not she brought her own ghost with her. This was where it happened, and it didn't seem to happen much to others.

Well, Cook said that she wasn't alone, at least. He had known this before, this hauntedness, in other people and himself. And then there was Flight Lieutenant Barker, something dreadful had most certainly happened to him. So it was the house, not her. Not just her. But not everyone, that too. Not Michael. Something in her, then – her depth of loss, perhaps, or the way she had craved death, or both together if they could ever be separated, if they weren't in fact the same thing anyway – had drawn whatever it was, the spirit of the house, to weave its spells around her. And something in her was drawing the patients too, as though she had a spark that others lacked; and that was either a monstrous coincidence, or else deep down it was somehow the same thing.

Or Aesculapius was playing mind games with

her, perhaps, planting seeds to see what came of them, what fruited. Of course he would do that, it was his profession and his purpose here.

She shook her head sharply, and took the stairs at a trot. Heading straight for Major Black's terrain – uninterrupted, she was sure: he'd be avoiding her, the coward – and so through to her own corridor and her own task.

The ballroom was empty, as expected; and what must have been the supper room, that too. The main hall, not a soul about. The corridor beyond, lecture rooms and suchlike, their doors standing wide and the rooms all empty. Except that here was one, Herr Braun's workroom, and the door was closed but the room wasn't empty beyond it, Ruth could hear that. Above the sound of her own clicking heels, she could hear strange noises, some violent disturbance, the crash of falling furniture and softer thudding sounds, as it might be a body crashing into a wall, again and again, as though men were fighting and blundering about in there.

She hesitated only a moment, before she opened the door.

And stood on the threshold, staring; and hesitated only a moment more, before she screamed.

FOURTEEN

Screamed and screamed, and could apparently not stop screaming.

Nor move: neither to go in and help, nor to run away.

Not all horror happens in the dark, or in a rising fog. Life is not always kind that way.

Ruth had windows at her back, all along the corridor; in Herr Braun's workroom the electric lamps were blazing, unshaded. Good tailors always want extra light to work their tiny stitches.

She could see all too clearly what had been done in here. She would have welcomed a little veiling shadow.

She couldn't remember his first name. He was Herr Braun in her head, with labels like dog tags hung around his neck: *refugee* and *Jewish* and *gardener*, *internee* and *tutor* and *tailor*, any or all of those, with a query over *friend*. She had thought he might become one. She had thought she might pursue that. Then she had thought again, when she realized quite how dedicated he was to Major Black's pursuits. There was a grim devotion beneath his urbanity that was cold at best. She wasn't sure how close she wanted to place herself to that. Nor whether she would ever want to debate it with him.

Now – well, now there would be no debating, and she didn't want to go anywhere near him, even if she could have managed it. Her feet wouldn't shift from where they were planted like stone; and he, he would be the devil to catch. He was careering unpredictably all about his wide room, slamming into walls and stumbling over fallen sticks of furniture. Never quite falling, though he made no obvious effort to save himself. Fear somehow kept him on his feet, as pain must keep him moving.

Ruth screamed on his behalf, because he could not.

His head was thrown back, too cruelly lit. If Ruth had thought him gaunt before, he was utterly fleshless now, as though his last trace of comfort had melted in the furnace of extremity. He could be nothing now except the bare man, skin and bone quite unrelieved.

The tailor, at his fitting.

His eyelids glittered in the light, where scores of pinheads held them closed. His narrow lips the same, except that it was needles that held those: the curved needles he would use on leather, a long rank of them, in and out.

She wondered – distantly, almost dimly, as though she could not quite see, or not quite think – why he did not try to pull them out, why he just cannoned off walls in his agony and made no effort to help himself.

Then she saw how he held his hands up before

him, blind and begging. She saw how needles erupted from every fingertip, and no, he would not be using those hands in a hurry. Not for anything, perhaps not ever again.

Horribly, there was no blood on face or hands: only the fine cold steel piercing and piercing, sewing his dry flesh together. Blood would have been a mercy, hiding the worst of it, and there was no mercy here.

She screamed for him, until her throat was raw; and might perhaps have told herself that she was only trying to summon the help they both so obviously needed, because she could not fetch it, because she could not leave him even if she could not get close. Her simple presence was something, she might have thought, something at least. Not a comfort, exactly, but a gesture. Like sitting at the bedside of the dying, long after they had lost all awareness. A gift, given in ignorance to the dark.

If she were accustomed to being dishonest with herself, she might have thought such things.

As it was, she only stood and screamed, until at last people came.

Competent people, who could take care of things: of Herr Braun, and of her. Matron, who might have slapped her if Judith hadn't reached her first, hadn't put her arms around Ruth's shoulders and spoken unheard things until at last the imperative of screaming wore away, and she could stop. Could be quiet, could gulp and sob in the blessing of other people's noise.

Major Black, who could organize men to take charge of Herr Braun: to grip his wrists and shoulders and frogmarch him away to Colonel Treadgold, to the promise of anaesthesia and absence.

Matron lingered long enough to be sure of Ruth. 'Done with the hysterics, then? Hmph. Good enough. I'd send you to your bed, only that I can't imagine anywhere worse for you right now. Don't worry about your ward, I'll see to that. You get yourself cleaned up, then find something to do, make yourself useful. Don't make me be ashamed of you, you're better than that.'

And then she was off, chasing strays away, patients and staff both. Ruth saw Michael but too far away, too many others with him, they couldn't even share a snatched glance. Besides, that wasn't safe now. What Aesculapius had seen, so might others see it too. Perhaps they already had. Judith's shoulder, there to be wept on, there to be leaned on – was that for comfort or for confidences, consolation or confession?

Ruth straightened slowly, shook her head, shook herself free of her friend's embrace.

'She's right.' Her voice sounded hoarse and painful, even to herself. But that was good, a reason not to speak much. A reason for people to give extra weight to what she said. 'I need to be busy, not sobbing all over you. My boys won't listen to me again, if I don't show them a stronger face than this.'

'Ruth, what – where are you going? What's going on, who did that to Herr Braun? And where are you *going*...?'

'To theatre,' she called back, over her shoulder.

'To assist the colonel, to undo all of that.'

She had found him; she had a claim.

She could make the case with even more dishonesty – *I found him, and I called until help came* – but she didn't need to do that. None of the surgery nurses really wanted to be there. They were only too willing to make room for her when she came in scrubbed and ready, to let her be the one who stood close beside the colonel, far too close now to little Herr Braun.

Unconscious and stripped, he seemed smaller than ever, and what had been done to him more cruel.

'Well,' Colonel Treadgold rumbled. 'This does not seem so bad, actually.'

The anaesthetist – Captain Folsom, she remembered – made a choking noise, as if he had accidentally breathed in a lungful of his own gases.

'No, I'm serious. I wanted him out for the count, but that's mostly for the man's own comfort, and to keep him quiet while we examine him. Don't let him go too deep, there's no need. Unless these pins are hiding worse damage than they seem, to his eyes or his tongue – but there's no blood, d'you see? I do believe he's just been ... sewn up. As it were. Major Dorian will have more work than we do, piecing his mind together afterwards. Unless I radically miss my guess, we have the easy part today.'

Indeed, after a little while, after the first careful extractions, he sent the other nurses away. He and Ruth could manage quite easily, sliding needles and pins one by one from slack skin and collecting them scrupulously in a kidney dish. By unspoken consent they freed Herr Braun's eyes first. The colonel spent a little time checking each eye, to be sure they were no worse than scratched by so much sharpness, going in or coming out; he spent longer on the eyelids, above and below.

'See, they're like stamp paper, perforated so close and so often the skin's ready to tear at a touch.' Indeed, they were ragged already. 'He's lucky, he'll keep his sight, I think, unless there's some deeper hurt I'm missing. We won't know that until he wakes and can tell us how he sees. But I may need to rebuild his lids.'

Lids and lips and fingertips, like many another of his patients. That couldn't be significant, surely? It must just be a coincidence. Happy chance, that the right man was on hand to repair the damage. If Herr Braun stayed, if they kept him here. Major Dorian might feel that it would be better for him to be moved somewhere else. Anywhere else. Might well feel that.

Might well be right.

They worked on, mostly in silence. Ungagging Herr Braun, unstitching his mouth one needle after another, checking his tongue and not talking, because there were only questions – *who?* and *how?* and *why?* – which nobody wanted actually to ask, for fear of whatever answers might emerge. It was better just to work, to deal with what lay under their hands, the next immediate need. The next immediate needle. The pins had been easier with fingers, pinching the heads between her nails, but they both used forceps for the needles. Grip the eye of it, grip and twist and slowly, slowly draw it loose. One down, one done, one fewer still to do.

But there were many, so many. His lips were ruined; his fingers – well. He would sew no more uniforms, never set a pin in cloth again. Never hold a needle. Never want to, more than likely. She hoped he might find peace in a garden somewhere. Somewhere else. Though he would need to work in gloves.

At last, 'That's all we can do for now,' the colonel said, stepping away from the table. 'What more he needs must wait on his waking, but no need to hurry him into that. Sleep is the best healer. Give him something, would you, Folsom, to keep him under until morning? Then have the orderlies take him to a room. On his own, I think, for now. Sister Taylor, with me if you would, if you're free...?'

She was free, entirely. She was also exhausted. The effort of fine-focused work, the need to be so terribly careful not to let steel points do any further damage on their way out, the need above all to keep the gates of her mind locked tight against the battering of horror while she held the thing itself in her sight and under her hand ... She had never felt so drained.

And yet she went with him, of course she did. He was her superior officer, or else her boss, or both. Also, she thought, he was a man in need.

Whether she had what he needed, that would be another question.

Up to his room again, then, and no sign of

Aesculapius now. Something to be glad of. Someone had lit a fire in the grate; that was a blessing too. For the comfort of it, more than simple warmth; for the colonel, more than Ruth herself. He slumped into a chair looking ten years older, his ebullient moustache suddenly a giveaway rather than a disguise.

'Sit, sit,' he said, wafting a hand towards the other chair, patting the air as though to pat her into it. Then, recovering himself a little, drawing himself up as if half inclined to rise, the training of a gentleman just a little late to kick in, 'I do beg your pardon, I just felt it, all of a rush there...'

'Nonsense,' she murmured meaninglessly, sitting down. 'We're all tired, I think. That ... was slow work.' Slow and terrible, and the pace of it not the worst of it, not by a long chalk.

'It was. Slow and fiddly. What I'm good at, by and large. But that, well. That's overdone me, I don't mind admitting. And left me with a headache.'

'Do you have any aspirin? I've none with me, I'm afraid. I usually carry a bottle when I'm on the ward, but—'

'No, no. Not to worry. It'll pass.' He frowned into the fire, then stirred himself abruptly. 'Time for a beverage, I do believe. That'll pick me up. Can I tempt you, Sister Taylor?'

'Thank you, no. Too early for me, and I'm still on duty.'

'Of course. Well, if you'll excuse me...'

Cider, frothing into a tankard. In honesty, she thought it was probably a little early for him too;

305

and as senior surgeon and commanding officer he was always on duty, or at least on call. Still, a single bottle would do him no harm, and possibly a power of good. Aesculapius would approve, she was sure. Men were great believers in the restorative power of a swift drink.

Herself, she was more inclined to look for food. Come to think, she hadn't eaten for ... how long? A while. A long while. She would dearly love just half an hour down in the kitchens with Cook. Or a tray, only a tray by herself, that would do.

She was caught here, though, for the duration. Until the colonel dismissed her. He had fallen back on gazing into the fire, weary and wordless. Froth on his moustache.

Looking to perk him up, she said, 'This'll finish Major Black's ... endeavour, won't it? They'll shut him down now, surely.' Shut him down and save all those boys, stop them throwing their lives away. Save Michael.

It was a horror, but it brought a blessing too.

'Not they,' the colonel said. 'Not yet. One inexplicable event? That's not enough.'

'It'll look like sabotage, to Whitehall. A fifth columnist in the house. More than one, maybe. They'll have to investigate, and they can't send anyone abroad until they're sure of them all. It means a delay at least.' *If you weight your report properly, and not let the bias show. I could help you with that, perhaps.* 'And it's not the first inexplicable event. Flight Lieutenant Barker...'

'Yes. He counts against me, though. One for the other side. It may have saved his life, even at

306

appalling cost, but it won't save the others. If anything it encourages the others, if they think my work may fall apart. Their faces, fall apart...'

'It might encourage the men,' she said slowly, 'I can see that, but not Whitehall. Not if you play it well. Leave them worrying that a man, any man, all the men might go through that same ... disintegration ... before they've done what they went to do, might find themselves in German hospitals giving up all our secrets...'

'Mmm. Mm-hmm.' That was neither agreement nor the other thing, just the noises of a man mulling things over, staring into flames. Ruth found herself doing the same, albeit without the noises. Fire was hypnotic, though she wondered if Michael would find it so, or any of his brother officers. Brother patients. Their memories and experiences of it were different, and so might their feelings be.

Peter had always been afraid of fire, of burning to death in his plane. He'd seen a fellow pilot die that way after a training accident, running across the landing field ablaze. It haunted his dreams ever after, and stoked his anxieties. Sometimes she drew comfort from the thought that perhaps he didn't actually choose to die. Perhaps he wasn't thinking that clearly. Perhaps it was only the fire and his terror, and the wind of his falling that put the fire out, and his not wanting to pull the ripcord because the parachute would slow him down and then the fire would erupt again and he would come down burning.

Perhaps.

It was a pity, to lose a love of fire. So pretty it

307

was. Even in this strange, ugly house, where ugly things went on. Incomprehensible things, hauntings.

She watched figures, dancing in the flames. Stretching, reaching, joining and combining...

Oh.

After a minute, she said, 'Do you ... Have you heard any other tales, about strange goings-on in the house here?'

He stirred, shrugged. 'Any old house must always have its stories. Human beings and architecture: between them, they breed fantasy. Boys, especially. Put a group of boys into a building and let them romance, let them talk after lights out, let them run around in the dark – of course they'll weave tall stories about hobgoblins and spooks. Of course they will.'

'Yes, of course.' *But what's your story, Colonel Treadgold? Do you actually know what you're doing?*

Right now he wasn't doing anything. Just sitting with his hands curled around his tankard, no longer playing mentally with the flames. She thought it had been subconscious, or nearly so, but she was absolutely clear in her own mind; it was no fantasy. She had seen shapes in the fire, artificial, manufactured. Not her work, not Peter. He was afraid of flame, and would never think to play with it.

'Let's change the subject,' she said. 'Where do you come from, Colonel?'

'Me? I'm a Devon man. Squire's son,' he said, and she could bless the legacy afforded such a start in life, such rank: good English manners, beaten into him at public school before the army drilled them deeper. He wouldn't leave a woman struggling under a burden of conversation. He'd shoulder his share, and follow where she led him. 'Little place on the edge of the moors. Do you know the county at all?'

'We had our honeymoon at Moretonhampstead.'

'Ah!' He brightened visibly, as though clouds had been blown from the face of the moon. And then it was easy, almost: firelight and soft voices, nostalgia and storytelling. Talk of the moors, the Hound of the Baskervilles, strange apparitions, noises in the night.

'Worst thing I ever saw,' he said, 'wasn't a ghoulie, nothing supernatural. It only sounds like it.'

'Worse than Barker, worse than poor Herr Braun?' She wasn't interrupting; he had lapsed into a meditative silence. She wanted to keep him going, and to keep bringing him back to D'Espérance. Everything connected. She was sure of that. It was only a case of digging out the links.

'Oh, yes,' he said. 'Worse for me. I was a boy, you see, fifteen. At that age, a thing goes deep. And this, this thing...'

'What did you see, Colonel?'

'I saw a man on fire, astride a blazing horse... . You see? It ought to be a ghost story, but it's not. He was my father, and we had a fire in the stables. He was trying to save his best mare, riding her out through the flames; but he was too late, the beast was too much afraid, it took too

309

long ... All his clothes were alight when they came plunging through the smoke, straight at me. I've never forgotten it.'

No, of course he hadn't forgotten it. How could he? The memory would sit in his head like a burning coal, all his life long smouldering. And now he had brought it here.

'And now you work with burns victims,' she said gently, obviously.

'Yes. Even before the war, this was my work. I saw him, you see. After he fell, I put the fires out, I sat with him. I went with him to the cottage hospital. He was still alive, but there was nothing they could do: not then, not there. Now, here, I could save him, but not then. Not there. So I watched for three days at his bedside, I saw how the burns developed, I saw what the doctors did for him and how useless it all was. I saw him die ... I still do see him, here and there. Here, sometimes, in the house. A figure of smoke in a doorway. It's foolish, but I don't much like going into the stable yard.'

'Not foolish at all,' Ruth said. It all made a grim kind of sense to her – *Peter is all fog, all falling; you, your father is all flame* – except that she still didn't have an answer to the last question in her head. *Do you know what you're doing?*

The house ... reacted differently to different people. To the strength of their own private hauntings. Hers was fresh and intimate, and all she could do was share her fear of falling, her vision of Peter's last moments. The colonel lashed out in his frustration, and stranger things happened, worse things, irrecoverable. Flight Lieutenant Barker, Herr Braun. But was he lashing out blindly, or did he know? She thought not, surely not. It would take a cold, savage mind to see any gain in such exquisite sufferings. She thought that was just the house, taking the energy of his rage and transmuting it into cruelty, in ways that might somehow advance his cause. He barely even gave that credit, seeing disadvantage everywhere.

Even so, could he truly be quite ignorant, as well as innocent in this? She wanted to excuse him utterly, but wasn't sure she could. Something in him must be seeing some connection – *everything's connected* – even if his rational mind declined to acknowledge it.

The clock on his mantelpiece struck the hour, delicate silver chimes.

'I must go,' she said, 'I'm sorry...'

'No, no. Of course. Duty first. I have my own rounds to do, in any case.'

It wasn't the needs of her ward that pulled Ruth away, it wasn't work of any kind, though she did allow him to think it.

This was their time, hers and Michael's: between morning surgery and lunch, an hour when they could both of them hope to slip away for a few snatched minutes. When those who were busy should be too busy to look for them, when those who were idle should be too idle.

It didn't always work out that way, but they would always try. Always hope. Always know that if nothing else, at least the other would be

311

thinking of them exactly now: a warm touch in the mind, a shiver at the base of the neck as though his good hand were holding her, just there.

Today was extraordinary, appalling, but still. Perhaps she was greedy, wanting more after so much. It didn't feel like that. Rather, she wanted less. No more shock, no more horror; no more cold, intense focus; no more doubts and questions. She wanted to be still in her body, still in her head too. Still in his arms. No passion now, only contentment. Taking comfort from the quiet warmth of him, giving comfort too, giving it back. He must be as needy as she was. More, perhaps. She at least knew what had happened, and had some notion why. She at least had seen the truth of it. He would be all at sea, with nothing to go on but hospital rumour and the terrible tensions sweeping through the house.

She could be slow to start, but at least she was quick to learn. Walking along the corridor from the colonel's office, she saw a stretch of bare painted panelling that reached from floor to ceiling, rather than stopping at waist-height like any self-respecting wainscot. Immediately she was looking for the hint of recessed hinges, any sign of a latch in the tongue-and-groove joints.

She saw what she was looking for, and paused like a conspirator to check back and forth, each way along the corridor before she worked the latch and stepped through the hidden door.

Of course it wasn't a secret, this network of servants' ways behind the panelling. What the patients knew, their nurses knew. And what the nurses knew, more or less the doctors knew: not so well, perhaps, not so intimately, but none the less. It was not beneath their dignity to explore a secret passage, only to be caught at it.

Still, there were reasons of pride not to use these passages. *We are nurses, not servants. We have no cause to hide.* And there were reasons of practicality too, because the passages were narrow and cramped and awkward, not really fit for hurry nor for carrying awkward trays even though that was of course what they were meant for. Servants in former times couldn't protest, but nurses these days certainly could. The taller bulkier orderlies would mutiny if anyone tried to force them out of the broad corridors that their seniors and superiors used. They didn't mind stepping aside, they were all trained to salute, but that was respect enough.

So, no. Secret or not, the servants' passages went largely unused. Which left them open for Ruth in her privacy, convenient in her urgency. She could slip out of sight here on the first floor and find her way unseen, unworried, through squeezes and up tight runs of steps so steep they were almost ladders, all the way to the attic floor. She felt like a mouse living within walls, scurrying about on errands utterly unconnected to the world beyond: as she was, as they both were when they came up here. This was a place apart, a space held between two hearts, inaccessible to strangers. Small wonder if the ways that brought them here were just as narrow, just as private, just as dark.

She almost didn't trouble with lights any more.

313

Soon enough she'd be able to find her way by fingers' touch along the walls. Or by smell, like a mouse. By whisker-twitch. If she were a man she might grow whiskers, just to see what they told her in the dark. Peter had tried a moustache once: not for long, only until she'd laughed at him. He hated that, poor dear, but it was no use. Whatever he'd been trying to achieve, an aggregation of fluff on his upper lip wasn't the way to do it, and so she'd told him.

The colonel, now, his magnificent facial hair would find him his way along these passages with no trouble – but she didn't want to think about the colonel just now. There was rather a lot, indeed, that she didn't want to think about. Michael was the perfect remedy, sufficient unto himself, enough to fill her mind even when he wasn't gratifying her body. Today, at this hour, she only wanted to be with him. To rest her head against his shoulder and feel encompassed as his arm closed about her, to hear his voice lightly muffled by her hair, to see glimpses of the pure soul that underlay the man within the boy. Crystal and iron, green growing things and sweet water, all of England under one skin. One skin that would blush terribly if she said anything so difficult, so of course she wouldn't. Think it, though, she could do that. England was no mind-reader: too gauche for that. Too young. Not like Aesculapius. *Nothing* like Aesculapius. That was something to be thankful for.

Here the steep stair ended, here was the door into the dormitory. She stepped out knowing already what she would find, by that strange other sense that lovers develop that is not quite telepathy and not quite foreknowledge, only an utter certainty. No lights on and the blackout still in place, because who would ever lift it now that they had so scrupulously shielded all the windows from the world outside? So it was all shadows in here even at this height of the day, and yet she knew before she looked that she would see him standing at the foot of their bed, their nest, waiting for her. Just a line of darkness in the softer dark, not even an outline, only an impressionistic dash, and utterly still and silent too, and yet...

And yet she knew that he would be there. And in the first moment of her looking, she knew that he was not Michael. No.

No.

And her world came crashing down, her little private construct, as the world beyond flooded in through inadequate defences, a tidal wave, destruction.

'Well, well. You, is it? Of course it's you. I should never have believed that farrago you fed us before. You're a quick worker, Sister, I'll say that for you.'

'Please don't.' She didn't want him to speak at all. His voice could only soil things further. Like a slick of engine grease laid down over ruin. *Please don't, sir,* she should probably say, because he was, of course, Major Black. There seemed small point now in the niceties, though, and she really couldn't be bothered.

She expected him suddenly to knock a light on, to expose her in her shame. That was what men did, she understood. Throw a cold clear light on what should always have stayed subdued, wrapped in the shadow of its nurture.

She had her own gift that she could weave in shadows, up here especially, where she had done it before at need. Her own man, a moment of clarity in her dizzy head, a point of light like a glimpse through a distant doorway. Falling and falling. A weapon falling straight into her hand. *I could make you fall from here, Major Black.* She trembled on the edge of it, poised to call Peter to save her as he had before.

'I came up to see what had left my men so ... confused,' he said, quiet and deadly, 'so off-balance that a woman armed with a torch could take them on and defeat them roundly. I found this little love-nest – you really shouldn't have made yourselves so obvious – and once I knew what to look for, it was easy to spot whom.'

Among his own men, he meant. He might have guessed about her, he must have guessed, but he had waited until now to be sure. Which meant that at least he hadn't interrogated Michael. At least she hadn't been betrayed, except by her own body and the instincts that compelled it.

Even so. It was hard to speak. He was almost courteous, waiting for her to catch her breath and her courage. She had fought his one man physically and his other more mysteriously, snatching at a power she ought not to possess; she ought surely to be ready for this, face to face and a simple battle of words.

Readier, at least. She ought surely to have expected it.

She ought to have anticipated it and put the bedding aside, cleared away any sign of occupation. Tawdry occupation, assignations. She could look at this through his eyes and feel his disgust, almost share it. She really ought to have seen this coming.

She ought this, she ought that. It was too late for regrets now; they were here.

She ought to feel stronger. He wasn't about to hit her; she was the one with the weapon, he was the one unprepared. He didn't know what she could do.

Even so. It was perilously hard to speak, harder yet to sound cool and unconcerned as she finally said, 'Well, then. What are you going to do about it, now that you – as you say – know whom?'

'Yes. That is the question, isn't it?'

He was enjoying himself, she realized, stretching out the moment for the simple pleasure of it. Wanting to watch her squirm on the hook of his hesitation. Pretending to be indecisive, just to drag it out longer.

All unknowing, he had perhaps never stood in so much danger. Never been closer to the edge. She trembled with the desire to push him over. *Oh, Peter, are you there?* But no, not for this. Not for her own petty temper. Not quite. She had her pride, as well as her principles. She would defend herself, yes, and Michael too – but not take simple vengeance, even on a cruel man.

She said nothing, then, waiting for him to convict himself. Soon enough, surely, he would say something that was not only unforgivable but irrecoverable. *Of course I must tell the colonel, and my own authorities.* Something like that. Then – for Michael's sake, more than her own – she would have to strike. He was sure to do it. Safe to. Even knowing that something uncanny had happened to his men, right here. He couldn't help himself. There was nothing in him that would allow him to wonder if perhaps she had been responsible for that. Despite what he'd been told, despite the obvious coincidences. One young woman, what could she do? What could she achieve, to threaten him? It wouldn't cross his mind. No, he would gloat at her from his high moral ground, his unimpeachable authority, and he would say something that she could not endure, and then she would have him. Yes. *Oh, Peter. Be ready...*

He said, 'Oh, for God's sake, woman, do you really think you matter that much, that I'd be slavering to expose your sordid little *affaire*? I'm only interested at all because you're a distraction to one of my men.'

'I won't let him go,' she said, meaning *I won't let you take him.*

'Oh? And how do you imagine you might stop him? The King's shilling, and all of that. He's a man in uniform, in time of war.'

'Whatever he owed this country, he's paid back already. With interest.'

'Oh, he's a hero. Indeed he is. This is the thing with heroes, that they don't stop. They don't know how to stop. Stopping is ... unheroic. You couldn't stop him if you tried. Which is why I don't need to stop you trying.'

318

An awful thought rose in her mind, like some creature rising in dark water. 'What ... what have you done with him?'

The major laughed briefly. 'I sent him cross-country on a paperchase, hare and hounds; he's the hare, with half the strength baying at his heels. Oh dear, did you think I'd had him posted? Shipped out early, to protect him from your influence? Again, Sister Taylor, you're not that important. I don't need to send him away until I'm ready. I don't need to hold this—' a gesture that encompassed their bed and the shadows and herself all at once – 'over your head like a threat, because you are no threat to me. I don't countenance threats.'

She couldn't quite work out whether that was a warning after all, a threat even. He was hard to read in the dark, in his overweening confidence. *I could trip you, Major Black; I could make you fall and fall* – only she didn't think she could in fact, not now. Not if he meant no harm, if he was only laughing at her.

No harm except the one great harm, of course, and that would come if he wanted it to, if he chose to make it so. But she couldn't destroy him for that either. Not for serving his country, the best way he knew. She had done the same thing, after all. Dressed herself in uniform and sent her man to fight. It was what people did. Men, officers did it on a larger scale, that was all. Women did the same thing individually, personally. Once, twice and again.

Oh, Michael...

* * *

319

She still wanted to frustrate the major; she still dared to hope that she could. Hope was what she had, so she clung to it.

Michael was what she wanted. She would have clung to him, only she couldn't come near him suddenly, or else he wouldn't come near her. They were used to leaving signals for each other, *I can be in the attics after elevenses* or else *I cannot*, a book left lying heedlessly this way on a sideboard, or else that way on a chair. She didn't know how to interpret the book's abrupt absence. Nor Michael's, from the piano and the dining hall and the sacred Friday dance.

That last, at least, she could ask about.

'Judith, where in the world is Bed Thirty-Four? How can he not be here?'

'That imp? Oh, I expect Major Black has him out somewhere, purging his native indolence. Luxurious little beast, that one. But the major's been sweating them hard, all his favourites. All the likely lads, and some of the less likely too, like your sweet Michael. I think something's due to happen, any day now.'

Your sweet Michael. Had she too noticed something, had she worked it out? If so, she wasn't saying. Wasn't even dropping a wink in solidarity. But then, Judith was a company girl. Hook, line and sinker. Perhaps she thought that any boy about to sacrifice his life for the greater good was entitled to a little fling before he went, no questions asked.

Perhaps she thought that's what the women were here for, to supply a degree of comfort to the troops. The condemned man's last meal, his last cigarette. His last night of pleasure, the soft playground of a woman's body.

Perhaps she was right. In Major Black's mind, at least, if not the colonel's. That might be an explanation, why he wasn't pursuing Ruth further: if he thought she was only doing what she had been fetched here to do, what lay out of reach of the orderlies. A war widow, still attractive and experienced with it; who better? At least she'd be practical, they could depend on her not to throw a fit at the first suggestion...

She was sure that some such thought had crossed Aesculapius' mind, at least. Whether or not the major thought that way.

Even if he did, even if he took it for granted and assumed that she did too: even that didn't explain his choosing not to threaten her. He wouldn't make empty threats, of course, but he didn't need to. Hospitals were full of widows fetching bedpans. She could be replaced in a week if he had made the other choice, to expose her.

She must really be as he had said, negligible. Of no account, no interest.

Something in her roused at that, stiff with determination to prove him wrong.

It wouldn't be easy, if she couldn't come near Michael. He wasn't the only one missing from the dance that night; she wasn't the only nurse looking about her, trying to spot a favourite, failing.

At breakfast next morning, there was a litany of not-quite-complaints. 'The squadron leader wasn't in his bed last night, neither the one they

321

all call Prosser, although that's not his name. They came in filthy, absolutely filthy at first light, along with half a dozen others who are not, I am pleased to say, on my corridor, not my responsibility. Those two used half my bathwater between them, and they're still not what I would call clean. I'd have sent them back out to the bathhouse if I'd had fair warning, sooner than let them carry all their muck onto my ward. If they hadn't looked so done-up, poor dears. They could barely keep their eyes open. I'm sure Prosser was asleep in the water, half submerged, like a whale.'

'Mine were no better. Half the forest under their fingernails, those that have 'em. And who is it who has to clean young Master Tolchard's nails for him, because of course his own right hand can't do it? Muggins here, that's who...'

Ruth was absurdly jealous, and tried to swallow it down, tried to be curious instead with all the other girls. What *were* they up to, these boys of theirs who were not quite patients, a little less like patients every day?

The answer emerged, little by little, from the wood. Trunk by trunk. They had been finding and felling trees: in the dark, because no doubt that was good for them, for their training, a useful skill for saboteurs. Now, by daylight, washed and fed and rested, they were getting grubby again. They had stripped off bark and branches, with hatchets and saws and apparently their fingers, either last night or this morning. What they had left were long bare poles, tolerably straight and tolerably clean. They might have

322

served to carry telegraph wires, if the GPO were less fussy.

As it was – well. Six or eight men carried each trunk out of the wood and down to the lakeside. They made a stack there and then set about digging a hole, it might have been a grave, man-deep. It took all of them all day, working in shifts, their various handicaps rendering them not good with spades and picks. They came in muddy, almost mired, exhausted again; grumbling that the ground by the lake was too wet for a proper saw-pit, they should have split the timber where it fell. Too late now.

'Well, you'll know for next time,' someone said brightly, into what became a lengthening silence. Not even the men quite knew what they were doing this for, to judge by their cryptic bafflement. But one thing was for certain in everybody's mind, that there would be no next time. This was a last hurrah, exercise and training and examination all in one. From how they performed under Major Black's eye in these days, he would choose the men for his missions.

The splitting and sawing, the shaving of planks was more test than necessity: as came clear next day, when trucks rolled in heavy-laden with great baulks of seasoned timber. More men, too: REME sappers, fit for digging post-holes and rigging A-frame cranes and raising the first pillars of an open framework.

'What are they *doing*?'

It was the question everyone was asking; the only question worth asking, and even that was a waste of time. Those who knew weren't saying, or more likely weren't asked. Only Major Black knew for sure, and for sure nobody was asking him. If he had any kind of conversation, Ruth had never seen it. If he had friends, she simply couldn't imagine it.

The rest of them, staff and patients both, they had nothing to do but watch and speculate.

'It's a tower. Tower of Babel.'

'Well, *ob*viously it's a tower. Or else it's a self-supporting ladder. Jacob's Ladder, reaching all the way up to Heaven.'

'It's a scaffold. They're going to hang an effigy of Hitler.'

'They're going to *kidnap* Hitler, that's what all this training has really been for. Then they can hang the real man.'

'Nothing worth getting so excited over, it's just a bridge. Some sort of pontoon bridge they're learning to build.'

'My dear dim thing, it goes *up*, don't you see? A bridge would go *over*.'

'And so it shall. How to build a bridge and not get your feet wet: build it on one bank, upwards, and then topple it. Let it fall across the water. That must be what all those ropes are for, to control its falling so that it doesn't break itself apart when it hits the opposite bank. Or splashes down, if they haven't quite built it high enough to reach. Why else would they be putting it up right there, right next to the lake? It's a bridge.'

It was not, of course, a bridge. It went high, too high, higher than it need be to cross all that width of water. The engineers were sent away and Major Black's men finished it off themselves, if finishing meant swarming up and using their hand-cut planks to make a stable platform at the top. If you could call it stable, with the planking so inherently uneven and its carpenters so ill-suited to their task, driving home the necessary nails with more enthusiasm than skill.

'Bags me not go up it,' Judith said firmly. 'Even so, who called it a ladder? Betsy? You win the prize,' a hand-knitted tea cosy that had apparently been intended for the front until it had been laughed into retirement. 'I think it is a ladder. At least, it doesn't seem to lead anywhere except the top of itself. If there's a better definition of a ladder, I don't know what that would be.'

So of course they called it Jacob's Ladder after that; which meant that of course Major Black became Jacob. There was a pleasure in that, but still no satisfaction so long as the great scaffold tower stood in the corner of their eye all day and all night, and no one who knew would say what it was for.

For some days it stood alone, abandoned, a perilous high structure, all beams and angles, with hanging ropes rove through pulleys in some complicated fashion more suited surely to the navy, and the navy of a hundred years before.

Then all unexpectedly, Jacob himself, Major Black came into the hall at teatime, beer-time, to interrupt the sing-song; and called for attention and waited – not long! – until he had it, and then said, 'I know you've all been wondering what it's for, that great excrescence I've had erected by the lake. I thought it only fair to tell you now.

You'll all know tomorrow anyway, you'll see it at work, but still. You're entitled to hear it from me, after all your good work nursing these young men back to health and fitness. Fitness to serve.

'What that thing is, it's a parachute training tower. In a few days' time I'll be having the men jump – on ropes, it's perfectly safe! – from both sides, so they'll be coming down alternately on land and on water. That way I can truly judge their fitness to jump, and hence their fitness for the missions I've been charged with. That's all, so you can forget your more lurid fancies, ladies. It's just another obstacle course, only more specialized. Oh, and there'll be no exeats for anyone this week, no leaving the base for any reason. And no locals coming in, so I'm afraid we must manage by ourselves, whatever needs doing. The gates are sealed, as of now.'

Behind Ruth, someone whistled softly under their breath. 'The colonel won't like that. He's been waiting another shipment of his cider.'

The colonel, of course, would not like any of this; his cider would be the least of it. Ruth liked it even less, and was just as powerless. This was the military machine at its most efficient, its most inhuman. A shell in the breech and the mechanism all locked down, ready to fire. A hand on the trigger, the last human touch – but it was Jacob's hand, and he was almost part of the device. Spring-loaded, dedicated, built in. He wouldn't falter.

He was, presumably, just what the war effort needed.

She found that – at this distance, in this state of mind – she almost couldn't care about the war. It had been different in London, with the bombs falling all around, that sense of being absolutely under Hitler's eye. There was none of that out here, it all felt distant and apart, no longer immediate: somehow more appalling and less significant both at once. How could the major, how could anyone send these young men off to their certain, deliberate deaths? How could the colonel, how could anyone let it happen? How could she?

How could Michael, how could any of them *go*...?

She still couldn't come near Michael. She saw him sometimes, distantly – playing one-armed monkey on the scaffold, high, clinging with his legs and swinging all his body down as though he knew that she was watching and wanted to alarm her, teasingly, like a boy – but whenever she happened to pass close to where he ought to be, he never quite was. Not at breakfast or supper, not in the line for pills or a packed lunch or a pint, not cheering on a hectic game of rugger or fiddling with his motor in the stable yard or dozing in the unexpected sun. Not on the colonel's list for future surgeries, although that was supposed to be his proper job, as guinea pig for others. And not her patient, of course, not on her corridor, so she really couldn't go to his ward or ask for him directly.

At her worst, at her most desperate she even thought that she might write to him. It would be stupid, but safe, at least. The post was still reliable. And he could open a letter discreetly, read it, reply to it with no risk to either of them. She needn't even sign it; just an *R* that might mean anything or nothing to anyone else. And no return address, of course. The next best thing to anonymous. Or better than that, because he would know and no one else could possibly guess.

Except that she didn't know where this avoidance came from. Was it Major Black keeping them apart, or Michael being deliberately elusive? He had so wanted this chance to fight again, never mind that he was so ill-made and ill-prepared for it. He knew that she would do nothing but work against it, that she was hellbent in opposition. Perhaps it was his own choice not to spend time with her, not to talk to her, not to have to listen.

Perhaps love was not enough. Perhaps it never could be.

She didn't know and was frightened of humiliating herself to no purpose, even repelling him further. Too much sentiment could drive a man away, especially in these circumstances, if he was already struggling with himself and his emotions.

So, no. She wouldn't write: too absurd. And she wouldn't lay an ambush, lurk on the stairs or by the bathroom doorway, somewhere he couldn't hope to avoid her. That way lay catastrophe. There was nowhere he was likely to go that others wouldn't. She would all too likely be caught by someone else, caught waiting, if they weren't actually caught together. She wasn't a schoolgirl any more, to stammer out excuses that were patently false. No.

She tried to lose herself in her work, in this big house, with the patients who needed her nursing and the staff who wanted her friendship. With all of that and her own curiosity, so much to learn, so much for Colonel Treadgold to teach her, then surely...

It was impossible. Not her fault, but patients and staff both couldn't stop talking about the tower by the lake, the guards at the gates, the lorries that came and did not leave. She had thought they were just delivering timber and ropes and whatever else was needed to erect such a scaffold, tools she supposed and bolts and steel brackets. Now it was clear they had another purpose. One had taken away all the superfluous sappers; only the drivers remained, close-lipped and patient like their kind, waiting out these days with old newspapers and greasy packs of cards. The lorries were parked up in the stable yard, silent and expressive, ready to take Major Black and his final team of volunteers. All his chosen men, with all their baggage, too: their guns and uniforms and explosives, their knives and radios and maps, assassin's kit or saboteur's depending on their individual particular missions.

Somewhere not too far away would be an aerodrome or perhaps just an improvised strip in a field standing fallow, a runway shaved from the turf and marked out with oil-barrel flares, camouflage nets on poles for a hangar. It would have planes and pilots, a minor armada, waiting with that same bored driverly patience, those same papers and dog-eared cards. Flight plans and fuel at hand, last-minute briefings prepared, parachutes stacked ready.

As soon as these boys could jump, as soon as they'd convinced the major, they'd be off. Ready or not.

Of course the staff had to talk about it; of course so did the patients, those who weren't going, those who couldn't leave their beds or their treatment yet. They were all of them invested, and all seemed to feel invested in the fate of one young scamp in particular, the little friend of all the world, would he or would he not pass muster. 'That Infant, I heard he's really going all out to convince old Jacob. Sworn himself to silence for a week to prove that he can do it, and you know how unnatural that is.'

'See now, I heard it the other way, that Jacob is really leaning on him to show that he's up to the job, or else stop wasting everyone's time...'

It was no secret, which way they wanted that particular skittle to fall. There was only one person keeping secrets, Ruth thought, in this entire hospital, and that was herself. Everyone else wore their emotions right out front, on their sleeves, in the public eye.

It was almost a relief – almost! – when Major Black made his second announcement, equally public, equally unexpected.

'You've all seen us testing the equipment all morning, with a kitbag filled with sand. You're all talking about nothing else, I know. Wondering when we'll chance it with the first live body, whether we'll wait till after dark just to deny you the pleasure of spying from the windows of your ward.

'Well, I've decided just to tell you, to save you hanging out of the windows and crying curses on my name.

'We'll be trying the rig ourselves from fifteen hundred hours this afternoon. I'll be first man up and first man down, twice over: once onto dry land, once in the drink. That way I'm first man to the towels, too.

'After that my good lads all get their chance. This isn't a popularity contest, you people don't have a vote and I'd rather you weren't all clustering around the lake there, getting in our way and cheering on your favourite. But if you want to come out and watch from the terrace, be my guest. Wheel out your less mobile friends; it's going to be sunny, and I'm sure they'll enjoy the show. Nothing better than watching your mates make asses of themselves.'

It all seemed wonderfully unlikely. Nothing she knew of Major Black could paint him as this good-humoured generous soul, standing halfway up the staircase at lunch to proffer the invitation. She cast her eye wider, and yes, of course there was Aesculapius. Leaning in a doorway, watching. Playing Svengali now, apparently, as well as Machiavelli: using the major to manipulate them all, mind and body.

It was all too easy for him. They made it too easy, she thought. Isolated and vulnerable, trained to trust authority, bored and a little desolate, they would leap at whatever offered. The

331

staff no less than the patients, the women no less than the men. Any chance of a change, even if it was only an hour or two of spectacle. Playing audience, letting go of tension.

The hour after lunch was all dash, then. Fetching wheelchairs for those patients who could sit but not walk, rolling beds on their casters for those who could not even sit, couldn't be moved from their mattresses. Out of the wards and along the corridors to queue more or less impatiently for their turn in the old steam-driven paternoster, an open platform in a shaft like a vast dumb waiter, that brought them slowly and wheezingly down to ground level with no hint as to its former purpose, why on earth a country house should want such an industrial machine.

Beds and chairs both went out on to the terrace, crunching over gravel and flagstones until they were braked by the balustrade. Then for their willing haulers it was back into the house and up again for the next, riding the paternoster again in chattering groups, excited, anticipatory.

Ruth was neither, but she pushed and pulled and hauled anyway. It was good to keep moving, good to have no time to stand and stare. Down there, to the margins of the lake, where the candidates were gathered: two dozen young men in the shadow of their tower, bare sketches at this distance, smudged figures against the dazzle of sun on water. One among them, she couldn't possibly tell any from which but there he was, no question in her mind, standing just a little apart from the others, *oh, Michael.*

Was he looking up here, seeing her just in this

instant before she turned to go? That she genuinely couldn't tell: whether he was a prisoner of discipline or an eager participant, yearning for her or keen to be away.

Turning, going back one more time, she saw one man genuinely solitary, startlingly on the high flat roof of the portico like some kind of emblematic statuary, coloured marble. It was the colonel, standing utterly still, hands behind his back, on parade. Even his moustache, she thought, was at attention. Paying tribute. *Oh, Colonel.* It was probably shocking, some form of military *lèse-majesté* to feel pity for one's commanding officer, but she couldn't help it. More than popular, he was adored almost on every corridor of his hospital, he held every man's heart in his hand and all the nurses were devoted to him, and yet he was more alone than anyone. More alone than Ruth was, even. And more haunted.

She had felt Peter hanging over her all day. Almost literally, as though there were no sun and he were up there in the cloud base above her head, falling and falling. If she would only allow it, she could see him in glimpses all about her: in a window's reflection, in the blade of her scissors on the ward and the blade of her knife at lunch, in her own little mirror and every mirror else all through the house. *Something is building*, his presence said to her. *A storm is gathering, and never mind the sky.*

Well. She would indeed not mind the sky; she didn't need to. Clear and blue like the dream of an English summer, it held no horrors for her, no

333

falling airmen. No blazing planes, no work for the colonel, no last-minute recruits for the major. Either of the majors. She didn't, wouldn't look around for Major Dorian. He'd be somewhere: framed in a doorway, no doubt. Watching the terrace, not the tower. Reckoning responses, making assessments. Taking notes.

So many directions not to be looking in. Not down to the lake for Michael, not up at the portico to see how unhappy the colonel was, not around for Aesculapius. It was a surprise to realize that she had nevertheless noticed who was absolutely not here. No sign of Cook coming up from his kitchen, despite a cluster of white-clad kitchen orderlies in one corner of the terrace.

Everyone else seemed to be here, though. Everyone who was coming, which meant almost everyone fit enough to come. There weren't many left behind, in the wards or anywhere. It was a circus, she thought: a slightly shabby circus with only one act, but any entertainment, any distraction was better than the other thing. And any opportunity to see your friends take a fall, as the major had said. As the other major, she guessed, had prompted him.

She had nothing to do now, no one more to fetch. She could run away, she supposed. Make the few remaining bed-bound patients her excuse to hustle back into the house, *someone has to watch them, be there in case of need.*

She could, but she seemed not to be doing that. She was standing here, one hand on the lichen-crusted stone of the balustrade, others pressed all around her but entirely alone, quite as alone as the colonel up on his promontory. He must have climbed out of a window, she thought, to achieve that high solitary place. There was no door that opened onto the portico roof, no obvious intention to use it as a balcony.

She wasn't looking around, though, at the colonel in his loneliness. Like everyone, she was looking down to the lake. If she watched, if she concentrated hard enough, perhaps she could force wishing into truth and make Michael flunk his test, make an idiot of himself over land and water, be transparently unable to handle a parachute or go to war.

It was sheerest superstition, the law of contagion, the worst kind of magical thinking – and yet, and yet. Here she stood, watching, focusing, yearning for disaster.

There was something happening at last. Not Michael, not yet, but one figure swarming confidently up the scaffold, up and up. As he'd promised, the major was going first to show his young charges how the thing was done, what he expected to see from them.

Up and up. He reached the narrow platform at the top of the high structure, the eye of the needle, with only pulleys in a framework overhead. He clipped ropes to the harness that he wore, called down – his voice thinned by distance, but still clear – and stepped confidently to the edge, the landward side.

She saw him stand, thought he rose up on tiptoe as the ropes tightened, as the men below drew in the slack. He gripped the harness above his head, for all the world as though he hung beneath a parachute; he poised and crouched and kicked the world away.

In that moment, thinking about it, seeing him fall and yet not fall, held by ropes and men and a counterweight, she thought—

Oh!

Magical thinking. The law of contagion. She had, almost, forgotten. He had been in her head all morning, and still she had almost forgotten. Not thought about it properly.

She could do this. Actually, she could.

She could wait till Michael was just exactly there, roped up and ready to leap. Then she could set Peter on him.

Even from this distance, she was confident of that. It wasn't really Peter – stubborn, self-willed Peter, who might not reach so far for her, for this – but some aspect of her own self, using some aspect of the house. The house loomed at her back, massive and potent; what she called Peter, her own haunted driven mourning soul hung poised, somewhere between the sunlight and the water. She could reach out and dizzy Michael's mind, make him fall all out of control. He'd be perfectly safe, with men watchful on the ropes beneath; and he'd fail his test comprehensively, and have no chance of being sent away. Yes.

And then she could pull Peter out of his mind again, swiftly, far too swiftly to leave any damage behind. She knew how to do that. Yes...

She watched almost with equanimity, as Major Black came to ground.

Almost. Not quite. He was coming down too

fast, surely? A man on a parachute ought to drift in the air, she had always thought, idle as thistle-down. This was ... not like that. The major seem-ed to plunge to earth, as though those men on ropes were pulling him down, not holding him back. The counterweight rose within the tower, dark and brutal.

He hit hard and crumpled, but seemed to be in control after all. He rolled and came easily up on to his feet again, and shrugged away the harness and seemed fine. Strolled among his men, talk-ing, pointing. Thinking it through, she supposed that drifting idleness was not ideal, for military men who might be shot at on the way down. Of course they would want to come in fast, their parachutes would be designed that way.

Which would make it doubly hard for dam-aged men, and all the easier to persuade the powers-that-be – even Major Black himself – that Michael was not competent. Michael and others, perhaps. She might be able to save more than one. If she could just fuddle their minds without getting fuddled herself, without letting it all overwhelm her.

Peter, be ready. Be true...

Major Black was climbing again, ready to do it all again, this time into the water. She supposed the men might have to ditch into the sea en route, if they ran into trouble, and he'd want to be sure that they could manage. Or their mission might require them to drop into a lake rather than a field, with a boat standing by for pickup.

There he was at the top again, clipping himself to the ropes again. This time facing the other way, towards the water.

Stretching up, crouching down, ready to kick off like a diver in fine form...

It was odd: he seemed suddenly to be surrounded by light.

It was as though the sun had pierced at last through clouds on a grey and rainy day, except that the sun was out already.

The major glowed, brighter than any sun; and capered strangely, a shadow in a nimbus; and threw himself all ungainly over the edge.

At some point – about the time that he stopped falling and started dangling, tried to swim down through the air against the ropes' refusal, started screaming – Ruth understood. At least a little, she understood.

That light that enveloped him? That was fire, flame in sunlight. He was aflame, and he'd tried to jump down into the water, and the ropes prevented him.

The men on the ropes understood, she thought, sooner than she had, but there was nothing they could do. The ropes and the counterweight were rigged not to let him down too swiftly, no more swiftly than a man on a parachute should fall. It had seemed dreadfully fast before. Now suddenly it was appallingly slow, and he was screaming all the way.

They could slow him further, but there was nothing they could do to speed him up.

He must have seen the water below as an offer of blessing, salvation held out. Like many an airman before him, plunging towards the drink, yearning to fall faster. Salt water is healing, but any water will kill the flame and suck the heat away and bring relief. A burning man will always run to water.

Unless that water is itself on fire.

It was the seaman's nightmare, burning oil on the surface as they jumped from sinking ships. But a seaman has a chance, perhaps, to think again. He can run from port to starboard, from bow to stern. Not jump yet. Hope for a lifeboat, a lifting wave, a limit to the oil. Something.

A falling man has no chance, no choices. Nothing he can do but fall.

Fall slowly, in Major Black's case: down to where impossible flames reached up, to clutch for him like bright petals eager for a feed.

Now the men were hauling on their ropes, trying to draw him back from that. *Better to burn in air,* they must be thinking, *good honest air, as we did. Better that.*

People could be saved, they knew, despite the fire and all its malevolence. Colonel Treadgold had saved them; he could save the major too, if they could only bring him safe to land and put that fire out.

They heaved, and his descent was checked. He hung aflame, a separate flame above the sudden blazing of the lake. Separate and screaming.

Then their ropes began to snap, smoking ends flailing in the turmoil. Burned through, perhaps, or—

Colonel Treadgold. Yes.

No one else, Ruth thought, was wondering yet how all this could be. No one was piecing together some difficult mythology of spilled kerosene

339

and sparks, of accident or sabotage or murder. That would come, but this wasn't the time.

No one, certainly, was turning around to look the other way. Up at the house, at the portico.

At the figure who bestrode the portico, stiff and vengeful and deliberate, fists clenched.

Oh, she thought. *You, Colonel – you do know. You know exactly what you're doing. Don't you?*

That wasn't a question, it was an accusation. She was only sorry he couldn't hear her. She wanted to shout it in his teeth.

She twisted away from him just in time to see the last rope fail and the major fall for true. Down into the inferno, the leaping flames of the lake where it was alight from one stone margin to the other.

She had no notion how deep it was. *Not deep enough* was her only thought. She thought it was fire all the way, all the way down.

And turned again, stared up at the colonel, wanted to scream at him and did the other thing instead, screamed inside herself.

Screamed for Peter.

It was a day, apparently, for falling. All the way, falling and falling.

The major fell into the lake. The colonel – well. The colonel was falling in his head already, falling and falling, before ever he fell off the roof.

Let him fall and fall, Peter. Take him with you. I'm letting go.

FIFTEEN

After the shock of silence, after the shock of shouting comes the relentless buzz. Low voices talk and talk in every corner, every corridor. In the dark of night and in the daylight, at mealtimes and make-work and all times else. People need to put their world together, somehow, anyhow that will hold. They have only words to do that with. They talk and talk.

Ruth tried hard not to listen. She tried very hard. Truly, she didn't care what the people decided, what consensus rose between them. Whether the lake had really been on fire, whether that had been spilled fuel or ordnance or optical illusion, some gift of sun-dazzle and reflection and the falling flame. Whether the major would live or die, or want to. Whether the colonel had slipped and fallen in his hurry to come down, or whether he'd actually jumped. *It was too high, he was too heavy; but of course he tried it, he had to try. He had to come and help, take charge, it was his duty...*
They could tell each other whatever stories they preferred. That didn't matter.

The colonel and the major lay in one small room together, separately unconscious. On her corridor, her ward. That didn't matter either. She could nurse them both. It was her duty.

Not nurse them back to any kind of health, she couldn't manage that. The major needed the colonel's care, and couldn't have it. There were other doctors here, but none so senior or experienced, none so innovative, none so bold. There were better doctors, all elsewhere and far away, all overworked already, not to be summoned for a single catastrophic man.

The colonel ... needed something that she had denied him. By her choice.

He had broken bones from his fall, and of course everyone assumed that his coma was part and parcel, came hand in hand: that he had knocked his head on the way down or else on landing, jumbled his brains if not cracked his skull.

Ruth knew better. In his head, she knew, he was still falling. Hand in hand, he and Peter, down and down.

She had let go, let him go. Coldly, deliberately, finally. She couldn't draw him back, not now. He was too far gone.

She didn't need to hear what people said, she didn't want to.

Sometimes, she had no choice.

Now, she had no choice.

They were gathered in the dining hall, everyone who could be: squashed up at every table, not a seat to spare. Ruth had an orderly on

342

one side, she hadn't learned his name yet. On the other side, she had Michael. Him she was holding on to. Hand in hand and not letting go, not now.

Major Dorian stood on the stairs, where he could be seen by all. Where Major Black had stood before him, which they were all thinking and no one was going to say.

He said, 'People. I know the war has been the last thing on your mind in these last days, we've all had monstrous shocks to contend with, terrible events. You've done remarkably well, the staff in particular, keeping everything together. I can't sing your praises loudly enough.

'But the war goes on. It may seem far from here; that isn't really so. Hitler's reach is long.'

Was he trying to suggest that Hitler had reached this far, that his hand lay behind the major's calamity, or the colonel's? Sabotage, fifth columnists, betrayal? Ruth wasn't sure. He was moving on already, leaving it to lie there in her mind, in everyone's, unexamined.

'Gentlemen, the major's special troops: you've trained this long and this intensely, and you're so close to ready, your missions are so urgent, it would seem criminal to let all that go now because of one accident in training. One double loss. The major would want you to follow through, and so, I'm sure, would the colonel.'

Well, he was lying, then. That was no surprise. The first casualty of war is truth; Aeschylus said that, and men had been repeating it ever since. And providing more evidence to support it. Whatever best suited their purposes at the time.

343

'We have the trucks,' he said, 'we have the drivers. We have the targets. We have another place that we can take you, for intensive parachute training. We have limited time, and a forecast of good weather. Gentlemen, who among you is still willing to go? I won't bludgeon you with talk of king and country, or appeals to your patriotism; that stands in no question. You honour those uniforms you wear. Neither will I ask you to do it for the major, for the colonel; that would be disgusting. I'm not even going to urge necessity. We can likely win this war without you. Just, not so soon and not without more cost. Every blow struck now, struck high against the head, will count for more further down the line.

'Oh, but you know this, you know all of this; we've talked it out before. It's time to call an end to talking. Gentlemen, the trucks stand ready for the road. Who will ride? On your feet now, if you're still willing.'

That was all. Well, that and the silence after, his expectant silence. His waiting.

And then the scrape of chair legs on the parquet, the shuffle of feet, the slow rise of bodies in the hall. One after another, men and more men, alone or in little groups together.

At her side, Michael's hand squeezing hers, then letting go.

Michael rising.

She sat there, head down, dizzy. Faint again. Too heavy to move, too numb to speak.

Distantly, she heard voices. 'You, Tolchard? Aren't you a little ... borderline?'

344

'I don't believe so, sir. I can keep silence when I need to–' his leg pressing against hers would attest to that, *I never said a word about us, did I?* – 'and if I can manage that car I can manage a 'chute one-handed, with just a little work on the harness. I'd like to try, at least. I'd like the chance to prove it.'

For king and country. For the major, for the colonel. For himself, perhaps. Perhaps still that, at least a little. More, though, this was for her. Stupidly, self-defeatingly, he would leave and fight and die for her.

And she couldn't say a word. For all the reasons that put him on his feet, she stayed in her chair and let him go.

SIXTEEN

Ruth stood on the back step with her case at her feet. She had missed the last coach to the railway station. Deliberately so. She'd been quietly, selfishly adrift in the almost-empty house, saying goodbye. To Peter, or perhaps to Michael. She wasn't clear about that. She didn't expect to encounter either one of them again.

A car made a wide sweeping curve out of the stable yard, drew up with a hiss of gravel.

It should have been Michael's landaulet, surprising her again; but of course it wasn't. No chance of leaving as she had come. Not this house, not her, not now.

The passenger door swung open, and there was Aesculapius at the wheel, leaning over. There was his teddy bear too, in the passenger seat.

'Get in, Sister Taylor. There won't be a better offer now.'

'Cook's still here, I think,' though she had skipped the opportunity to say goodbye to him. Some conversations she was just not ready for.

This was actually another of those, but she wouldn't dodge it now. He said, 'Indeed, but he's staying. I don't believe there's anything for you to stay for.'

There's nothing for me to go to either. That was more true than even she had realized; it sat in her head like a revelation, that she was no longer in pursuit of a bullet.

'Come with me,' the major said, 'I want to talk to you.'

'What, will you offer me another job?'

'If you'll take it, yes. Not like this. Another kind of nursing. Will you come? I'm driving down to London, all the way.'

'I ... have nowhere to go, in London.' It was a shock to realize that too was true. They'd only ever rented, she and Peter. She'd let that house go, of course, when she came north with no plans to return.

'Don't worry about that. We'll find you a bed. And a life, if you'll take it.' And then, once more, 'Will you come?'

Apparently, she would. He was out of the car, lifting her case into the back. She was in the car, moving the bear, getting settled. Being prepared. For what, she couldn't imagine and wasn't going to ask.

'What will happen to the house now?'

'D'Espérance? Oh, the Ministry will rescind possession, I imagine. No further use for it.'

As he pulled away, Ruth caught one last glimpse of the back door in the wing mirror. Standing wide, with a figure outlined in the doorway. He wasn't wearing whites, but still she rather thought it was Cook: her first glimpse of him outside his own domain.

Or not, perhaps. If Cook wasn't leaving, if the

house was reverting to its former ownership...

Well, that was another question not to ask. She might dance to Major Dorian's tune, she might have done that all along, but she was damned if she'd start before he whistled.

She sat still, then, and waited.

Soon enough, he'd tell her what he wanted. Soon enough, she thought she'd probably say yes. Make a promise of it. Yes.